THE BROKEN FEW

SHELLY JARVIS

The heart will break, but broken live on.

LORD BYRON

CONTENTS

CHAPTER
ONE

I look at the book's pages, but I don't see the words. They are a swirl of black, like clouds before a storm, merging and separating as my mind drifts. This is when it's safe to think; the book is a shield, my brain is a weapon.

"Can you even read?"

Crack, I think.

I don't look up. If I did, I'd start imaging my guard's head smashed against the floor. Like Rek—. I don't think her name anymore. When I think of *her*, of my time in the City of Trials, I want to fight.

But I can't. So I listen to Doctor Okada's advice on repeat in my mind: avoid focusing on whatever, or whoever, is bothering you and instead focus on what you can do about it. That is one of the keys to maintaining control.

I can't do anything about Tinora.

That's what I call her, inside. I don't know her name—I haven't asked and she hasn't offered. The only thing she offers is vitriol. The only thing I ask is—

Where is Thoa? How is Krew? When can I leave?

—nothing. I don't ask anything anymore.

"I can read," I say, though I don't know why I acknowledge her. "Thank you for asking."

She chuckles, but there's nothing joyful about it. I let my eyes drift to the edge of the book and watch her from behind my shield. Tinora is running her fingers along the edge of the bed, checking the imaginary cracks in the wall, walking to the desk they gave me to check the pens. She's checking my room because the doctor is coming to visit today so she wants to make sure I'm not going to stab him. Honestly, it's been so long since I've tried that, I don't know why she bothers.

"You're holding the book upside-down," she says.

"Just trying to challenge myself," I say, but I flip the book around.

Stop paying attention to me, Tinora.

Thinking of the name I've given her always makes me smile. It's a Raider word that translates to the old tongue as "jerk."

The old tongue? I think, shaking my head. *Why do I still call it that?*

Everyone here speaks it. Most of them speak three or four languages, things I've never heard of like *Russian* or *Swahili.* Doctor Okada has taught me a little of the language of his ancestors —*Japanese,* he called it. I can say words of greeting or farewell, but when he writes it out I can't understand how words are formed from the characters he draws. They are beautiful, broad strokes in black ink, but they are a secret kept behind a locked door and I get only the barest glimpses.

Tinora stops and stares at me. I try to pretend I wasn't watching her, but it's too late. I lower my shield and meet her gaze. Her thin lips curl at the corners and I can already tell she's about to piss me off. She says, "I'm going to tell the doctor you're not really reading, *Little Star.*"

I'm off the bed and on my feet before I can stop myself. I advance on her, stopping only when she pulls out the little black shock-box. I have to force my jaws apart to say, "Do not call me that."

Her grin is full now, wolfish. It makes her look wild and dangerous and I hate her more than ever. "I'll call you whatever I want. You're *my* prisoner."

"Actually, she's *my* patient."

Both of our heads whip around to Doctor Okada standing in the doorway. Tinora forces a laugh and steps towards him, saying, "Of course, doctor. We were just having a little battle of wills and I wanted to make sure she understood her place."

He purses his lips. "Your job is to guard her and protect her, not antagonize her. Your presence here could be why we're progressing so slowly."

"Doctor, I hardly think—"

"Yes, I can see that. That's why you'll be reassigned."

Tinora stares open-mouthed at him for a few seconds, as if she can't decide whether or not he's serious. Her eyes follow him as he steps past her; with one last hate-filled glance towards me, she leaves my room, slamming the door behind her.

Doctor Okada takes off his jacket and places it over the chair at my desk. He rolls up the sleeves of his pale blue shirt, meticulously, and doesn't speak until he's finished. I watch him as he moves, surprised at how quiet he is. Most people are loud, even when they aren't speaking or doing something—their very nature is loud—but not the doc.

He's had a haircut since his last visit. Thick, black hair is parted to the side and full of something that holds it in place, but makes it look wet. He's a handsome man, dark eyes, dark lashes, looking out from skin as smooth as a river rock. He has a moustache and beard, both kept trimmed and pristine at all times. He's younger than I thought at first. Late twenties, I would guess, though he carries himself like a much older man. Perhaps that's why I haven't noticed how handsome he is before now.

Normally I don't get to look at him this long, but today he

seems distracted, like he can't look at me, so instead I look at him. When his eyes do meet mine, I flinch, afraid I'll be in trouble for how I reacted to Tinora.

"Why didn't you tell me?" he asks, his voice softer than I've ever heard it.

I shrug. "I can handle it."

"Oh, Nova, you still don't get it. You shouldn't have to handle it. This is supposed to be a safe place for you to gain an understanding of what it means to be a human. Civilized people do not behave like that."

I drop my gaze. *Stupid, Nova. You should've known.*

"I see what you're doing, and I need you to stop."

"Stop what?" I ask.

"Blaming yourself. It's your go-to. But this isn't your fault."

I nod, trying to let his words mean something in my muddy thoughts.

"Do any of the other guards treat you like that?"

All of them. "No."

Okada sighs. "We've been at this nearly seven months now, Nova. I know when you're lying." When I don't answer he says, "I'll take care of it."

Then we fall into the rhythm of his visits. He checks my temperature, my blood pressure and heart rate, looks in my ears and mouth with a light. Okada listens to my back with a weird tube called a tetherscope. I still don't know what it's for, but I don't bother asking. I don't want to risk him stopping when it's the only physical contact I have with another human. Instead, I lean into the touch. I know he understands, for though he doesn't say anything about it, his hands linger longer than they need to on the top of my back.

"I planned to take you for a walk today, but after what I walked in on—"

"Please?" I cut in, hoping he hasn't changed his mind. He takes me out of the room every fourth visit. Those short trips around the ship are the only bit of exercise I get, the only respite from these white walls, this black floor.

He smiles. "Okay, we can still go. But I'm not happy with how you handled that situation, even if Jane was antagonizing you."

Jane? I feel my lips curl into a sneer involuntarily. *After all these months, it's so anticlimactic.*

"You're right, of course," I say. "I'll do better next time."

As he leads me out the door, he says, "There won't be a next time, Nova."

My heart hammers so hard in my chest I'm afraid it's going to break free. I force my words out as steady as I can: "What do you mean, Doctor?"

"Well, I can't let you move to your own place yet, but I'm going to petition the Règle to release you into my care."

I bite my lip to keep from screaming. Being released to the doctor might not be ideal, but it would be better than being stuck in the single room all the time. I'll need everything to be perfect during this walk. I don't want to risk him changing his mind.

As we turn down the corridor away from my prison, I can't help but smile. My chest feels lighter with each step. The corridor is metal, narrow, but there are windows where I can see outside or into different parts of the space station. I wonder if the whole place is like this or if it's different when you get away from the holding rooms. The doctor *tells* me it's different, but I don't know if I believe him.

He's been kind to me. He's the closest thing I have to a friend in this horrible place. But he works for the Règle. He takes care of me because that's his job.

"Ready?" he asks.

I stop moving at his words. I wasn't paying attention, lost in my own thoughts, and I'm not ready for his game. I think about trying anyway, faking my way through it, but he'll know. He always does. So I say, "I'm sorry, Doctor, but I was thinking."

He laughs, a booming sound in this small place, and I find

myself taking a step away from him. "You're allowed to *think*, Nova. We want you to be an educated, informed citizen. These last few months have been to train your brain to think correctly. And I believe we're almost there."

"I hope so," I say. And I mean it.

"Okay then," he says, "Instead of telling me what we passed, tell me what you see now."

I look around at the metal above and below. There are no windows here, nothing exciting to see, but I know that's not a good answer. I've tried it before and received the Okada frown.

"Pipes," I say, pointing up. "The big one—I think it carries air. That one with the blue stripes, it moves water. But I don't know what the other one does."

He smiles and leans over conspiratorially, whispering, "Me either."

I return his smile as I continue to look around. "The corridor intersects in fifteen yards. If we go left, we'll pass the window that shows the farm owned by the...Swedes?"

He nods. "What happens if we go right?"

I swallow hard, but I don't think he sees. "We pass the rooms where the doctors operate." *Where Thoa died.*

"And?"

"And the medical students line up to watch and learn."

He lets silence stretch between us for a moment, but I dare not break whatever he's trying to do with words. After a moment, he says, "Anything else?"

I keep my face clear, or at least I try to, and pretend I'm trying to recall. "I don't think so. We haven't gone far that way. I think you prefer the left."

"I do," he says. "Good observation."

"Why?" I ask. I know it's a gamble, asking something that isn't on the script we've been perfecting these many months, but I'm curious.

His smile broadens and he says, "That's the first time you've shown interest in me, as a person."

"Oh, uh, I'm sorry?"

"No, please, don't be. That's a big step. I'm glad you asked."

But he never answers. Instead he starts walking again, leaving me to trail in his wake, wondering what drives him as we turn left, wondering what he's running to, or running from.

CHAPTER
TWO

Doctor Okada doesn't come to see me when he's supposed to. At first I try to tell myself he's running late, or something came up and he had to change his appointment, but no one tells me this, or anything else.

On the day after Okada missed his appointment, my door opens and I see Tinora standing there, hands on hips and a smirk on her face.

"What are you doing here?" I ask.

"Did you really think you could get me in trouble by tattling to your doctor pal?"

"He caught us fighting, Jane." Her head jerks back like I slapped her. It dawns on me that in addressing her by name, I've taken away some of her power. She's not a mystery, or incognito, she's just a woman with a bad attitude.

"Doesn't matter what he saw. I told the boss you seduced him and he should be removed from your case."

My eyes go wide, rage boiling in my gut. Doctor Okada is the only person who has shown me kindness here, the only decent one among them. For her to do that...

My hand is around her neck before I realize it. I step her back against the wall as I feel her pulse thrum against my fingers. I use my other hand to pin down her arm as it tries to grasp her weapon. I stare into her beady eyes and say, "Doctor Okada is the only reason I haven't already snapped your puny neck. You have the heart of a monster and all I want right now is to rip it out to see what color it bleeds. But I won't. Because thanks to Okada, I'm better than that. I'm better than you."

I release her neck and step away from her. She sputters, gasps for air, then coughs when it hits her lungs. I relish the sound of her pained breathing. Okada hasn't changed me *that* much.

From the hall outside my room I hear a slow clap. A figure comes around the door: the doctor. Not the one who's been helping me all these months; no, this is the doctor who was trying to save Thoa. The one who let him die instead.

I clench my fists at my sides. It takes every ounce of restraint I have not to pounce on this man, this intruder. He's come into my home uninvited and only brings *bad*.

"That was impressive. Truly. Such self-restraint. You've almost made it to the point we expect children to be at before we let them socialize with others. Very, very good."

Tinora says, "You see, Shaw? I told you she's a nightmare."

"So I see. The reports made it seem like she was much further along."

"Like I told the boss, Okada has something weird with her and he's flubbing the reports to get her out of here."

"Your demonstration has definitely been eye-opening, to say the least. I'll report this to Clemont and let him make the decision on what we need to do next."

"Next?" I ask. "You need to let me go. I've cooperated with you, I've learned how to manage my anger, and now I'm ready to leave."

Tinora and Shaw laugh together until Shaw says, "You *actually* believe that, don't you? Your delusions are spectacular, I must admit. But honestly, Miss Kennedy, you shouldn't expect to merge with the general populace for some time. Your work with Okada has produced minimal results, so it's time to take it to the next level."

OVER THE NEXT THREE MONTHS I DISCOVER THAT THE "NEXT LEVEL," according to Shaw, involves torture. He doesn't actually call it that, none of them do. But when they come to take me to the room where they shock me until I'm drooling, I can see in their eyes that they don't like what they're doing. Except Tinora. Escorting me to the torture chamber is probably the best part of her day.

One of the guards has the decency to look ashamed whenever he comes for me. He's older than me, probably close to his fourth decade. I wonder if his age has made him softer than the others. In his eyes is kindness, even as he's tying my wrists.

He's my favorite and in my head I call him Vivon. *Alive.* Because he's the only one who will be when I'm done.

I haven't yet decided how I'm going to kill the others. But I spend hours and days and weeks thinking about it, daydreaming and planning and *wanting.*

It's easier to think on death, to plan and prepare for when it comes, than to think of the life I could've had on-world. I lived with the Raiders; alas, they weren't always the nicest people around, but they were the family I made for myself. I had Rego, my father for more than a dozen years. I had Thoa, though I didn't know it at the time, and he could've been the great love of my life. I had warm nights in the desert, cool mornings by the mountain streams, walks through dappled forests and hikes beside sheer rock walls that led to vast canyons. We traveled it all, and it was beautiful.

But it wasn't enough for me. I wasn't satisfied as a hunter, dealing death to bring sustenance to the Raiders. No, I just *had* to be a life-bringer. And Krew had to put himself in front of me and give me the opportunity.

My step falters and I stumble. The time from finding Krew through the trials flashes in front of my eyes and the real world parts to show me all the things I try to avoid. Finding Aunt Rachel, saving the children, befriending Coco, learning I have a half-sister —the good floods in and my breath catches in my throat. But I know what comes next and I brace myself against the wall as my vision fills with blood.

Nukiki. The sky pirates.

The man in the marketplace. Nigel's guards.

The mazulla fighter and all those bodies on level one.

Morian and Heinrich. Borah. Clea. Allon.

Rekka.

Thoa.

The bodies pile up in my mind. Maybe the weren't all at my hand, but some of them would be alive if I hadn't captured Krew. Thoa would be alive.

I let my fingers trace along the paper star on the inside of my opposite sleeve. I keep it with me all the time now. Tinora almost found it once. I can't let them find it. It's the only thing left of Thoa. I will protect it with my last breath, protect it in the way I couldn't protect him.

I pause. Vivon turned right when he should've turned left. I step around the corner, afraid of what this means. He is standing there, waiting, smiling. My eyes flick from him to the other man in the corridor, surrounded by dark gray metal and stale air: Doctor Okada. I can't stop my feet from running to him, throwing myself against him. I want to hug him but my hands are tied.

I feel him shake with laughter as I press against him. He asks, "Did you miss me?"

"What are you doing here?" I ask, verging on tears.

I stop myself before they fall though. No matter that he's the only friendly face I've known these long months, he's still a stranger. A wonderful, kind, perfect stranger and I'm so happy to see him. But part of me remembers, hold it quietly inside, keeps it secure to remind me—this could all be a trap. Okada could be the bait. I'm on their ground and they make the rules here.

"Get out of here, Jackson," Okada says.

"I could help you," Vivon says. *Jackson*, I correct myself but it doesn't feel the same on my tongue, doesn't have the reminder that he is untouchable, that he lives.

"That wasn't the deal," Okada says. "You're already going to be in a lot of trouble for this."

"For what? What's happening?" I ask, turning to Jackson.

He says, "We're getting you out of here."

His voice rumbles, like deep waters. I've never noticed. Hell, maybe I haven't heard it before. I smile at him, the widest, brightest smile I have, and then I swing my tied wrists towards him with all my strength.

He stumbles back, his hand going to his face. With a busted lip he asks, "What the hell? I'm trying to help you!"

"I'm trying to help you too. Now it looks like I attacked you, obviously." I turn to Okada, who looks nearly as horrorstruck as Jackson. "Did you really not think of that?"

Okada shakes his head. "We don't really do that here. Fighting, I mean."

"I've gathered," I say.

Jackson laughs, a slow chuckle at first, that gains speed with each second. "She's right. It should be believable."

"I mean, I've had the area cloaked with a privacy field. No one will know what happened to you anyway," Okada says.

"Right, but if I look like I put up a fight, maybe I can avoid the punishment."

I laugh, unable to control it. "I can't believe you planned a rescue without thinking about this."

Okada's cheeks flush. "Well excuse me for not being an expert in prisoner extraction."

They laugh at that. I chuckle with them, a little too late and a lot too disingenuous. I don't know why it's funny. But after a second, my laugh almost sounds real to my ears. A little too loud, too high-pitched, but at least I know I can still do it. For the first time in months, I let a glimmer of hope slip into my heart. I almost feel human again.

"Okay," I say, after a moment, "let's do this right. Jackson, you need to get on the floor. I'm going to tie you up."

He slides down the curved wall and slumps expertly. If I didn't know better, I'd guess this wasn't *his* first prisoner extraction. I rip off a strip of cloth from my pants and tie his wrists.

"Jeez, Nova, not so tight."

I look at him for a moment, right into his soulful brown eyes. He's never used my name before, never indicated he knew it. But of course he does. He probably sat in his quarters watching me almost die, betting on who would survive longest in the trials. Or maybe he didn't. Maybe some of them are good.

"They have to be tight to be believable," I mutter, pulling my eyes away from him.

The thought that some of the star-people might be good has suddenly put me in a strange mood. It's easier to think of them as terrible. *Just like they think of the on-worlders as animals.*

When I stand, Okada hands me a change of clothes. The knee-length robe is smooth and colorful, a multitude of greens. I put it on over the prisoner clothes I've worn since I got here. I slip out of my torn pants and put on the slim black ones he's given me.

"You sure this won't draw attention?" I ask, pointing at the bright garment.

He smiles. "Not where we're going."

I look down at Jackson and he gives me a smile. "Give 'em hell, kid."

"Thanks," I say, smiling back. "For this. For caring. For not being like everyone else."

He nods. "There's more of us than you might think. Don't forget that."

I feel like he's reading my soul, pulling out each terrible thing I want to do like it's written on my face. But he doesn't hate me for it; instead, he reminds me that even here there are people, not just extensions of the Règle.

Okada takes my arm and leads me away down the corridor. As we walk, he touches his ear and says, "We're moving. Keep the screen until we get to the parade."

"Parade?" I ask, my heart hammering wildly. "Won't that be full of guards?"

He nods. "Calm down. We'll be invisible to them."

Trust him, I tell myself. Because what else can I do?

I hear the parade before I see it. Voices filter through the corridor, rising and falling in a wave that pulls me under the current. I'm compelled to move faster, to run towards the sound, but Okada keeps me steady. His hand on my arm is a reminder of where we are, who we are, and I slow my steps to mirror his. He is not worried.

When we turn left at the next intersection, I see why. The corridor widens into a vast room, bigger than any I've ever seen, full of people moving and dancing haphazardly. They're drunk, they're happy, and they're all dressed in clothes as bright as mine.

Okada stops just before we enter the room. He takes off his coat and turns it inside out, revealing his own bright costume. He touches his ear again and says. "Give us to the count of three."

We start off again and I count it off in my head. We're in the crowd as I get to three. There's a *pop-pop-pop* followed by an explosion overhead. I throw myself to the ground, my head swiveling as I search for somewhere to hide. My eyes land on a table at the edge of the room and I start crawling towards it. I'm certain the guards have found us and I need to find a weapon. Anything to use against them, to give us a chance to get away—anything so I don't feel powerless.

But then I hear the people around us laugh, *ooh* and *aah*. I look over my shoulder to see Okada in the middle of the crowd, staring up. I follow his gaze to the showers of light sprouting and dying overhead, streams of fire crackling and dancing above the windows.

I find my feet and give a look around me. No one seems to be paying attention to me. I step close to the doc and whisper, "What's happening?"

"Fireworks," Okada says. "To celebrate Chinese New Year."

I knit my brows, trying to work out what he's talking about but the words just don't make sense. I don't bother asking again. I jump with each fresh *pop*, but I continue walking, directed by his warm hand.

When we get to the other side of the room, Okada says, "I'm going to put my arm around you. Lean into me and keep your head down. This is the worst of it."

I do as he says, though my eyes still look up, searching the space around us. It's full of people milling about, though not as crowded as the room before. There are people in fancy clothes pushing their way through the crowd, groups of friends and families laughing and eating as they walk towards the celebration, guards patrolling and trying to control the throng, couples perched against the walls, absorbed in this moment with each other.

The sight of them sends a rush of pain through my chest. Who are they that they should be able to live happily while I watched my love die?

Then we've turned a corner and the traffic dies. There are still people roaming through, but not nearly as full or as loud. A few more turns that I don't keep up with and we've reached a door. Okada swipes a card in front of it and it opens. He pushed me in and closes it behind us. He flips up a small panel by the wall and slides his hand over a key panel. I watch the panel flash red and he puts his hand on top of it, releasing a hiss of breath when it then turns green.

"Yosh, is that you?" a voice calls from the other room.

I recognize that voice. *No*, I think, shaking my head. *There's no way...*

But then he comes around the corner and with a chuckle he says, "Nova, so glad to finally—"

His words are cut off by my hands around his throat. I shove him against the wall, my face a mere inch from his. My voice comes out in a growl: "Baz, you prick. What is this?"

I dimly register Okada at my arm, trying to pull me away. But he doesn't, he can't. New hands are at my other side, jerking my elbow. Stronger than Okada. The person's hand stretches over mine, prying at my fingers curled around Baz's throat.

Dark skin, absorbing all the light around it to make it glow.

My grip on Baz loosens, slips to nothing. I let him go so I can turn around to look at Krew.

Krew.

I'm in his arms and we're both crying and holding each other and laughing before I've fully registered that it's him, that he's really here. We embrace so long I lose track of everything else. When we break apart far too soon, he puts his hands on my face and smiles at me in a way that lets me know I'm safe. I'm loved.

He whispers my name, so soft, so tentative. It's almost like he's afraid I'm not really here, like I'll disappear if he's not careful. Or maybe he's not sure all of me is here. He's not wrong; part of me is on-world, part in the room where Thoa died, part in the white room, part on the torture table. I don't know if those parts will ever find their way back to me or if there will always be jagged cutouts where once I was whole.

I smile at him and ask, "How is this happening?"

Krew takes my hand and leads me into the room I haven't seen yet. The walls are a muted gray—not the cold color like the corridors, but deep and warm. There's a red sofa and accents of red and white throughout the room.

This isn't Krew's home, I'm certain; he is bright yellow and orange, the heat of summer on your skin, the tickle of sand between your toes as you sit by the lake after a swim.

I don't think it's Okada's either. The doctor is mountain streams and frosted heather, the icy wind still lingering at the start of spring when life is first starting to bud on the trees.

That leaves…

"Baz," Krew says.

My eyes cut from Krew's gaze to the man standing across the floor rubbing his raw-red neck. Baz can barely speak, but still manages to sound sarcastic when he croaks, "You're welcome."

I nearly start for him again but Krew pulls me down on the couch and puts his arm around me. Though my eyes are still on Baz, I see Okada wince from the side of my vision. I don't know why, don't know what's happening, but I don't like seeing that look after all he's done for me.

I take a deep breath to steady myself and tear my eyes from Baz. I sit up and put a little distance between me and Krew so I can see him properly. The look he gives me makes it clear he isn't sure if he should let me have more than an inch of space.

I say, "I'm fine. I'm not going to hurt him. Not yet, anyway."

Krew chuckles and glances to Baz. "That's the best you're going to get."

"Wouldn't expect anything else," Baz says.

I feel the fire ignite in my gut again as soon as I hear his voice. I'm in the trials, listening to his taunting as he leads us to death, one by one. The star-people were faceless, nameless as we fought for their entertainment, but they had a *voice*.

I shake away the chills his voice sends through me. I want to hurl myself at him, crack his head against the floor until he looks like Rekka. But I stay put. I need to know what's going on and I won't get answers if I kill him.

I take a deep breath and ask, "Where are we? Why is *he* here?"

Baz smirks and says, "*He* is here because *he* lives here."

"Yeah, obviously," I say. "The place is a clear reflection of you —gross."

Krew chuckles and says, "Now, now, Baz is helping us. Probably not the best idea to insult him."

I nod. "Fine. But why is he helping us? He's terrible."

Doctor Okada says, "He's not as bad as you think. Everything you know about him is based on the game. It's all for show."

"And you know him well?" I ask. I don't know why I find it so hard to believe that a kind person like Okada could befriend someone like Baz. Then I remind myself, Okada could be just as bad.

Baz steps across the room to stand by the doctor. And then I see it. Their eyes, their chins, they're jet-black hair. I whisper, "Brothers."

Okada nods. "I know you think of Baz as the face of the trials, and after all you went through, I understand how you feel."

I growl, "You have no idea how I feel."

The doc presses his lips into a thin line, his eyes going soft. "You're right. I don't. But I know Baz. The whole time he was directing the show, he was trying to keep you safe."

"Bullshit," I spit.

"It's true," Krew says. "He had to be careful and make it look like he was messing with us, but he's been on our side the whole time."

I narrow my eyes as I look at Baz. He may have Krew and Okada fooled, but not me. There's nothing he can say that will convince me.

Baz kneels in front of me. "I'm truly sorry for all I put you through. It was the only way." I shake my head to argue but he presses on, saying, "And I'm sorry that we had to continue to hurt you these last few months when my brother would visit you."

My eyes flick to Okada, but he doesn't meet my gaze. I look back to Baz and ask, "What are you talking about?"

"We needed you to seem reformed and they insisted you cut ties with your old life. So we forced you to say it, over and over."

The hammering of my heart in my chest is so forceful, I can barely manage to breathe. *Thoa is dead, Krew is in prison. Thoa is dead, Krew is in prison.* But Krew is here. I stare into Baz's dark eyes and barely manage to whisper, "Say it."

"Thoa," Baz says. "He's alive."

CHAPTER
THREE

I jerk awake on Baz's couch, the sight of snapping teeth fading from my mind. The nightmares never change. Someone has covered me with a blanket as soft as a jumprat pelt. The room is dark aside from a row of tiny orange lights running along the top of the wall. I don't know how I got here. I sit up as quietly as I can, replaying the evening in my mind. I must've fallen asleep while we were talking. The last thing I remember is learning that Thoa is alive.

Of course he is, I think. If he was dead, I would know. I would *feel* it.

I hear the rasp of voices in the other room. I move as the Raiders taught me, the practice coming back as easy as breathing, though my muscles are weak from disuse in the white room.

I creep to the edge of the next room, peeking around to see Okada and Krew at a table, heads bent close as they whisper. I can't make out their words, but I can see the worry on Okada's face. Krew reaches forward and places a hand on his cheek, caresses it. Okada closes his eyes, seeming to relish the touch. Krew closes the gap between them, presses his forehead against Okada's. The movement tips Okada's lips greedily towards Krew's and they press together, softly, then with urgency.

I slip back towards the sofa, careful not to be heard. I don't want to disturb the moment between them; also, I don't want them to know that I saw them. Knowing what I know about the star-people, the way they take private moments and turn them into entertainment, I don't want to be like them.

I think back to the trials, to the dinner party and the secrets. It was months ago, but every moment is etched into my brain as if it was yesterday. Krew's secret was that he came to meet me, despite what his fiance said, or perhaps because of it. Could Okada be that fiance?

It would explain why he smiled when he heard Baz's voice over the speakers that first time, why he looked up and said he was sorry...it also explains why he trusts Baz—the brother of his lover. Has he been working with them this whole time? To what end?

I lean my head against the arm of the sofa as the questions swirl around inside my head. Nothing makes sense, no matter how much I think about it, and eventually I resolve myself to uncertainty and let my mind slip into a much-needed sleep.

A KNOCK ON THE DOOR ROUSES ME FROM MY SLUMBER, WAKING ME before the dream-teeth could get me. Baz walks past, bare but for the striped shorts covering his rear. I follow him with my eyes, tracing the contours of his shoulders, the muscles in his back, the hard lines of his calves.

I let a hiss of breath between my teeth, cursing myself. I refuse to be attracted to him. He may be pleasing to look at, but his insides are rotten.

He comes back into the room, Okada trailing him from the door. I assumed the doc spent the night here with Krew, but he must've left at some point to refresh himself. Unlike his brother, Okada is dressed in a suit, his hair combed to the side, his eyes bright and eager. Baz scrubs a hand through thick hair, making it stand on end. He barely looks alive, much less awake.

"Why are you here?" Baz mumbles.

Okada furrows his brows. "To get her ready, of course."

"Ready for what?" I ask.

Baz ignores me, squints at his brother. "It couldn't wait a few hours?"

"It's a quarter past second bell. How late do you normally sleep?"

Baz shrugs. "I'm not on a schedule."

Okada rolls his eyes and says, "You should get dressed. We've got a lot to do. Where's Krew?"

"Bedroom," Baz says, wagging his brows. The jest sends a smile across his face, waking up his features. He crosses to the bedroom and leans inside. A few seconds later he says, "No, sorry, he's *not* in the bedroom. I don't know where he is."

"You let him leave?" Okada asks, fear coloring his voice.

"I didn't *let* him do anything. He's a grown-ass man. Besides, aren't you the one in charge of knowing where he is? Or are you still...iffy?"

"Why can't he leave?" I ask, unsure I want to be privy to the status of their relationship.

Okada glances down at me as if he'd almost forgotten I was there. He grimaces for a second before saying, "He can, but he shouldn't. At least not for awhile. Not while they're searching for you."

"I still think keeping them here together is a bad idea," Baz says. "If he's a suspect, they'll follow him. And if they follow him here..." He waves his hands in my direction.

I frown. "Baz has a good point." They both look at me like I sprouted an arm from my forehead. I smile at their expressions, unable to help myself. "Believe me, I never thought I'd agree with something he said, either."

Baz smiles at me, and it's the first time his face has seemed genuine. I hate it.

"So maybe Krew could stay here and I could go somewhere else," I say, smiling back.

I expect Baz to be annoyed, but he just laughs. "You're spunky, I'll give you that. It's easy to see why everyone likes you."

My eyes flick to Okada, but his face remains impassive. It bothers me that I can't read him. Even the slight changes on his face are unreadable. He's closed off, not just from me, but from everyone. I wonder if he was always that way, or if it's new. I don't know which is worse.

"It's fine," Okada says as he moves to sit beside me. He lowers a bag to the floor and adds, "We don't need him for this anyway."

I look between them, trying to figure out what's going on. Baz shrugs and walks to the bedroom. While he's gone, Okada dumps the bag's contents on the floor. I don't recognize most of the stuff, but I do see a mirror and comb in the mix.

When Baz returns, he's dressed in a plain white shirt and loose tan pants. He sits on the floor and runs his hand over the stuff Okada brought. Baz picks up some scissors and says, "Let's start with the hair."

I DON'T RECOGNIZE THE GIRL LOOKING AT ME. HER HAIR IS SHORT, shaved on the back and sides, with longer white-blonde curls piled on top. I reach up and touch the hair, following the movement of my hand in the mirror to make sure it's really me.

Raiders don't prioritize looks and I've never given much thought to my appearance. But now, looking at this stranger, I miss my long red hair. The Okada brothers are right, though; without my hair, I'm unrecognizable.

Baz walks into the small room where I'm sitting and staring at myself. He hands me a small cup and says, "Wasn't sure if you like tea or not."

I hold the faintly brown liquid to my nose and inhale notes of cinnamon and cardamom.

"Chai," he says. "It's Yosh's favorite."

"Yosh? That's Doctor Okada's name?"

He smiles. "Our parents were traditionalists. They researched our on-world heritage in the archives and came up with Yoshinori and Tsubasa."

I nod, though I only understand part of what he says. Instead I ask, "Where is Yosh?"

"He went to find suitable clothes for you."

I feel a shiver run up my spine as I realize they've left me alone with him. They trust him to keep me safe, and they must trust me not to hurt him while they're gone. I take a breath, suppress the thoughts of the trials that come unbidden to me at the thought of hurting Baz.

I meet his eyes in the mirror. He's watching me, a frown tugging at the corner of his lips. I wonder if he knows the struggle happening behind my eyes. After a moment of silent staring, he looks away. Like his brother, I can't seem to read the expression on his face. If I had to guess, I'd think it was remorse.

"While Yosh is out, I'm going to work on your face."

I look back to the mirror, run my hand over the face before me. "What's wrong with my face?"

"Nothing," he chuckles. "We're just trying to make you blend in better until we figure out what our next step is."

He spins my stool until I face him. He withdraws a small tube from the drawer of the vanity and presses a button. A gentle *whir* comes from the device and he presses it to my eyebrow, saying, "Hold still."

"What does—"

"Shhh," he says. "I said be still."

I try not to move while he runs it over and under my eyebrows before moving it above my top lip. When he turns it off, I turn back to the mirror. The change is minor, but I can see the difference. The tiny hairs above my lip are gone. My brows aren't as thick as before. They're still full, only the shape looks purposeful instead of random.

"You're going to learn makeup now." I must give him a discouraging look because he presses a hand to my shoulder and says, "Don't worry, it's easy. It will help you look more like an offworlder."

Baz rummages through the bottom of the closet in his washroom until I hear a faint, "Aha." He brushes off the screen on a strange circular device.

"What's that?"

"Only the greatest invention of the twenty-ninth century." He holds it out to me and I look at my face on the screen. I look mostly the same, only my cheeks and lips have a pink tint. He pushes an arrow on the screen and my face changes—neon yellow eyeshadow, a trio of thick black lines trailing from the corner of my eyes, and fuschia lipstick making my lips into a square.

Another flick of the screen and the top of my face looks like a spotted pouncer, thick circles of black surrounded by tan and yellow. I laugh. "That looks wild."

Baz smiles, shrugs. "Some people are into the wilder looks. It mostly depends on which part of the station you're from. This quadrant tends to be a bit more conservative, but there are parts that consider the animal prints mild."

"Really?" I ask, squinting at my reflection. "Do you think I should wear something like this?"

He laughs. "Oh, stars no. It would hide your face, but that's what they *expect* you to try to do."

I nod. His logic is sound. "What do you recommend?"

Baz flips through a few screens, then several more. Finally he stops on one that still looks like me, only elevated. My face looks contoured, taking focus from my sharp chin and drawing it to my eyes. My lips are glossy, a shade darker than their natural color, and a thin wing is drawn out from my lined eyes. A dusting of gold above my eyes and a bit of mascara give me a sophistication I would've never achieved on my own.

"Yes?" he asks.

"I love it," I say.

He flips the device to the opposite side from the screen and holds it against my face. I feel a tickle against my skin and the device beeps. Baz pulls it away and I'm staring in the mirror at this new girl in full makeup. The image takes me back to Aeroport, when Permilla fixed my hair and makeup before we went to the Mayor's party. She helped me fit the role of Thoa's wife. What I wouldn't give to be back there right now, Thoa by my side.

The thought of Thoa sends a spasm through me and it's all I can do to keep from crying. I try to think of something else, anything else, but Thoa has taken root in me and nothing else will fill the space.

Baz kneels in front of me and wipes at the tears I was trying not to shed. "You okay?"

I tense at his touch. He is not my friend and I do not trust him. But I hurt, I hurt so much, and I need to feel the touch of another person. I lean against his hand on my cheek. The tears are falling in earnest now and I'm not fooling either of us. Baz pulls me against him until we're both kneeling on the floor. My tears soak into the white cloth on his shoulder, smearing the black mascara we just used. He rocks me back and forth, cradling my head against him as he soothes softly into my ear.

I don't know how long we sit that way, but at some point the tears start to subside and I realize I'm shivering. As I pull away, Baz reaches up and pulls a robe from a hook on the wall. He drapes it over me, then hands me a wad of tissue.

"I'm sorry," I say, pointing to his shoulder as I dab at my face.

He presses his lips together in a smile, shaking his head. "Don't worry about it."

"I'm usually better about controlling my emotions."

"You want to talk about it?"

I shake my head. I can't talk to him about Thoa, not without remembering all the things he put us through in the trials. That version of Baz doesn't reconcile with the man sitting in front of me, and I don't want them to. This Baz is kind.

He swallows. "I can't imagine how hard it must be for you. Taken from your home, separated from everyone you know, tormented, afraid for your life."

"Thanks for the recap," I say with a chuckle.

He puts his hand on mine and says, "I'm serious, Nova. You've been through it. It's okay to take a minute and let yourself hurt and cry and whatever else you need to do."

"Thanks," I nod. After a moment I add, "You know, you're pretty good at being a friend when you're not being an ass."

He smirks. "Don't get used to it."

Baz helps me up and cleans my face, puts cream under my eyes, then has me practice the makeup on my fresh face. I'm too heavy with the blush and he wipes it away with a laugh, but I do okay with the rest. When I'm finished, we stare at my reflection and Baz seems satisfied with the results.

"Not bad for your first time."

"You're a good teacher."

"Well, I had a lot of practice," he says, his smile turning sad. He looks at me, and seeing I don't understand, he explains, "I was born wrong-bodied."

The wording is unfamiliar, but I know what he means. "Mazu-lyr," I say. "It's the Raider word."

He tries to word on his tongue and smiles at me. "I'm glad you understand. I wasn't sure you would."

"Of course," I say. "But I don't understand how you became...right-bodied." I think to the Raiders, to Leer and the way he would bind his chest. We knew he was a man, no matter what his body looked like.

I stare at Baz's chest, though it is covered. He wasn't wearing a shirt earlier, but it was not bound as Leer's.

He catches my eyes in the mirror. I'm suddenly filled with guilt, though his face bears no anger or hurt. He says, "It's easier here, to change, though not everyone does. I can't imagine it's easy on-world for something like that."

I shake my head, but I don't really know. Leer was a Raider—nothing is easy for a Raider.

CHAPTER
FOUR

K rew returns shortly after we finish our makeup lessons. Baz and I are settled on the couch sharing a bag of crunchy things called chips. He stops in the doorway, his eyes shifting between our faces. I watch a look pass over his features, but I can't place it.

He clears his throat and says, "Well, you two look cozy. Thick as thieves now?"

I furrow my brows, unsure what he means. I know thieves, most of the Raiders, in fact, but they are not thick. They are muscled sometimes. Perhaps Krew is complementing our muscles.

I lose the thought when I see someone peer out from behind him. "Ivy?"

I jump to my feet and run to her. My sister and I haven't known each other long, but the sight of her delights me. The last time I saw her was ten months ago when I slipped her a piece of paper in the market to ask for help distracting the guards in the City of Trials. She did, but I never got a chance to thank her.

"I can't believe you're here," I say, pulling back to look at her. She's taller now, still not as tall as me, but closer than she was.

"Me?" she asks. "What about *you*? You're the one who's been in hiding for months."

I bite my lip, holding back the retort that pops into my head. I don't want to talk to her about my time in the room, locked away from everyone except the voices that crept into the silence.

She runs a hand over my new blonde locks. "But girl, this is working. Maybe I need to hide out here for awhile."

I wince. I know she's trying to make things light, but my insides squirm at her words.

Baz says, "Let's get back to where you tell us why you're here."

He's looking at Krew when he asks, not Ivy, and his words send a prick of worry through me. I was so happy to see her, I didn't think of the trouble we might be in if anyone saw her come in. But Baz did.

"Don't worry," she says. "I hacked our trackers so no one knows either of us are here."

"If someone saw you—"

"They didn't. We were careful," Krew says.

"Besides, you need me," Ivy says with a shrug.

Baz raises his brows but doesn't say anything else. Instead, he and I watch as Ivy sits in the floor in front of us and fishes into her bag. She withdraws a thin bracelet like they're all wearing. The sight of it starts my stomach doing flipflops.

I don't realize I've stopped breathing until Krew sits down and puts his arm around me. "You're okay," he says. "It's not a real one. It's just to help you blend."

I focus on the circles he's rubbing on my back and let my breathing match the rhythm. Ivy's words drop into my ears like bricks. "I mean, technically it's a real one. It will monitor where she is and all that, it just won't have her name on it."

"Wait," Baz says, "we're giving them a way to track her?"

"Nope. We're giving them a way to track whoever she becomes."

"That seems like a bad idea," he says, brows raised.

Ivy smirks. "A worse idea is to let them see her moving through the halls and not be able to check her deets like they do everyone else."

"How often does that happen?" Krew asks. "I mean, we're citizens."

Ivy chuckles and shakes her head. "You're a smart guy, usually. But damn, that's a foolish question."

Krew and Baz look at each other, then back to Ivy. I want to laugh at them, at the situation, but there's something very un-funny at what she's trying to tell them. I say, "They watch you. They keep track of everyone, citizens or on-worlders. Living up here doesn't make you special."

Ivy nods and I watch the realization set in for the guys. Krew's face grays, turns to ash. Baz's mouth is a small circle, his eyes wide. It would be comical, if it wasn't so sad.

"What name do you want?" Ivy asks, drawing my attention back to her.

I stammer, "What?"

"For your bracelet," she says, not looking up. She has a rectangular device attached to the bracelet and she's typing away on the letters. I couldn't guess what any of it means, except that she's fixing it for me. She stops typing and looks up at me. "We need to give you a name so I can fill in your background and establish a history for you."

I think of the name I used to get into the tower, the name of Hoshi's mother. "Alexis the Huntress," I mutter.

Ivy shakes her head. "Already on the radar. Once you used that to get into the tower, it was tagged as an alias on your profile. We need something new."

Most of what she's saying goes over my head. I glance to Krew, who seems to be coming back to himself. I shrug at him and he says, "We need a name that's common enough on the station to sound normal, but not so common that it sounds fake."

"What heritage are you giving?" Baz asks.

Ivy shrugs. She looks up at me and says, "Don't think it matters. There's not a lot of traditionalists anymore. Most people don't pay attention to what the earth was before."

Baz smiles and says, "I have an idea."

He gets up and goes to his bedroom. I hear him fumbling around for a minute before returning with a thick book. Krew asks, "What's that?"

"My dad used to collect old books about the world before the cataclysm."

He puts it on my lap and starts flipping through the pages. I've seen maps before, scratched on hide or cut into stone, but these are something else entirely. These maps are brightly colored blues and greens, lines criss-crossing where rivers were, land masses bigger than anything I know.

I stop on a page when I see a word I recognize. I trace my finger to the middle of the page, confused by what I see. "Dallas is a port. We traded there once. I mean, I didn't go into the city, but I know there wasn't this much land beneath it."

Baz says, "This is what it looked like hundreds of years ago, before the water took over the land below it."

I run my fingers along the land under it, wondering what those places were like so long ago. I stop on a town's name and say, "Cameron."

"I like it," Krew says. "It's not common, but I've heard it before."

"Cameron," Ivy says under her breath. She looks up at Krew and asks, "What was that guy's name that used to work for dad, with the big curly hair?"

"Liam?"

"Yeah. What was his last name?"

"Forsberg," Krew says.

She says, "Perfect," and goes back to typing.

I look at the guys, but they seem as lost to what Ivy is doing as I am. Baz keeps flipping pages in his book while she taps out a rhythm on her device. Krew looks around at us, his brows creasing. "Where's Yosh?"

"He went to get clothes for Cam," Baz says, not looking up.

I jolt at the new name. I've spent more than twenty years being *Nova*. How do I change and become someone else?

"Cam," Krew says, trying out the name. His lips turn up the edges. "I like it."

"Good, because she's stuck with it now," Ivy says.

She reaches the bracelet towards me, but all I can do is stare at it. I don't want the thing, I don't want to be part of this sick world they have up here, and that damned bracelet is a symbol of this whole messed up place.

Baz puts down his book and takes the bracelet from her. He turns to me and says, "Putting this on turns you into a different person, but you're still the same inside. You might be stuck in the wrong body for awhile, but it doesn't change your heart, and it isn't forever."

I turn towards Ivy as she sucks air against her teeth, like she thinks he's lying to me, but Baz puts one finger against my cheek and turns my eyes back to him. I say, "I'm scared."

"I know, I am too. But this will help keep you safe."

Everything in me screams against the cage that is Cam's body. I don't want to be trapped as someone else—hell, I don't want to be trapped at all. I want to roam and be free and live and die on-world, among the Raiders, among my family.

But I'm not among the Raiders. I'm sitting on the cold floor of a cold space station, orbiting my home. I look from face to face, weighing my options. I can run, but I won't make it far. And even if I somehow escape the guards, where would I go? I don't know how to get home.

Or I can trust them. They're mostly strangers, and one of them was actively my enemy until yesterday.

Despite everything in me—my instincts, my Raider training, my gut—saying this is a trap, I press my lips tight and lift my hand towards Baz. An overwhelming dread fills me as he slips the bracelet over my hand and I watch a tangle of sensors worm into my flesh until the metal is snug against my skin.

CHAPTER
FIVE

My name is Cameron Forsberg.
My name is Forsberg. Cam Forsberg.
Cameron. Cam to my friends.

I smile, point my finger at my reflection. It...doesn't work. I don't know how to be this girl. But I need to figure it out.

I step back to the front room. Ivy is curled into the corner of the couch tapping on her device while Baz wears black goggles over his head and seems to mime shooting a gun. I peek around the corner where Krew and the doc are making dinner. It's strange to watch them. They're tentative with one another, unsure.

I understand that. It must be hard for Yosh to reconcile his feelings with the man who left him to go on-world to meet someone else. Flashes of our time in the woods fill my mind without warning, sending warmth crawling up my skin. I shake my head, shake away the memories. I glance up at Okada, realizing he must've watched what happened. And Krew...

He knew about the cameras.

When we were together, he knew his fiance would see it. What does that mean? Is that a sign of his feelings for me or his disregard for Yosh?

I sigh. It doesn't matter. My feelings for him weren't real. At least that's what I keep telling myself. I love Thoa. Thoa is alive. So Krew is out of the picture. I can't have both. Thoa told me that himself.

But I lean against the doorframe as I watch them. Krew's dark skin seems to shimmer under the kitchen lights. His fitted shirt shows off the lithe figure underneath, the curve of his biceps and ripple of abs. His face is glass—sharp, but fragile—and I wonder how his cheekbones didn't cut me when I ran my finger across his skin.

But he is more than the handsome man before me. He is quick and funny, finding joy where none should be. He is kind and generous and *better* than the other star-people.

Or maybe I've only seen the worst of them. Maybe there are thousands like him aboard this station and I'll learn to love them.

No, I think, *that's not why you're here.*

I turn from Krew and Yosh, my fists clenching at my sides. There is kindness here, yes, but it will not sway me. I've come to destroy this place and make them pay for what they've done to the on-worlders, to my people.

My name is Nova Kennedy and I am a death dealer.

CHAPTER
SIX

W e walk through the Pœwani market and I count my steps. Four-hundred and thirty-seven from Baz's apartment to the center of this place. The market is steady, but not busy. I will not waste any steps avoiding the crowd today. Cameron does not like crowds. They make her nervous. So we try to come to market when there are less people.

Even with less people, I estimate there are around six hundred people moving around us, searching through the vendor's wares. We try to blend with them, though I'm not sure why. It's been seven weeks since my escape and there seems to be no pressure to find me.

Occasionally I'll see my picture flashing on the holograms in the corridors, red letters under my face spelling out their warning in dozens of languages. I see it in the old tongue—English, as Okada calls it—but there are many more I don't recognize. Yosh and Baz speak seven languages between them, Krew another three, including French, the tongue of Kavis the homesteader, and Ivy speaks six on her own. According to them, all the warnings are the same. I'm violent, dangerous, and any sighting should be reported with haste.

But no one looks at the holo-warnings as they pass. The longer they're there, the easier to ignore. I ignore them now, too.

We're shopping for *fun* today. That's what Baz says, anyway, but I don't see anything fun about it. Cam hates shopping. Nova does, too.

But we're here, moving from vendor to vendor. He says we need to find something for Krew to celebrate his upcoming birthday. I remember the tradition from my childhood; there was a cake with candles and a gift. A dolly. The one Rachel still keeps for me. I hope.

"How about this?" I ask, holding up a shirt.

It's weird, seeing all these things so readily available. I wore the same copper robes for years, and before they were mine they belonged to Rego's husband, Jasper.

Baz shakes his head and with a chuckle he says, "Cammy, no."

Cammy. He's the only one who has taken to calling me that. I hate it.

"I know you," the vendor says, wagging a finger. "You're Baz Okada."

Baz flashes his biggest, fakest grin. The man melts. I worry that we might not be able to get his tongue back in his mouth. Baz says, "That's right," and proceeds to weather the storm of compliments as everyone around starts to ask for autographs and pictures.

I slip away, out of range of their cameras and out of earshot of the praise. This is a regular occurrence when I go out with Baz. It was weird and a bit frightening the first time, but now I'm used to it. While he does his thing, I'll head off to my favorite bar in this district and he'll find me when he's done.

It wasn't hard to pick a favorite bar around here. There are only two in the market. The first is near the center, near where we are right now, but it's loud and crowded and well-lit. Horrible place to brood. The other, the one I like, is on the edge of the market where the less-scrupulous spend their credits. The name is in one of the languages I don't know, but when Baz screwed up his face and translated it to mean "Dirty Onion," I basically fell in love with the place.

The Dirty Onion is dark. Not just dimly lit, it's impossibly dark. The counter has a neon sign above it, a glowing teal glass that barely illuminates the cases of alcohol lining the shelves. Each table has a single spark on the table encased in something that keeps it flickering all the time. I don't understand that part, but I don't need to. The important part is that I can go there without worrying about who's watching, because no one can see anyone in the place.

The drinks, well, they're terrible. Probably because the bartender can't see what she's doing. I head over to order anyway. Bets is cute, from what I can see of her. She's tall and broad, thick in her shoulders and hips, with a roundness to her that makes me think she's warm. She never smiles, but her eyes smolder enough that I don't really need her to.

"Bets," I say, sidling up to the bar.

"Cam," she replies, tipping her chin at me. "Usual?"

I nod. She turns around to grab a couple bottles, giving me a prime view of her ass. I've never wanted to be a pair of pants as much as I do right now. I smirk. Nova never thought about things like this, but Cameron does. Cam thinks about it more than she should.

When she turns back to me, her eyebrows are doing that thing they always do when she catches me checking her out.

I blush, thankful the neon teal lighting hides it from her. She pushes my drink across the counter as I slide my bracelet to her credit-reader. After it beeps, I head towards a table in the corner. A crash echoes from somewhere in the room and I instinctively turn to look, despite the darkness.

I press into a wall—nope, that's just a very hard body—and turn around to see the stranger I've bumped into.

"Sorry about that, miss," he says, his deep voice rumbling through the chest I'm still pressed against.

My mouth drops open, but I can't find any words. Even in the blackness of the room, his eyes seem to glow with their strange, enchanting blue. His hair is long again, not as long as it was before we left camp, but the dark curls fall nearly to his chin.

His brows knit together. "Excuse me, but have we met before?"

My voice hitches and I'm unable to answer. I want to grab his face and pull it to mine, to whisper against him, "Yes, we've met, we're in love, I love you, you are part of me, my heart aches when I'm away from you, don't leave me again."

But I don't. I can't. I just stare into eyes of brightest blue, eyes that have known me better than anyone else, eyes that don't know me at all.

"Tabarus," a girl says, coming up beside him. She wraps her arm through his and says, "Watch where you're going, baby."

I turn away at her approach, press back into the room, craving the darkness. They don't follow. I watch their outlines as they reach the door, letting in the light from outside.

Twenty minutes later, the seat beside me droops as Baz sits down beside me. "Sorry about that," he coos. He must get a glimpse of my face in the flicker at our table because his tone changes and he asks, "What's wrong?"

"I—I just saw Thoa."

"What?" he asks, turning to search the dark room.

"He's gone. With a girl. His girl."

Baz sucks air between his teeth and says, "Damn. Sorry, Cammy."

"I know her," I say, my voice cracking. "She was one of my guards. Jane."

Tinora.

She tortured me for months. Now she has Thoa. One way or another, I will get him back. And I will make her pay for all she's done.

CHAPTER
SEVEN

The walls are white, the floor is black, when these guards leave, the man comes back.

No, no. I shake my head. These walls are gray. ~~The guards will~~ there are no guards. The man is Doctor Okada and he is my friend. He's my *friend*.

Crack, crack, crack.

Blood blooms at the edge of my vision, but when I turn towards it there's nothing there.

This is what they've done to me. This is who I am after a year in their care. I stare up at the ceiling in Baz's apartment. He has painted it black, trying to disguise the part of the ship he can't hide. A laugh bubbles out of me, shrill, tangling with the sob I'm working to hold back. Everything on this ship is a lie. Including me.

I close my eyes and take a deep breath. I count in my head, as Rego taught me, until my pulse slows and the tension in my muscles slacken. I'm safe, I'm fine. Everything is fine.

Except they have Thoa.

I clench and unclench my fists, tangling them in the soft blanket Baz has put over me. It must've been Baz. He must've got me back to the apartment. I don't remember the walk back, the trip through

Pœwani, the four-hundred and thirty-seven steps back to Baz's apartment.

Maybe it isn't his apartment. Maybe they've decorated a room to look like it. Maybe I'm in custody again. Baz and Yosh, Krew and Ivy, all of them could be—

"Hey sweetie," Ivy says, entering the room and sitting on the edge of the bed. "Baz told us what happened. How are you feeling?"

My lips are so dry they're sticking together. My throat aches from the desert that lives inside me, dry and empty. But there are tears at the corners of my eyes, an oasis in this parched land.

Ivy puts her hand on mine and says, "Yeah, I get it. One time, I caught my girlfriend out with someone else when she was supposed to be at home sick. Ugh, I was so mad at her. But also hurt, ya know?"

I nod along as she talks, but her words are floating past me like whispers on the wind. My sister is sweet, she wants to make me feel better, but she doesn't understand. She wasn't there when Thoa looked me in the eyes but didn't know me. He didn't *know* me.

I toss the blanket aside, forcing Ivy to stand. She stops talking and just watches as I rise from the bed and stumble to the front room. I feel like a ghost haunting this place. Yosh and Krew's eyes turn to me as I pass them, but seem to travel through me, unseeing.

I reach the front door as Baz steps through. ~~He's going to hit me~~ He looks startled to see me there, but I shove past him into the corridor. He grabs my arm and tries to pull me back inside, but I'm strong. Even after all these months without exercise, without walking the land and hauling beasts in my skiff, I'm still powerful.

Baz is behind me in the doorway of the apartment yelling for the others. I run. I can't let them catch me. They want to protect me, they want to keep me safe, they want to leave me locked away. I try to remember that it isn't their fault, that they're doing the best they can. I'm sure it isn't easy for them either. But each step that carries me away from them makes it harder to remember their motives. Makes it easier to remember what freedom tastes like.

"No running!" a man bellows.

I slow my pace and glance over my shoulder. A guard is standing at the intersection I just passed, his eyes following me as his hands drops to the taser at his belt. I smile and throw my hand in the air, calling, "Sorry."

He nods, his hand still resting near his taser, but without the hardness on his face.

I keep going, twisting my way through the corridors. I wasn't paying attention when I ran, wasn't counting my steps. Probably doesn't matter anyway. They've never taken me more than five hundred steps from the apartment anyway. I need to keep going if I'm going to…

What? If I'm going to what? What the hells am I doing?

I look ahead to the markers of the next intersection. Blue-nineteen-square. Pœwani market is at blue-fourteen-square. I can go there. I don't know why I *should* go there, but I guess it doesn't really matter right now. I just need to keep moving. Get out of sight. Get away.

I follow the signs through the corridor until I reach the throng of people going into Pœwani market. They're everywhere, swarming the vendors like ants on a piece of fruit. I take a deep breath and throw myself into them. I move with the crowd, letting the press of bodies push me further in, away from the entrance.

The crowd winds through the market until we reach the edge. The Dirty Onion is a dozen yards away. I step towards it, but hesitate when I realize Baz will probably think to look for me there. I start to turn away when I feel a hand on my shoulder.

I freeze.

My instincts spring up, begging to be freed. I want to grab the hand and twist it off me. I want to bend it, break it, ruin the fine finger bones. I want to grab the knife that should be at my belt, whirl around and slash, release blood from flesh.

But I don't. I can't. To do so would most definitely draw attention, and of all the things I want, I don't want that. I plant a smile on my face and turn towards the hand.

"Bets," I stammer, surprise and relief flooding me when I see the bartender.

"Hey, Cam. Thought it was you."

She looks from my face to her hand, still on my shoulder. A blush creeps up her neck, coloring her pale skin pink. She pulls her hand away, strangely awkward in her movements. I've only ever seen her in the bar where she portrays confidence and ease; somehow, outside of her normal domain, she comes across as timid and unsure.

Bets brushes back a strand of her brown bob, tucks it behind her ear. "So," she says, her mouth curling into the closest thing to a smile I've seen from her, "headed back to the Onion? You left in a hurry earlier. Didn't even finish your drink."

"I was thinking about it," I say, shrugging my shoulders. "Unless you have a better idea?"

Her brows raise and her eyes return to their familiar smoldering gaze. "I could think of a few things."

She extends her arm to me and I take it, letting her lead me out of Pœwani in a direction I've never been before. I should count steps. If I need to get back here in a hurry, that's a sure way to know how far I've traveled. It's the only way I've been able to calculate distance on the space station. The intersections are marked to help with navigation, but they're not evenly spaced, so distance isn't trackable.

I should be counting steps. But I'm not. Instead, I listen to Bets tell a story about one of her customers. She laughs, and I join in a second later, hoping she didn't notice the hesitation. I don't want her to know that my laughter isn't easy, like hers. It feels nice talking to someone who doesn't know that I'm broken.

I'm not surprised when Bets takes me to her apartment. We both knew that's where we were going, though neither of us said it. Part of me knows I shouldn't go in, that I'm here because I need a place to escape from ~~the people who've been holding me hostage~~ my friends. But another part of me wants to go with her. We've been dancing around each other for weeks, but my heart was still tied to Thoa, tied to the love I feel for him. Seeing him today—seeing what's left of him—released me from the obligation. He doesn't remember me. Whatever has happened to him over this last year, he's lost to me. As much as it hurts, there's relief, too.

Bets leads me into her place. The door opens into the kitchen like at Baz's apartment, but unlike his, there's only one room attached to it. It's narrow, with bunkbeds pushed against one wall and two clothes chests against the other. Her apartment has none of the splendor or fine things that Baz's does, but it does have one thing his doesn't: a window.

I feel myself pulled to the rectangle of space between the chests. It's small, only about as big as my head, but through it I can see swirling white over blue waters, patches of land, a perfect sphere that sends a pang of homesickness through my gut.

"It's kinda cramped," Bets mutters.

I turn to her, unable to keep the smile from my face. "I like it."

I return my gaze to the window and feel her step up behind me. She's looking over me, staring at the world below, but now I'm finding it hard to concentrate with the way she's pressed against me. I feel the press of her breasts at my shoulder blades, the round-ness of her belly low on my back. She puts a hand at my waist and slides it down to my hips, sending a shiver through me.

There's no longer a thought of whether or not I want her; now, I *crave* her. I *need* her touch. In the window's reflection I see her smile.

WE ARE A TANGLE OF NAKED LIMBS ON HER BED WHEN HER ROOMMATE comes in. I startle, unsure of who he is, but she doesn't stop what she's doing. He smiles down at us and I smile back, twirling my hands in her hair while he watches. He raises his brows with a question and I tip my head in a nod.

He takes off his shirt and tosses it to the side of the room. He is tall and thick, not muscled, but still firm. His dark hair is shaved, with only a bit of stubble showing, but there are curls of black hair on his chest and a trail leading down into his pants.

His eyes are still on me, still making sure this is what I want. I reach towards him and grasp the button of his pants, pulling it loose and unzipping them. He smiles as they fall to the ground. He moves his hand to Bets, letting his fingers trickle down her back. She looks up, and when I smile, so does she.

I relish their touches, their skin on mine, the connection that comes from being touched, the pleasure of being wanted. We spend hours this way, resting and switching and sharing each other's bodies as if there will be no tomorrow. And if we're lucky, maybe there won't be. Just an endless night of being everything and nothing, wholly satisfied by another's touch.

I SLIP INTO MY CLOTHES IN THE NEAR-DARK OF THE ROOM. BETS IS curled on the bottom bunk, a soft snore whispering from her. I watch her while I zip up my boots. She is not what I expected. I thought her tough as a Raider, and perhaps on-world she would be. But here, in the quiet, in this intimate place, she is gentle. She is timid to act, but ferocious when given permission. She is a generous lover, taking pleasure in the pleasure of others. In another time, I might love her.

But this is not that time.

I glance to the top bunk, surprised to find her roommate watching me. There's something in his gaze that still feels hungry. I briefly wonder if he is ever satiated, or if his desires are forever-burning.

"She'll be sad in the morning," he whispers.

I don't know if he means because I'm leaving or some other reason. I don't ask. It wouldn't change anything either way. "Tell her..."

He nods. "I will."

I step out into the corridor and stalk off in the opposite direction from whence we came. I know I should go back to Baz's place, but I can't. Maybe I'm being cruel by making them worry, but I need to be away from them to figure things out. With Thoa lost to me and no way home, I need to figure out how to be Cameron.

There's no difference in the lighting, nothing to indicate that it is early morning. Station time is the same, no matter which quadrant you're in, and there are always people moving about on their own schedule. I pass a man with a raven tattoo stumbling down the corridor, drunk off his ass, while also passing a fetching mazulla mechanic on their way to work.

I'd never considered all the jobs that must occur in this place. There are vendors and bartenders, guards, mechanics, doctors, and...Baz...whatever he is. Ivy works for my dad at a security company that tracks anyone going from the station to the planet, but she also does hacking on the side without his knowledge, hence my fake tracking bracelet. How many more thousands of people are aboard doing thousands of other things, living their lives as best as they can?

I'm stuck on this thought when I get a sudden chill, a cold finger trailing down my back with the realization that someone is watching me. I glance around as casually as possible, but there's no one in front or beside me looking my way.

Turning right at the next intersection, I kneel down by the wall and pretend to adjust my boot. Dozens of people swerve around me, but none seem concerned with the frazzled girl at the edge of their sight. Except one. As I glance around the corner of the main corridor, I see him stumbling there, doing his damnedest to pretend he isn't following me.

I turn back around, my pulse quickening. The drunk I passed two corridors back. There's no way he could've kept up, except that he's clearly not drunk. But I know it's the same man, the same raven tattoo on his wrist.

My eyes flick around the corridor, looking for another way out. I could go back the way I came, try to find Bets' apartment again, but I made too many random turns and I don't think I could find it again. I can stick with the main corridor where there are more people around, but there are also more guards and more chances that I'll be noticed. Or I can try to get away. I don't know where any of these paths lead, but my instincts are telling me to make a run for it.

I finish with my boot and stand. I stretch a bit, cross back into the main corridor, then take off running down the path opposite. My boots clang against the metal, pounding in time with the thump in my ears. I skitter down another hall, and another, taking turns at random in the hopes that I confuse him.

He's still behind me—I can *feel* him—so I throw out a burst of speed and round the next corner. It's a dead end.

I slide to a stop in front of a curved glass window. For a second, I stare out into the black, searching for pinpricks of light that I know are there. I take a deep breath and turn to face him.

He's close to my height, with a thin frame built for running. Like Krew. His grayish-purple hair is long, pulled back from his face, but a couple strands have come loose while he chased me. He moves a hand to push back the hair, again showing the raven tattoo on his wrist. He looks up with eyes as green as summer grass, and panting a little he says, "Damn girl, you're fast."

"Not fast enough," I mutter.

Half of his mouth hooks up in a smile. The other side stays flat and I see a scar that seems to be holding that side of his face hostage. "Well, you didn't need to run from me anyway."

"A strange man starts chasing me through the corridors and I shouldn't run?" I ask, pursing my lips.

"I'm not that strange," he says with a shrug. He pulls a pair of gloves from his pocket and slides them on. "Besides, I'm here to help."

"Help with what?"

"Your plan. Your escape. Whatever you're planning."

"I don't know what you're talking about," I say.

He smiles that strange smile again. "Yeah, okay Nova."

I squint at him. "You're confused. My name is Cameron Forsberg."

"I'll call you whatever you want, as long as I get to help. You're not alone, Nova. There are several of us who want to help."

"This is just a misunderstanding," I say, holding my hands up to him.

He sighs. "I was afraid you'd say that."

He tosses something at me and I catch it. It's small, the size of a marble, but I don't know what it is. But I do know the air is suddenly thick. My head feels heavy and I'm struggling to stay upright.

As my body tips forward, the man steps in front of me. He catches me in his gloved hands. From faraway, like my head's under water, I hear, "I'm really sorry about this. It isn't how I wanted this to go. But don't worry. I'm going to take good care of you."

CHAPTER
EIGHT

In my dreams I am a bird. I am a raven, trapped on the wrist of a man. I flap with all my might, but I cannot escape. I claw at the man, at the veins at his wrist, until a red river pours from him. Still, I can't get away. As the life flows out, I feel my own strength fading. His blood tangles around my legs, my feathers are slick with it. He takes his final breath and it's then I realize that I am the man, and I am the bird, and I am the blood. We die together.

I gasp and sit up, eyes popping open. I gulp air greedily, thankful for each breath. As I start to come back to myself, I look around and try to figure out where I am. It's dark—no running lights here. There's an echo of sound that seems to be coming from overhead. I look up, but the darkness hides what's above me. Still, the heavy thumps sound like footsteps and I think I may be under the corridors.

The only thing I can see with any certainty is the chair I'm in. It's big and fluffy, brown, or maybe green. It's softer than it should be, than it looks. It's lying back with a footrest popped out of the front of it. That's when I realize my feet are strapped to it.

Amateurs, I think. They didn't even tie my hands.

I let my fingers crawl over the bindings on my legs, feeling for a release. But there isn't one. The strips aren't rope or cloth, not metal chains or something with a lock; honestly, I don't know what they are. As annoying as it is, I'm impressed. A little, at least. Raven-dude knew what he was doing, or he got lucky.

A light flickers at the edge of my vision and I turn my head to see a boy standing there. He's young, nine or ten, with light shaggy hair he shakes out of his eyes. He smiles at me with a strange brightness I've never seen before. *Unburdened*, I think.

He turns his head and yells, "She's awake."

I hear footfalls stomping towards me and raven-dude comes into the room. He ruffles the kid's hair, though the boy swats at his hand. Raven-dude's eyes are locked on me as he tells the boy, "Thanks, Miles. Go tell Alexis we'll be along shortly."

He opens his mouth to speak, but I don't give him a chance, "What is this? Why am I here?"

He smiles, a chuckle rocking him though he doesn't make a sound. "I told them this was a bad idea. You're not exactly the most understanding person around."

"You don't know a thing about me," I spit.

He nods. "I know way more than you think, but that's not important. This isn't about me, it's about you."

"What about me?"

He steps a little closer, blocking out the little bit of light so I can no longer see anything but a silhouette. "You're here for a purpose, Nova. And we want to help you figure it out."

HE TIED MY HANDS BEFORE RELEASING MY LEGS, AND NOW WE'RE walking in a dimly lit passage about a third of the width of the corridors. Raven-dude is behind me, urging my steps on with his presence. When I stop walking, he just stands there waiting. I can practically hear him smiling, though he doesn't say anything.

Fifteen minutes later the passage opens into a wide room. It's not vast like the markets or the gardens, but it's bigger than Baz's apartment, so that's something. There are more lights here, but not many. Instead of the electrical lighting like the rest of the ship, they have lit candles encircling the room. Within the circle of candles there are half a dozen people. There are others wandering around outside the light, but it's clear these six are the ones who matter.

Raven-dude leads me into the circle and someone brings me a chair. I stand there, refusing to sit, but he just smiles that half smile at me and I get annoyed that my resistance doesn't bother him.

When I sit, he bends to tie my legs to the chair. I kick up, my knee catching him in the face. He falls back, blood trickling from his nose. I smile at him now, treasuring the look of surprise on his face as he wipes blood off his top lip.

A slow rumble starts to come from him, a deep belly laugh, and soon each of them is laughing. My smile slides into a frown, then an all out scowl. What is wrong with these people?

"Might as well untie her hands," a soft voice says.

I look around the circle, finding the woman who spoke. She's old—like, really *freaking* old—with short white hair. She's small in stature, but I can feel everyone else in the room go still when she speaks, deferring to her. When my eyes meet hers...

I've seen them before.

As raven-dude unties my hands, I say, "We've met before."

She shakes her head, sadness creasing her brow. "You know my name, dear girl, but not me."

The raven-dude's words come back to me: *Go tell Alexis...*

"Alexis the Huntress," I breathe. "You're Hoshi's mother."

She nods, presses her gnarled hands together across her belly. "And who are you?"

I press my lips together, unsure what to say. After a moment I say, "You know who I am."

She shakes her head. "I know who you *were*, before they got ahold of you. I don't know who you've become."

"I'm still me," I grind out between my teeth.

"Who is Cameron Forsberg?" the man to her left asks.

I glance to him, to the thick puckered scar where his left eye should be, down his cheek. His skin is nearly as dark as Krew's, but it doesn't have the same glow. His right eye is brown, lovely, but not the same light-consuming darkness that Krew's is.

I bite my lip for a moment while I watch him. He's fidgety. He scratches at his hands, moves his fingers up and down along the mottled gray overcoat he wears, digs so hard at his thumb that it's rubbed raw and red. Everything about him makes me feel jumpy, like my body wants to imitate his. I don't like him.

I turn back to Alexis when I say, "Cameron helps me survive. Cameron is not a threat."

Alexis huffs. "Cameron isn't you."

"So what?" I ask with a shrug.

She sighs, but it's a different woman who speaks. She's sitting closest to me, her long legs spread in front of her chair like she's claiming the space around her. Her lips are painted bright red and turned in a sneer. "Told ya."

I take her in, the long black hair braided down her back, the muscled arms and broad shoulders, the massive chip on her shoulder. She's confident in a way that tells me she's not. Everything about her is there to intimidate others. I bet it works on most people.

"Listen sweetie," I say, turning up the honey in my voice in a way that makes me certain it'll undermine everything she's trying to do, "I don't know what you told them, or what you think you know about me, but trust me, you don't know a damn thing. I have been through hell this last year and I guarantee you don't know anything about it."

She pitches forward and is in my face faster than I can react. Almost too late I jump up, thankful that Alexis told them to untie me. She presses her chest against mine and tries to take another step to push me backwards. I don't budge.

"What is your problem?" I ask, pushing right back.

"You think you're the only one who's been through it? We've all been through it."

I roll my eyes. "Please," I say, stretching out the world. "You off-worlders don't know anything about what it's been like for me."

"Karina, sit your ass down," Alexis says, getting to her feet. She walks over and stands in front of me, and though I'm a foot taller than her, I flinch at her closeness. Karina doesn't scare me, but Alexis does.

"I'm sorry," I mutter.

She shakes her head. "What Karina is trying to say is that we all know what you've been through, because we've been there. We're not off-worlders. We came up through the trials. All of us."

Shit.

I look around at them, meeting each person's gaze. Alexis' has a hard glint in her eyes, but there's compassion as well; Karina glares at me, raven-dude is all smiles, the mazulla person beside him purses their lips and folds their arms, but doesn't openly hate me. The fidgety man with one eye has a question in his gaze that I can't answer. Beside him, a middle-aged woman gives me a sad expression out from under shaggy bangs; the guy beside her meets my eyes for only a moment before glancing away, uncertainty on his face.

I swallow hard against the tension building inside me. "What is this place?"

Alexis sighs. "You ask the wrong questions, girl."

She turns and walks back to her seat. To her back I say, "I don't know what you expect."

"We expect a warrior," raven-dude says. "We expect the girl from the trials."

I put my hands on my hips. "Why do you need her?"

The woman beside fidgety guy says, "For the same reason she needs us: to show the off-worlders that we aren't their toys."

"To break them," Karina says, smacking her fist into her other hand.

"How?" I ask, my voice cracking. "There are so many of them and this place is massive. What can a handful of us do against them?"

Alexis shakes her head. "Wrong question."

"Then what's the right question?" I ask, annoyance clear in my tone.

She smiles. "What *can't* we do?"

THE LITTLE BOY, MILES, LEADS ME TO A ROOM OFF THEIR MAIN MEETING area. There's a cot against the wall and a chair in the corner, a single candle and match on the floor by the makeshift bed.

He makes to scurry off but I stop him. "How do you fit into all this, kid?"

Miles smiles at me. "My grandma. The Huntress."

I raise my brows at this, but he just grins wider. I dismiss him with a nod and he skips away. He is a child of this place, and though he is a descendant of an on-worlder, he's never known the troubles of living on the planet.

I pace the room for a few minutes, unsure what to do. They haven't locked me in and I've seen no security, except for the fact that each of them made it through the trials and could probably put up a good fight. But just because they've given me faux freedom doesn't mean I'm allowed to leave.

With a heavy sigh, I plop onto the cot. Even if I left, where would I go? I ran from Baz's place, ran from Bets. I'm tired of running. Maybe these people can give me a reason to stand still.

Raven-dude is at the door of my cell-room, staring in at me. I roll my eyes and ask, "Do you ever give that smile a rest?"

Apparently he takes my words as an invitation, because he steps into the room and moves to the seat in the corner. He pulls it from the wall and spins it around so his chest leans against the back, his legs straddling it.

"What's the alternative? That frown that's always tugging your face down?"

I purse my lips. "I don't always frown. Only when I'm being held hostage."

His half-smile broadens on one side. "You're hilarious."

I quirk my brows in an appropriate "how so?" expression, but he just shakes his head. I don't get this dude. I ask, "So what's your deal? How do you fit in here?"

"Same as you," he says. "I won the trials, came up here, went through re-programming, but it didn't take. Osric found me stumbling down the hall one day and brought me here."

"Osric?" He scratches one hand against the other, imitating the fidgety way the man by Alexis had moved. I nod, "Ah."

"I don't know what I would have done without them. They helped me deal with my brain and all the things going on in it. The trials can really mess you up."

Tell me about it, I think. Instead I say, "How long have you been here?"

"Six years. I was the newb until you came up."

I feel my stomach plummet. All those deaths in that time and no winners. But really, winning feels worse than dying. At least if I had lost in the trials, I wouldn't have to think about it everyday, wouldn't have to see the blood on my hands every time I look at them.

"How did you deal with it?" I ask, unable to keep my voice from cracking.

He sighs. "Not well. For awhile I tried to pretend it didn't happen, but burying it didn't help. I tried to blend with the people here, but that didn't work either. So I started drinking, started using anything I could get my hands on. That dulled it a bit, while I was on it, but then there were terrible periods when I was coming down where my mind would grab the memories and I couldn't get away. When Osric found me, I was..." he pauses, swallows, then says, "I was on my way to kill myself."

I look over at him, but his eyes follow his fingers as they trace the lines of his palm. After a moment of quiet I ask, "How did this place help you?"

He shrugs, but his mouth is quirked up again. "They get it, ya know? They understand where you are, even if you don't. Believe me, I didn't know where my head was for awhile. But Alexis fights for each of us, makes sure we're okay."

"She's tough," I say.

Raven-dude nods. "Yeah, but she had to be, after everything that happened to her."

I lean towards him and lower my voice. "What *did* happen to her?"

He meets my eyes and shakes his head. "That's her story to tell."

I nod, but my thoughts turn to her daughter, Hoshi. She told us her mother won the trials, but died right after the games. Her winnings went to her children, giving them better lives. I wonder how much Alexis gave up for herself to make that happen for them. I wonder how much of her really did die the day she left them behind.

"I know they can be intimidating," he continues, "but they're good people. They want to make things better for the on-worlders, but they won't force you to help. They think you can help, though."

"They?" I ask.

"We," he says. "*We* think you can help. *I* hope you do. But you're the only one who can decide that. So what's it gonna be, Nova? You wanna break some governments and stuff?"

I smile, and somewhere inside me I feel a bit of my Raider self uncoil, coming back to life. "Where do we start?"

CHAPTER
NINE

I spend three weeks with raven-dude, Benjy, learning to travel through the station unseen. There are hatches and tunnels hidden throughout the place, mostly used when they were first building the station that would become humanity's home.

Benjy gives me a full history of the star-people. Their ancestors were on-worlders, but the world was on the brink of destruction. He doesn't know the details, says there were a lot of factors that led to the end of the world as it was, but whatever caused it, they had enough time to start the station. Nearly every country from the old world was represented in the beginning. No one believes in that separation anymore—now it's just on or off-worlders.

There were space stations already in orbit to start them off. Each new shipment of equipment was added to the old, until eventually they had this giant monstrosity surrounding the whole planet. It took hundreds of years to finish and work out the kinks, to build the passages and rooms and markets the way they are now. Benjy says the station is perpetually under construction in one area or another, but mostly it's cosmetic now. The old construction passages are forgotten.

We're climbing through a narrow place now, one I haven't seen before. I still have trouble navigating the place without a map, but Benjy seems to always know where we're going. He slips between two bulky tubes and I follow, coming out in a small room where a ladder leads up to the surface.

"Where are we?" I ask.

He smiles, and I can't help but smile back. After only a few weeks, I've come to appreciate the lightness he carries with him, the way he makes everything easier just by being around him.

But then he says, "Don't be mad."

My smile drops and my eyes narrow. "Where?"

"At the intersection by your dad's office."

I feel like he just punched me in the gut. I haven't seen Ledwin Kennedy in over a year. Before that, it was a dozen. I don't know why he would bring me here.

"Why?" is the only thing I get out.

"We're going to need his help, eventually. Thought it was time to figure out where he stands."

"He works for the Règle. That tells me everything I need to know."

"Come on, Nova," he says, rolling his eyes. "You know people are more complicated than that."

"I don't need to know his complications."

"Didn't he save your ass at the end of the trials?"

"How do you know about that? I thought they turned off the cameras at the end."

He smiles. "They turned off the public stream, sure, but we're tapped into the main controls. We saw the whole thing."

I frown. "Is he why you needed me, why you grabbed me?"

Benjy shakes his head and for once his smile is missing. "We came for you because you belong with us. We understand each other like none of these off-worlders can. I mean, your dad's role is a perk, for sure. But I grabbed you because we want the Raider girl who won the tower to be with us when we make our next moves."

"What are the next moves?" I ask.

I've been thinking about it these last few weeks, but didn't want to pry until they knew they could trust me. But now that they want to involve my father, I think I deserve to know what's going on.

"Don't worry, Alexis has it all lined out."

I bite my lip, unhappy with the dismissal but hesitant to push too far. Benjy has been the most accepting of me, the only one to volunteer to show me the ropes. I don't want to isolate myself from him, too.

Instead, I nod and ask, "What do you need me to do?"

HIS BLOND HAIR IS PARTED, SHARP AND PRECISE AS ALWAYS. HIS cornflower blue eyes match the pale shirt he wears, stark against his dark pants and shoes. I walk towards him as he punches in a keycode to his office door. He has a beard now, blond like his hair, with touches of strawberry like Ivy's hair, and a patch of gray.

As the door opens and he steps inside, I step behind him and place my hand on the door before he can close it. He startles and turns to me, his eyes finding mine. I watch his mouth form my name, but he doesn't speak. He simply moves to the side and lets me pass.

The room is not what I expected. There's a reception area with a handful of chairs and a leather couch that looks hard. Ledwin leads me past them, through the door by the glass window where the sign-in sheet waits, and around the corner to a small room with a plain metal desk. All the while, he doesn't speak. Neither do I.

He motions for me to sit in front of the desk, then steps to a panel in a back wall. He flips a switch and the movement seems to relax him. His shoulders droop a little, losing their tension. He puts his hand in his pocket as he walks past the desk to sit beside me, taking my hands in his. Something scratches at my palm, but I ignore it when he speaks.

"I'm so happy to see you. I've been worried these last few months," he says, then mouths, "since the escape."

His words surprise me. I thought Ivy would've told him she saw me, at the very least. The fact that she didn't is a bad sign. "I've been okay."

He nods, his smile broadening. He runs a finger over one of my loose curls and says, "I see you've figured out a disguise. I like you as a blonde. Reminds me of your mother."

My brows furrow. My mother had red hair. He knows that. Or he should. His smile has a strained expression, unnaturally tight. And his teeth...they're not smiling, they're flashing the same warning a wild animal does before it attacks.

"I shouldn't have come here."

I pull my hands from his grasp and rise, turning to the door. As I reach the doorframe, he puts his hand on my shoulder and spins me towards him. He mouths, "Hit me."

I don't hesitate, happy to have the chance. I swing, nailing him square in the jaw. He falls backwards, landing on the floor. I watch him, unsure what's happening. I hit him hard, but not *that* hard. He props onto his elbow and shouts, "You can run from us, hide from us, but the reach of the Règle is long."

Run from us, hide from us.

I dart from the office, back out into the reception area, out into the corridor. I run to the hatch where Benjy is waiting with a privacy field engaged. He pulls me inside and closes the hatch behind me. I stumble against him and he wraps his arms around me.

"Whoa, hey, what happened?"

I breathe against his shoulder, inhaling the clean smell of his shirt and the salty tang of sweat on his skin. When my body returns to normal, when my breath evens out and my jittering heart slows a bit, I pull from his arms. Our friendship is tentative enough without adding the requirement to comfort each other during emotional outbursts.

There's something in my hand.

I turn my back to Benjy and take a couple steps from him. There's a piece of paper folded into a tight square. I unroll it, stare at the tiny loops upon it. My father slipped me a message, a warning that rattle inside my head: *You're being watched. One at the apartment, one of the trial winners. Trust no one.*

CHAPTER
TEN

I sit in my tiny room on my cot, reading my father's note over and over until the words don't make sense. Then I reread them until they do. I try convincing myself this is a trap, that he's working to discount this movement, that he's trying to create doubt about my friends.

But something about the whole thing rings true.

I can't pinpoint what it is, why these scribbled words suddenly make me feel more solid, but they do. Despite the work they did to help me fit in with the off-worlders, something always felt off at Baz's place. And I'm certain the meeting with Thoa at the Dirty Onion wasn't a coincidence. Someone wanted me to see him, to know that he was lost to me.

The one thing that bothers me is the thought that one of the trial winners is a traitor. After everything we've seen, all the blood we've spilled and the horrors we've caused in the name of entertainment, how could they side with the Règle? *Who* would side with them?

I run through the things I know about each of them, lingering on anything that might give someone an excuse to turn on the other winners. Unfortunately, I haven't spent enough time with anyone but Benjy to really understand them. Even he confuses me some-times. Just when I think I understand what makes him tick, I learn something new that throws my theories about him into chaos.

Maybe it's an affiliate of one of the trial winners. I mean, there are other people down here—family, lovers, sympathizers—but no, the note says a trial *winner*. I want to believe Alexis is good, and from my time with him, I'm pretty sure Benjy is, too. That leaves fidgety Osric, bad-bitch Karina, mazulla book-reader Qen, the middle-aged woman, Grieva, or Drev, the young man who can barely meet my eyes.

I bolt up from my cot. How did I not think of him before? Some of the winners are civil, some are openly hostile, but Drev is *nothing* to me.

I find my way to my feet and peer out into the open area. People are milling about, joking with one another as they do chores and prepare food. Drev is nowhere to be seen. I spot Benjy across the way, sitting outside his own little room while Qen stands behind him rubbing his shoulders.

I head for them, trying to figure out what to say as I march across the empty space. If I'm going to accuse Drev of something, I'll need proof. If I'm going to get proof, I'll need Benjy's help. I know he and Qen are lovers, but I don't know how much I can say in front of them. Trusting them could be the right move, pushing them to my side. Maybe everything I say to Benjy will go straight to Qen's ears anyway.

Benjy is already smiling when I reach him, but something about it seems off. I meet his eyes, their bright green dulled in the shadows of this place. He says, "Hey. Feeling better?"

I nod. I didn't tell him what happened, didn't share my note with him, and he didn't press. He knew I was upset and was fine comforting me without needing to know the details. The simplicity of that made me trust him more.

I take a deep breath and say, "I need to talk to you."

"Shoot," he says.

"Not here," I say. I cast my gaze around the room at the many bodies, the many ears who I don't yet trust.

"Okay, let's get out of here."

Qen gives me a dark look, suspicious. I say, "You can come if you want. I trust you."

The glint in their eyes loses a bit of hostility, but I don't miss the way they tense at the word "trust."

Benjy and Qen follow me out of the living area and down a dark side hall. We walk for ten minutes before I feel like we've gone far enough away to have some privacy. I pull out the note Ledwin gave me and hand it to Benjy. When he finishes, he hands Qen the paper as he finds my eyes. Even without words, I feel like Benjy understands the weight of what is happening, the heaviness of what I'm about to say.

Qen's tone is accusatory, yet somehow also dismissive. "This is bullshit. None of the winners would compromise the group."

"Where did you get it?" Benjy asks.

"My dad," I say. My voice sounds weak to my ears and I wonder if it does to them as well.

"Do you trust him?" he asks.

I shake my head. "I don't know."

Qen folds their arms over their chest. "You can't be considering this."

Benjy tilts his head the tiniest bit. "It makes sense, babe."

"I knew bringing her here was a mistake," Qen grumbles.

"The real mistake would be ignoring this warning. Even if it has no merit, we should still investigate to be sure."

Qen purses their lips but says nothing. I swallow, ready my voice, and say, "We should start with Drev."

"Drev?" Qen scoffs.

Benjy shushes them. "Keep your voice down."

Qen looks around. "Because there are so many people around to overhear me?"

"Because Nova is entrusting us with this information, and as a trial winner, she deserves our confidence."

If his words surprise them, Qen doesn't show it. I do, though. My eyebrows feel like they're going to rise right off the top of my head. I don't know why it surprises me; honestly, Benjy has proven himself a good friend to me over these last few weeks and this reaction is what I'd hoped for when I chose to tell him.

"So, Nova deserves our confidence, but Drev doesn't? He's been dedicated to Alexis, dedicated to the cause, for nine years."

"Then we should be able to clear his name quickly," Benjy says. Qen purses their lips but doesn't say anything further. Benjy continues, "What about the other one the note mentions?"

I wince at the thought of one of my friends being a traitor. I'd finally come to like Baz, even if I didn't fully trust him, but he is the obvious choice among them. I grind my teeth and growl out, "I'll deal with that."

Benjy raises a brow, but doesn't press. Instead he says, "Okay, let's figure out how we're going to clear Drev's name."

I nod instead of asking the question I want to: What will we do if we can't?

FIVE DAYS LATER I'M ON DREV DUTY, TRAILING HIM THROUGH THE corridors as discreetly as possible. It isn't as easy as I want it to be. Drev is a young guy in his late twenties with an air about him that seems to render him invisible to others. He isn't tall or short enough to draw attention, his brown hair is simply cut, his clothes and features are nondescript—he's the perfect average person.

It works for his purposes. He's skimming credits from their bracelets, his modified device pulling a fraction of a percent from each person he passes within a certain range. I watch him slip in and out of the crowds, his movements matching the pace of those around him. No one even glances in his direction as he steals from them.

I have to admit, I'm impressed. There's an indefinable grace to him, his heists an artform. The more I watch him, the more certain I am that he's in a dance with a force I can't see.

The Raiders aren't against stealing when it's necessary. Though we didn't go to cities often, they taught me how to steal when we did. Rego taught me the classic tricks of misdirection and distraction, how to choose a mark and move in and around the crowds. Even now, I feel an itch in my fingers as I think back to those lessons. In a pinch, I could take what I needed if there was no other option.

And I guess there isn't another option in this place. Trial winners are given a sum of credits when they get here, put in a room of their own, and that's the end of it. Some of them ride their fame for awhile, but most can't handle this place. Like Benjy did, they turn to drugs and alcohol to dull the pain of their memories. Alexis tries to rescue them, but she hasn't been able to save them all.

Benjy won't give me the details of Drev's time here, even with his possible betrayal, but in watching him I've put together enough information to get a sense of who he is. If I'm honest, I no longer think he's the traitor. Someone working for the Règle wouldn't spend hours of his day walking the corridors, stealing from off-worlders. This is a man who has no other options, not someone in the employ of the Règle.

I follow him around the next corner and find myself at Pœwani market. I'd been so focused on Drev, I hadn't noticed where we were going. The place is packed and after only a few seconds I've already lost sight of him.

I curse under my breath and plunge into the throng. I watch the movement of the crowd and try to follow it, like swimming with the current. No matter where I look, I can't find Drev. With a sigh, I resign myself to going back to the down-under without any new information.

The crowd thins out as I get closer to the edge of the market. I can see the Dirty Onion in the distance and my thoughts momentarily turn to Bets. I could swing by to see her, I *want* to go see her, but I don't know how she would feel about it. We had a good time, could probably have a good time again, but it was kinda awful of me to leave without at least saying goodbye last time. Maybe I should go see her and start off with an apology.

I heave a sigh and take a step towards the bar when a flash of brown catches at the corner of my vision. I spin towards it and see a figure move behind a stall selling carpets. I'm certain it was Drev. I take off after him, peeking around the corner when I reach the stall.

He's there. Talking to...Thoa.

What the actual...?

CHAPTER
ELEVEN

Drev hooks a thumb over his shoulder and they both look to me. I pull my head back around the corner, but it's no use. I know they saw me. I take a breath and steady myself. I look down at my hands and find them trembling. I shake my head at myself, shamed that my body would betray me in such a way.

But there's nothing for it. I'm nervous.

I take a step around the corner. They're gone. I step towards where they were, my legs suddenly shaking as bad as my hands. I keep going, looking between stalls, trying to figure out where they went. There's no sign of them, and with the crowds, probably no way to find them again.

There's an exit ahead. The entranceway is smaller than some of the others and goes into a corridor I've never used. I head off in that direction, hoping to get myself under control while cursing myself the whole time. Thoa was there, feet from me, and I ducked away from him. Why? Because I'm scared? Because I can't handle seeing him? Or because I can't handle looking into the face of someone who no longer knows me?

I haven't gone far down the corridor when something presses firmly against my back. A gun? Surely not, but perhaps a different weapon. Before I can wonder about it further, a voice at my shoulder says, "Don't turn around. Understand?" I nod only a fraction. The voice says, "Go to green-sixty-circle."

I keep walking, waiting for more information, but there is nothing else. A little further down the hall and I dare to look behind me. No one is there. I'm mostly sure it was Drev. I've only heard him speak twice, his voice unremarkable. If it was Drev, why should I follow his instructions? If he's the traitor, he could be planning anything at the location looming ever closer. Then again, he could have guards grab me right here, right now, if he wanted to.

My brain runs scenarios of what he could be planning the whole time I'm walking, but I keep going. I was always going to go, no matter how foolish it makes me. Where Thoa is concerned, I'll always be a fool.

This hall is dimmer than the others. The lighting fixtures are older, the metal tubing and walls, too. There's no traffic this far away from everything. It must be one of the older parts of the station, one that hasn't been updated.

I reach the intersection marked with the number sixty inside a green circle. There's no one here—no guards, no Drev, no Thoa. Then I hear the *clang* of a door open and a broad-shouldered Raider sticks his head into the corridor and my world narrows to him, to his face, to the eyes that shine like beacons guiding me to harbor.

I move to the door and he steps aside to allow me in. He closes the door and stands there, staring. Neither of us move, a strangeness between us. My lungs seem to forget how to breathe, my chest falling still even as an ache fills me.

Two steps.

That's all it would take to be in his arms. But I don't take them and neither does he.

The door opens again a moment later, the scrape of metal deafening in the silence between us. Drev steps in and another figure enters behind him. It's a face I recognize, one I wasn't sure I'd see anytime soon. One I'm not sure I can trust.

"What's shakin', babes?" Baz asks.

I bite my lip to keep my retort in. Baz has been kind to me since I've been here, but he has a history of serving the Règle. He has a good life, paid for with money from the entertainment industry. There's no reason he should be on my side. But I still want to trust him. I want to believe he is good.

"I'm Tabarus," Thoa says.

"Oh, I know who you are big fella," Baz says with a smile. "We all do."

Thoa's brows furrow, but he doesn't say anything. He steals a glance at me, so quick it might not have happened. But his face clears and he plants a smile there, like a piece of armor protecting him from whatever is happening.

"I'm Baz, that's Cameron, and you know Drev," he says, flicking his hand towards each person.

Thoa nods. "Welcome to my home. Drev says we have something to talk about, but wouldn't tell me more." His smile falters slightly, right at the corners, but no one else seems to notice. "How can I help you?"

Baz smiles. "Let's start with a seat. You live in the middle of nowhere and my legs are tired."

Thoa's cheeks flush a little. Embarrassment? It's something uncommon for him. For the old him, anyway.

He leads us into the other room. His apartment is somewhere between Bets and Baz's in size. There's a bed against one wall and a couch against the other. I go to the couch, expecting Baz to follow, but instead he flops down on the bed, rolls over, and strikes a pose that somehow seems aimed at everyone in the room at once. It's one-hundred percent Baz, eliciting a smile from my lips that I hadn't expected. It dawns on me that I've missed him and I file that away to inspect later.

Drev joins me on the couch while Thoa moves to stand against the wall. I've seen the man in sandstorms and monsoons, heavy snows and hungry deserts; still, I've never seen him as uncomfortable as he is looking at the people assembled in his home.

"How long have you lived here?" Baz asks.

"About a year," Thoa says. A crease forms between his brows, like the answer he spoke wasn't the same one he was thinking.

"You live alone? Or are you hiding some secret lover under the floor?"

I glare at Baz, but he doesn't look at me. His eyes are fixed on Thoa. He's looking for something in his face, but I don't know what. I'm not sure he could find it even if it was there. He only knows us from the games.

Thoa nods. "My girlfriend lives a couple quads away. She wants to move in together, but I don't know."

I want to feel bad for the self-conscious way he's shrugging, for the worry that crosses his features, but I don't. I can't get my mind around the word *girlfriend*.

"Where did you live before?" Baz asks.

I feel my whole body tense. I try not to look at Thoa, not to search his face for any memory of me, but it's no use. Just as I've convinced myself not to look at him, I find my gaze drifting to his. He's looking at me, too, his eyes searching me for a flame of recognition.

We stare at one another for a long time, the room around us silent, waiting. Finally, still looking at me, he asks, "What's with all the questions?"

"I'm sorry," Drev says, drawing Thoa's attention. "I know it's weird, but I promise he's going somewhere with it. Trust me."

I'm suddenly struck by the ease with which Drev speaks for Baz. How do they know each other? What plot have they hatched together? For that matter, how does Thoa know Drev?

Thoa runs a hand over his face and shrugs one shoulder. "Honestly, I don't remember anything before the accident."

"Accident?" Baz asks, one brow raising.

"Nasty fall while I was at work," Thoa says, a frown tugging at his lips. "I woke up in a hospital room with no memory of my life. Jane was there and she filled me in with the basics, like my name, job, our...relationship."

His pause sends my heart skittering. Drev asks, "But it doesn't feel right, does it?"

His tone is so soft, the sadness so real, it's as if *he* was the one in love with Thoa. I look between them, waiting for Thoa to answer. The shake of his head is so small, I almost miss it. But it's there. He might not remember me, he might not know the truth about who he is, but he's not lost to me. Not fully. Not yet.

"You know her, though, don't you?" Baz asks, pointing at me.

His eyes find mine again. There's something shy about the way he looks at me, like he's afraid if he looks at me too long, I'll disappear.

"I saw her at the bar a few weeks ago."

"But it's more than that," Drev says. "Tell them what you told me."

Thoa scrubs a hand over his head while his cheeks blaze. "I shouldn't."

Drev nods, urging him on. "You won't scare her, I promise."

Thoa forces a smile and says, "It's nothing, foolishness really."

"Please tell me," I say.

"Um, well, it's just that I keep seeing you, at night, in my dreams."

His words hit me so hard I have to hold back tears. After a few seconds I manage to ask, "What happens in your dreams?"

His tentative smile cracks as darkness covers his face. "I don't like to talk about them."

"Because of the blood," Drev says. We all look at him, but he's staring down at his hands as if we're not there.

"Yeah," Thoa whispers.

"The tower battle," Baz says. "So it seems they didn't quite wipe everything out."

Thoa's eyes go wide. "You make it sound like it was real."

"It was," I say.

He shakes his head. "No. Absolutely not. I can't accept that."

"Why?" I ask.

He presses his lips into a grim line. "Because if it was real, if I was there, I did horrible things."

"Everything you did was to keep us alive," I say.

"No," he says, pushing away from the wall and standing over me. "I am not that person. I'm not."

"Thoa..."

He winces. "That's not me. My name is Tabarus. Thoa was some other person."

I rise to my feet, and though I'm several inches shorter than Thoa, I feel like I'm towering over him. "You were that person. You might not remember, you might not want to, but you can't erase who you were."

"I don't know who I was," he yells.

"I do," I say. "You were Thoa-gra, the Bonecutter. You were a Raider. You provided for your found family. You were a great warrior, greatest among us, and you were feared." He shakes his head in protest, but I continue: "You were kind, brave, with a generous spirit and a heart to help others. You saved people everywhere you went. Hells, you saved me. You saved me with your kindness, your love, and yes, with your hands and body covered in blood. You kept me alive and I loved you for it. I loved you, and you loved me, and that's supposed to be enough."

I'm sobbing, but I don't know when I started crying. My fist is against Thoa's chest, and I don't remember doing that either. I stare up into impossibly blue eyes, eyes that have given me life on so many occasions, and I search for that life again. I dive through the blue, hungry for even a flicker of recognition, but all I see is sadness.

I turn towards the door, tears still streaming down my face. He calls to me, "Wait, please. I'm sorry." I stop, hand on the door, hoping. His lips move as if he's searching for something, and he says, "Please, miss, I'm sorry."

Miss. He doesn't remember my name.

I push the door open and run out into the corridor. I run until my lungs burn, until my eyes hurt, until I can't feel my legs. Then for good measure, I run a bit more. I find a door to the underworld and slip inside, curling into a ball on the unilluminated steps. There I let myself melt into the puddle of emotions I've been fighting. There I cry away my last hope.

CHAPTER
TWELVE

I emerge as a block of ice. No more melting. Solid, cold, unyielding. There is no heat on land below or stars above that can burn hot enough to make it to my core.

I'm more than halfway back to the home of the trial winners when I hear the screams. They're faint, but I don't need to be close to know where they're coming from. I dart ahead, running through the near-darkness.

The clomping of boots stops me in my tracks. I duck between the wall and a dangling tube as thick as my waist and crouch as low as I can. A couple guards bypass me at a jog, but I don't move. The steady rhythm of a troop marches towards me.

Grieva is between the first two guards that pass. She doesn't fight, she doesn't scream, she simply walks between them, managing to look regal in her stained overalls. A row of non-winners, family and friends of those who've managed to have a life here, are marched through the corridors behind her. Behind them is Osric, with a guard on each side and a third behind him with a taser to his back. Another guard is carrying Qen over his shoulder while they spit and curse and call out to the traitor among us.

I watch Benjy walking a few feet behind. There are no guards on him.

He stops in the corridor, close enough that I could reach out and touch him. I could wipe that despicable smile off his face. I think about it, let the image of his broken corpse falling to the ground fill my imagination. But I don't. Instead I watch as they lead out Miles, the energetic, innocent kid with the bad luck to be related to Alexis the Huntress. He bites at the closest guard, showing the ferocity of the Huntress' bloodline.

A guard slaps the kid across the face and I feel my blood boil. It takes everything in me not to run for the guard right now and free the boy. I clench my fists at my side, fighting the urge to attack. It will do no good to save one boy and risk capture when there are so many others who've been taken.

They bring Alexis a moment after Miles passes and I watch her stop in front of Benjy. The guards stop, too. Even in custody, she's still in charge.

For a moment I think she sees me. But then she fixes Benjy with her rock-hard gaze. Though she doesn't speak, doesn't ask, his body seems to deflate and he mumbles an excuse. Even this close, I can't hear him. Alexis shakes her head and Benjy reaches for her. One of the guards knocks his hand away.

She says, "You've chosen wrong, Benjamin Besser."

He recoils as if she slapped him. "What else could I do? We're fighting a battle we can't win."

She purses her lips. "You should've kept your faith in me, in the winners, in the Raider. She's the key. She might not know how yet, but she's the one who will change everything."

Benjy scoffs. "She's in over her head."

"No, sweet boy, you are. And now there's no way out for you."

As she starts walking again, Benjy calls out, "I'll have the others soon enough, then we'll see who made the wrong choice."

He stalks back towards the area where he brought me a month ago, where he introduced me to the others and reminded me why

I'm here. I wait, backed into the corner, until I no longer hear the boots down the hall. I wait until there are no crying children, no screaming men or cursing women. I wait until my legs ache from crouching so long. Still, I don't move.

Until I hear someone coming down the corridor. Running.

I step out into the corridor just in time to grab Karina's arm. She whips it out of my grasp and swings a fist at me. I throw myself back, hitting my head against a pipe. She jumps at me, wraps her hands around my throat, and growls out, "What did you do?"

"Not me," I say, barely able to speak with her hands gripping me so tightly. "It was Benjy."

"Liar," she growls.

"I swear it," I say.

"He told me you were trying to turn us against one another. He said you were after Drev."

"I was wrong," I cough. Her hands loosen at my words, but she doesn't let me go. I gasp, sucking in a deep breath. I can see I've only got a few seconds to change her mind. "I got a tip that there was a traitor. I thought it was Drev and I told Benjy and Qen. But it wasn't. He's been trying to help Thoa."

"The other winner from your trials."

"Yes. I was with Drev today, and Thoa. When I got back, they were leading the others out. I hid until I heard you coming."

Her brows furrow. "Why not let me pass and keep yourself safe?"

"That's not what Alexis would want."

Her hands drop at the mention of Alexis. She says, "You barely know her. How can you know what she wants?"

"She told Benjy he chose the wrong side. Even now, she still thinks we can win."

I expect the words to encourage her, but instead she deflates. She's no longer the confident woman with the chip on her shoulder; in fact, she looks vulnerable. Weak.

Loose strands of black hair have fallen from her braid and

surround her face. She chews on the inside of her jaw. Whatever thoughts are rolling around behind her dark eyes, I can't read them.

Her moment of fragility doesn't last long. Her body coils back up, readying for whatever comes next. She nods once, deciding something within herself, and asks, "Who else is free?"

"Just us and Drev," I say, before amending, "Or he was a couple hours ago."

"We need to find him before they do. Thoa, too."

The thought sends a chill through me. She's right. If they're gathering all the winners, they might go after him as well. "He's at green-sixty-circle."

"Damn," she says. "There's a lot of entrances between here and there."

I nod. "One of us should go top-side."

She says, "I'll do it. I'm less of a target."

"Not anymore."

She curses under her breath. "You're right. We'll never get to Drev with every guard on high alert. We need new faces."

"I know where we can get them. I have a friend who can help," I say, thinking of Baz. But as soon as I think of him, I remember there's a traitor among my top-side friends as well. Even if it isn't Baz, he may be captured by the guards for helping the trial winners.

"You sure we can trust her?"

Her, I think. Bets. Of course. "Yes, I think so. But she doesn't know who I really am, so we'll need to be careful."

She nods. "Lead the way."

WE COME OUT OF THE UNDERWORLD A CORRIDOR AWAY FROM BETS' apartment. I have no idea if she'll be home or working at the Onion, but this is our only chance. Karina pulls her jacket hood up over her hair, managing to put enough of her face in shadow that she isn't immediately recognizable. I don't have a hood, and I'm pissed at myself for not wearing something inconspicuous.

We come around the corner of the intersection by Bets' place at the same time a pair of guards pass. I recognize one of them, though it's been awhile since I've seen him: Vivon, *alive*. His eyes catch mine and I know he recognized me, I know it as sure as I breathe. But he doesn't stop. I don't turn around to watch him, but part of me knows he's directing his partner away from us. Vivon is a good man.

I knock on Bets door. I hear footsteps approaching, the mechanism turning inside the door. Every second stretches on before me, promising my capture.

The door opens and Bets is there, the light from the kitchen creating a halo around her. Her lips part slightly, her eyes widen, and I'm suddenly very unsure about the choice to come here. Then she steps aside and waves us in. Karina and I slip past her, and I watch as Bets looks around outside her door before closing it.

When she faces me, I give her my brightest smile. She says, "What are you thinking?"

My smile drops and I blink at her, unsure of what to say. Karina must notice, because she says, "We're sorry for the imposition."

Bets holds her hand up to Karina and looks at me. "Explain."

"I'm sorry," I begin. "I shouldn't have left like that."

Bets says, "I don't give a damn that you left like you did. I mean, yeah, you suck, clearly, but it sorta pales in comparison with showing up at my door when there's a station-wide warrant for your arrest."

I hear Karina mumble a curse, but it doesn't seem to phase Bets. "I didn't know—"

"Didn't know you were a criminal?"

I swallow, searching for my voice. I don't know what I expected from her. No, that's not true; honestly, I expected her to be happy to see me again. It was unfair to put that expectation on her.

"We don't want to make trouble for you," I say. "We'll go."

"Are you out of your head?" she asks.

I flounder for a moment. "I mean, yeah, maybe."

There's a pause, a silent breath between us, and then she starts laughing. It's just a low chuckle, but it gives life to her eyes. After a moment she says, "You can't go out there, at least not looking like that. But we need to get you out of here before Xander gets home."

"Xander?" I ask.

She gives me a strange look, before her eyes turn to their normal smoldering gaze. "Yeah, I guess we didn't worry too much about introductions that night."

I smile, but my cheeks are on fire. I glance at Karina who is pointedly staring at me with the biggest smirk I've ever seen. I try to change the subject, point at Karina, and say, "This is Karina."

Bets nods. "Oh, I know who Karina is. Baddest bitch the trials has ever seen. No offense, Nova."

Karina shakes hands with Bets and says, "I thought you said she didn't know who you were."

Bets chuckles again. "She wasn't going by the same name last time she was here, but I knew. Xander didn't, and it's best to keep it that way."

Bets leads us into the next room and starts rummaging through the chests against the wall. She pulls out gray coveralls from Xander's chest and hands it to Karina, who immediately starts stripping out of her baggy clothes. Bets stops to watch her, unashamedly admiring Karina's body. Not that I can blame her— the woman is a gift to the eyes.

She zips up the coveralls over her underclothes and asks, "Where can I wash up?"

Bets points her to the bathroom tucked away in the corner. It's so small, I don't think I even noticed it last time I was here. Bets goes through two more drawers before she finds something I can wear. Her frame is bigger than mine, her hips and butt too full for me to wear most of her pants. But she has a pair of leggings that work and one of Xander's tank tops that's too small for him. As I lace up my boots, she pulls out a thin jacket the same color as Thoa's eyes.

Karina comes out of the bathroom without her braid. Her hair is chin-length and angled over one eye. She's washed away her standard red lipstick, and put on dark eye makeup that somehow changes her face in a big way.

It takes me a minute to take it in. She looks younger this way, but no less fierce.

"You're next," she says.

Bets ushers me into the bathroom. My hair has grown a bit since Baz and Yosh cut it and my red roots are showing. She grabs a razor and takes my hair down to the scalp. When she's done, she turns to the makeup machine, programs something in, and pushes it against my face.

I look in the mirror, surprised by the teal above my eyes, the dark lipstick, the black star pattern at my temples. Bets says, "It won't hide you forever, but you'll pass for someone else if they don't look close."

We head for the door. Karina taps her bracelet against Bets' and says, "A little something for your troubles."

"You don't need to do that," Bets says.

Karina smiles. "That's why I want to."

She moves away to give me a moment of privacy with Bets. I look into her eyes, into the strange kinship I feel for her. "Thank you for this. I know you didn't have to—"

She cuts me off, her mouth pressing against mine. It isn't a passionate kiss, or a loving one, or even the hunger I felt from her last time; this kiss is goodbye.

When she pulls away, there's a sadness in her eyes. I turn, unable to say anything to make it better.

But something stops me at the door. Something heavy in my gut. Without looking back I say, "There's a reckoning coming, Bets. Stay on the right side."

CHAPTER
THIRTEEN

We push through the corridors as fast as we dare, but there are guards everywhere. We stalk in silence, trying to blend with the dwindling crowds.

Out of nowhere Karina says, "I liked her."

"Who?" I ask, taken aback.

"Bets. She's good for you. Balances some of your wildness."

My mouth hangs open at her words and I'm glad she isn't looking at the blush creeping up my neck. "How can you think that after knowing her for twenty minutes?"

I glance over and see Karina shrug. "Time doesn't make things truer. Twenty minutes or twenty years, it would still be the same."

I bite my lip as I chew on her words. I don't know if she's seeing what she wants, a reflection of her own unmet desires, or if there's truth that I don't see. Either way, it doesn't matter. I whisper, "I won't see her again."

She stops and I think it's because of what I've said. But then she shoves against my shoulder, forcing me down a side hall. I hear guards pounding down the walkway we just left. We continue on in silence, thoughts of Bets replaced with actively avoiding the guards.

Twice more Karina pulls me down a side corridor just before we reach a checkpoint where they're scanning bracelets. The second time, the realization sends a cold chill through me.

"We're screwed," I mutter.

"No, we just need to keep going."

"They can trace us through the bracelets."

She shakes her head. "Mine's hacked with a different profile."

"Did Benjy know that? Did he know the name?"

She stops, her eyes going wide. "Shit."

"So even if we find Drev, they'll just track us down with the bracelets."

We turn another corner, silence falling between us. I steal a glance at her, certain she's trying to work something out in her mind. Finally, she says, "Why haven't they already?"

Her question stills my quaking inside. I fight the hope blooming in my chest, not because I don't want it, but because I won't be able to handle it if I'm wrong. "Ivy," I say. "My little sister. She's the one who hacked mine. Maybe she's doing something to help."

Karina's eyes tell me she doesn't believe it, but she doesn't say anything. I'm grateful she doesn't. I need to believe Ivy is on my side.

We're nearly out of the more populated corridors when our luck runs out. A guard spots us in the crowd, and though she doesn't seem to recognize us on sight, she approaches with her scanner.

"Arms out," she says.

I hesitate for a second, but she doesn't notice. Her scanner beeps over my bracelet. I don't know what it tells her, but she seems satisfied. She reaches forward to scan Karina's and I hold my breath. Even if Ivy was able to fix mine, she wouldn't know to hide Karina's fake profile.

The machine beeps. The guards reads the screen. Her lips pull down in a frown. Her gaze flicks up to us and she says, "Go about your business. Sorry for the delay."

We hurry away, neither of us speaking for the next dozen intersections. When we're only four stops from Thoa's apartment, Karina slows and pulls me against the wall. She says, "What just happened?"

"I don't know," I say, but a grin stretches across my face.

"Your sister," she says, "what does she do?"

"She works for the Chasseur. For my father. She tracks people who go on-world illegally."

Karina doesn't smile, but I can tell she is pleased. "Guess I owe her a drink."

The stomp of boots draws my attention. A squad of guards is marching towards us, prey in tow. Thoa, Baz, and Drev walk between them.

"I'll take left," Karina says.

She moves across the hall before I have the chance to object. Not that I would. We have to get them away now, or we may not get another chance. Still, attacking eight armed guards without weapons or backup is a bit daunting. I'd feel better about it if the poor guards at least had a fighting chance.

Karina's attack is so fast, even I'm taken by surprise. The first guard is down, neck broken, before I've made a move. But I won't be outdone.

I run up the wall beside me, using the momentum to propel my body at the guard closest to me. She hits the ground hard, but I grab her head and smash it against the floor to make sure she's out. I don't think she's dead, but close enough for me to move on.

I grab the taser from her hand and jab it into the leg of the guard beside me. The shock rolls up his body, sending his eyes back into his head. I drop the taser, jump to my feet and smash him in the nose with my elbow. He drops to the floor in front of me and I knee him in the side of the head. He falls next to the woman.

Karina is fighting her third and Drev has his bound hands wrapped around the neck of his second. I look for the eighth, but they're gone. At least one of them had the sense to run.

I rummage around in the soldiers pockets until I find a pocketknife. It isn't big enough to use in a brawl, but it's perfect for what I need. I help Baz to his feet. He threw himself out of the way when we attacked. Smart, really. He holds his wrists up for me and I cut them with my new knife.

Next I move to Drev. His shy, boy-next-door look is gone and there's something wild in his features. There's blood on his lips, dribbling down his chin. I look at the guard at his feet and see that one of their ears has been ripped off. When I slice his bonds, he greets me with a bloody grin and I have to suppress a shiver.

My hands move to Thoa's. He stands statue-still as I slice through the plastic ties at his wrist. I look up at him, wondering what this sight brings to mind. His lip trembles as tears trail silently down his cheeks. He wears the saddest expression I've ever seen.

I don't know what I expected, but it wasn't this. I guess I thought his instincts would kick in and he would fight with us. But he didn't. Instead, he mourns those who aim to hurt him.

"Hey," Karina says, snapping a finger in front of my face. "We gotta go."

"Yeah," I say. There's a numbness in me, holding my brain hostage, and I'm grateful there's someone else to make decisions for us.

"Everyone grab a weapon and let's get moving," Karina says.

We each grab something. We look around at one another for a moment before Baz says, "Follow me."

Karina says, "I don't think so, pretty boy. I know who you are. Your voice haunts us all, a harbinger for trouble. I will never trust you."

"I don't give a damn if you trust me," Baz says. "You can figure out your next move *after* I save your ass."

Her brows go high as she says, "Excuse me? Pretty sure it's your ass that just got saved."

I take a deep breath. "We don't have time for this. Baz, if you have a plan, lead the way. Karina, you don't have to trust him—but trust me."

She presses her lips thin, like she's not sure she can do that either. But when Baz starts walking, so does she. Drev walks behind her and I watch the fingers on his left hand as they drum the air at his side. I don't know what darkness he's trying to shake out, but I hope he does. We need him to be in control of himself for whatever comes next.

Thoa and I trudge along in the back, a heavy silence between us. This place has ruined each of us in different ways and I don't know how to bring him back from what they've done. Worse, I don't think he wants to be brought back.

After a few minutes, Thoa says, "It was Jane."

"Who?" I ask, distracted.

"My girlfriend. She's the one who came for us."

"Shit," I mutter. "Did we...did I...?"

He shakes his head. "She ran."

Jane was the eighth. *Tinora.* The one I long to destroy.

I let the weight of her escape settle over me. Of all the things he could say to me, this is the worst.

We've been walking for fifteen minutes, in and out of crowds but no guards in sight, before I notice Baz touching his ear. He seems to do it each time he stops. When I'm sure of what I'm seeing, I step forward and grab his arm, spinning him towards me.

"Whose directing us?"

He looks startled for only a second, then his trademark grin shines across his face. "I forget how smart you are."

"What's going on?" Karina asks.

I point to his ear. "Someone is giving him instructions."

"Yeah, and we need to move. There's two squads approaching," he says.

Baz turns down the side corridor and we follow. Whether there are guards approaching or not, we can't linger. I sidle up beside him and say, "If you're betraying us—"

"Damn, Nova, give me some credit," he snarls.

I flinch back from his words. There's never been trust between us, but there was friendship growing there before I left. Maybe that should be enough, but with everything I've seen, it isn't. Still, I've never seen Baz angry, not like this. Or maybe it's hurt that I'm seeing. Either way, guilt surges through me, knowing I caused it.

A wall panel slides open ahead of us and I see Krew's head pop out into the corridor. Baz makes for the opening and we file inside. Just as the wall closes, I hear boots pound past.

We're in a room barely as big as Baz's kitchen. There are tables against each wall with equipment I've never seen on each one. Ivy, Krew's sister, and an older woman sit in front of the tables, smiling up at us. Ivy hops up and throws herself at me, wrapping her spindly arms around my neck.

Her embrace sends me spiraling. I cry into her hair, weeping like a child. "I'm sorry I left. I'm so sorry, Ivy."

She shushes as she pats my head. "It's okay. You're okay. We're together now."

When I finally pull away and wipe my eyes, taking a shaky breath, I'm embarrassed by my outburst. She pulls the woman to her feet and says, "Nova, this is my mom."

The woman holds a hand out to me. "Wina."

I shake it as I survey her. She's thin, lanky, like her daughter. They have the same high forehead, their eyebrows arch the same way, their skin tone is nearly identical. When she smiles, I feel warm. Mothered. Loved.

Ivy steps between us and pats my cheek, saying, "I'm just glad you knew to find Baz. I wasn't sure how I was going to get you here if you didn't."

I look at him and he taps his ear. His smirk is turned down, disappointment mixed with his *told-you-so* expression. "I'm sorry I doubted you."

He nods, but doesn't say anything. I let it go for now. I'll need to make a grander apology when we have more time, but that isn't a luxury for us right now.

Karina steps up and extends a hand to Ivy. "I guess you're the one to thank for getting us past that scan."

Ivy nods. "No sweat. But I will take you up on that drink." Karina's quirks up one brow and Ivy says, "I patched into the camera and audio feeds."

"Audio?" Krew and Baz ask in unison.

She nods. "No one talks about the audio. Honestly I wasn't even sure they really had it. But when Nova left last month, I started digging, looking for a way to find her. That's when I found it."

"Damn," Krew says. He steps behind me and puts a hand on my shoulder. It joins us in heaviness, and I think he's just now realizing how bad things really are. "So they can see and hear everything that happens in the common areas?"

Ivy nods. "I suspect they've started putting them in newer residences, too, but I don't have proof yet."

I glance to Baz, realization hitting me like a fist to my windpipe. "How old is your place?"

Baz meets my gaze. "I moved in while you were still in custody. After a renovation."

I shake my head. "They've known all along. Every move we made, no matter how careful we were, they were watching."

"But then you left," Ivy says. She spins around to the table and starts tapping on one of her devices. "You were off the grid until a few days ago. What changed?"

"I went to see Dad," I say.

She spins back to me, eyes wide. "No! His offices are bugged, big time."

I nod. "He gave me a note, said there was a traitor at Baz's place and one where I was hiding out. Then he told me to hit him and I ran."

Ivy leans back in her seat and folds her arms across her chest. "They took him in an hour ago."

"What?" I ask, panic bubbling in my chest.

"I didn't know why. His offices only have video, but I saw the whole thing go down. I buzzed Baz, Yosh, and Krew to get over here."

Baz says, "We started wearing these communicators in our ears after you left, in case one of us saw you."

Ivy nods. "I searched for Cameron Forsberg's bracelet and found you."

"You could've done that after I left."

"She refused," Krew says. "Said you deserved to make your own decisions."

My heart swells as I look at Ivy. She's better than I deserve.

"Anyway, your tracker had an alarm set so they could track you, too. Not sure how long it had been there. I disabled it and gave you a new name. I saw Karina's bracelet traveling with yours, so I changed hers as well."

"Smart," Karina says.

Ivy nods. "Thanks. I waited until after you'd freed the guys before I changed theirs. But now everyone should be clear."

"Couldn't the cameras in the corridors track us here?" Karina asks.

Ivy shrugs. "Sure, if I let them. But I'm in their system so deep at this point, I can loop their feed so they only see what I want them to see."

"You're kidding," Karina says, a genuine smile spreading across her face.

"It's taken me years," Ivy says. "Dad knew we'd need it eventually, so he started teaching me to hack when I was ten. Honestly, it's not that hard. A lot of the security is based on tech from before the cataclysm. It's been upgraded, sure, but it's still old enough to be easily accessed if you know what you're looking for."

Baz says, "So the kid got us here without being seen, which is awesome, but that doesn't really help us in the long run. After what happened to that first squad, they're going to start sending out in force, with weapons other than tasers."

"He's right," I say. "We need a plan."

"I have one," Ivy says.

She pulls a box from under a table. Inside is a thick metal band a bit larger than the bracelets we wear. I ask, "What is it?"

"It removes the bracelets," Ivy says.

"Why would we do that?" Baz asks. "They're already changed so they aren't trackable."

Ivy says, "That won't last forever. And it definitely won't last once you're on the ground. The bracelets are what processes the transfer of our bodies from one place to the next, so we'll need to keep them until we get on-world. But after that, we should ditch them."

"Wait, what?" Baz asks, mouth dropping open.

Karina smiles. "Can you really get us on-world?"

Ivy nods. "I don't have all the equipment dad has at the office to dampen your body's sensory of the teleportation. So yeah, I can, but it's going to hurt like a mother."

CHAPTER
FOURTEEN

W e argue while Ivy preps her equipment. We feel bad for leaving people behind, we feel bad about involving those on-world, we worry that nothing will be changed if we leave. Everyone feels the heaviness of this, but there's something else in the air, too, like a shock of electricity jumping body to body. It forms a strange excitement.

Drev is mid-panic attack about going on-world when Krew pulls me to the side. He says, "I'm not going down there."

"What?" I ask, eyes going wide.

"Yosh isn't here and I'm not leaving without him. I made that mistake once and caused all this."

I bite my lip, afraid of my words betraying me. I've wondered what my life would've been if Krew hadn't shown up in the grasslands that night, blamed him for changing my future, but despite everything, I don't regret the way my life has gone. It isn't what I expected, maybe not what I wanted, but it's honest. I won't spend my life ignoring invisible wrongs.

I put my hand on Krew's shoulder and say, "Don't worry, he'll make it. He knows what to do. He's probably just holed up somewhere waiting for guards to pass."

"He hasn't checked in," Krew says.

"Stop. Ivy would know if he was picked up. She changed his tag already so they can't track him. Besides, we'll need you when we get to Coco's to help explain everything to them."

"Nova, I left him once and I still regret it."

"We aren't leaving him. He'll be here. He's just late."

The words are barely out of my mouth before someone knocks on the wall. Krew turns towards the sound, but Baz is already headed for the door. He asks, "Who is it?"

"Open up," Okada's voice whispers.

It's ragged—I can hear it through the door—and something about it seems wrong.

"Wait," I hiss, but it's too late.

Baz opens the panel and his brother steps through, hands raised. Tinora/Jane enters behind him, a gun pressed between his shoulder blades. Her eyes flit around the room, lingering on Thoa a moment before landing on mine. "Well, well, well, what do we have here? Lovers reunited after all this time? But you don't remember that, do you, poopsie?"

She turns her gaze to him again and I'm surprised to see her soften. Despite her cruelty, I think she might feel bad for what they've done to Thoa. When she turns back to me, it's clear none of that pity transfers to me.

"What do you want?" I ask.

She snorts a laugh at my foolish question and shakes her head. Then a spark lights her face as she asks, "Does it bother you that I've been building memories with him while he's forgotten you?"

I jump towards her, but Thoa wraps his arms around my waist and pulls me back. I don't know if it's to protect me or her. My rage boils to the surface and I spit at her, unable to do anything else.

She smiles wickedly and asks, "Has Tabarus told you about our vigorous sex life? It was definitely a perk of the job. Do you think he'll always think of me as his first?"

"I'm going to kill you," I growl.

My anger is so strong, I feel like I'm foaming at the mouth. I don't care about the things she says, about the way she tries to hurt me, but I will ruin her for what she's doing to him.

Thoa's arms tighten around me until I'm pulled back against his chest. He's warm, firm, reassuring. But he doesn't know me.

Tinora just stands there, smiling, her weapon digging into Yosh. "That's my favorite part about the whole thing. There's not a damn thing you can do. The guards will be here any second."

I hear a strange *pop* and realize Baz is gone. I want to look at Ivy, but I don't want to give her away.

Tinora asks, "What was that?"

"What?" I ask, drawing her attention.

I put my arms over Thoa's as they linger around my waist. I turn my head and look up at him. "I'm okay. You can let go."

He hesitates for only a second. I step towards Tinora, but the venom is out of me. My sister needs a distraction so she can do her part. I ask her, "Why do you hate me?"

She looks at me as I take another step towards her in the small room. There's only an arm's span between us now. She pushes Okada away and aims her weapon at me. I don't look at it, don't acknowledge the barrel pointed at my chest, keeping my eyes on hers.

There's another *pop* and she tries to look past me. I step forward until the gun is pressed against my body and say, "Answer me."

"You're a waste," she growls. "Of time, of space, of breath. You don't deserve the time they committed to trying to make you better, you don't deserve to occupy the same space as decent people, and you don't deserve the breath I'm wasting talking to you."

Pop pop.

I lean close to her and whisper, "You sound jealous."

She laughs and says, "Of what? You've got nothing left."

"It may seem that way—"

"It is that way," she cuts me off. "Anyone in your life would be better off without you, I mean, just look at Tabarus. Removing you from his life was the best gift Okada could've given him."

I feel my eyes go wide as Tinora asks, "What? You didn't know?"

Pop pop pop.

Tinora pushes me to the side, shifting her gun to Ivy. "What are you doing? Where is everyone else?"

"Gone," Ivy shrugs.

"How?"

Ivy holds up a small silver tube. Before another word can be said, she jabs it against Thoa's arm and with a *pop*, he disappears.

Tinora's brows shoot up, but her jaw tenses. "Give it."

Ivy tosses it forward and as Tinora moves to grab it, I dive for the gun. I knock it from her hand and it slides across the floor. Ivy's device clatters to the ground and I scramble for it while she tries to get the gun. I get to the device first and smash it against her leg just as her fingers graze the gun.

Tinora disappears.

There are boots behind me in the corridor, but I don't look at them. I step towards Ivy and she says, "Hurry, Nova, let's get out of here."

I put my hand on her shoulder and say, "You're strong, sis. Keep them together, keep them motivated."

"No," she says, shaking her head, "That's your job. You have to go with us."

"I'll find you again. I promise."

I shove the device against her arm and she disappears.

CHAPTER
FIFTEEN

I tuck Ivy's device as deep into my boot as I can and spin to face the guards I hear pounding towards the room. But they aren't in view yet. They must be coming from a different direction.

I shove the wall panel closed and turn to survey the room. There's nothing there to block the entrance—there's barely anything there at all. There's a handful of chairs, some tables holding Ivy's screens and gadgets, and a couple boxes stashed under the tables.

I pull out a box and rummage through it, hoping there's a weapon or two I can snag. I still have a taser I stole from the hall guards and now I have Tinora's gun, but I'd love to have a blade in my hand. The first box is useless, full of wires and shiny parts that don't seem to do anything. The second box is much the same and I'm about to give up when I see something behind where the boxes were stashed.

There's a hole cut into the wall and wires snake from Ivy's machines into it. I pull the wires free and shimmy inside. The opening was barely big enough for me to get through, but there's a hollow space inside the wall where parts of the ship converge and it's enough room for me to sit in relative comfort. I reach out and pull the cords from Ivy's machines back into the hole, pull the boxes back in front of me.

And I wait.

I can hear the guards outside Ivy's hideaway, stomping back and forth as they try to trace whatever signal they were using. Probably Tinora's. I wonder if they noticed when she blinked off the station and landed on-world.

Time is fluctuating for me, slow in the moments when I hear the guards near, quickly when they seem to be leaving, and I don't know how long it takes them to find the room. Several minutes at least, no more than an hour. I wish I could see their surprise when they find an empty room.

I listen as they tear away her equipment. I feel the tug of the wires in my hand as they pull at them and for a second I forget that I need to let go. But they tug harder and I release them, watching them slither out of my hiding hole. A moment later, a hand is gripping the edges of the hole. When it finishes inspecting the entrance, it moves into the hole, towards me.

My breath hitches in my throat as I watch the hand inch closer. I shift my body away from it as best I can, but the hole is small and there's nowhere to run.

The hand rakes across my leg.

It recoils, in surprise or uncertainty, I'm not sure which. I don't move, can't. But I slide the taser into my hand and ready myself for the next probe. But it doesn't come. Instead I hear the retreat of footsteps. The room outside this wall seems quiet, empty.

I count to ten, then a hundred, but there's nothing happening outside. Or they're all standing there with weapons pointed at the hole. I stifle a laugh as I imagine it. From what I've seen of the guards on the space station, they aren't patient enough to wait for me to come out. No, if they knew I was here, they would drag me out.

That means the hand that found me belongs to someone who doesn't want me turned over. There's only one person I can think of, one guard who showed me kindness while the others reveled in hurting me.

I maneuver myself through the hole feet first, finding it much more difficult to get out than it was to get in. The room is empty, like I thought it would be, but not just of people. Everything Ivy had built, every piece of her equipment, is gone. Even the cheap tables and chairs have been removed.

I move around the room, searching for anything I may have missed, anything the guards may have missed. I need a way out, but there doesn't seem to be any hidden compartments or panels that move. I let go of the last dregs of hope I was holding and my frustration buzzes around my brain with no way out. The only thing left in the room is a scrap of paper on the floor. I kick at it and the paper flutters weakly before dropping back on the ground.

I rub my fingers over my eyes until they water, then drop my hands to rest on my waist as I let my mind tick off all the things pressing against me. I'm a wanted criminal. I'm being hunted. I sent all my allies on-world. Everyone else I know is in captivity in a place I know nothing about. Except Bets. But I can't go back there and risk putting her in danger.

My head droops with the weight of my thoughts, heavy and lost. That's when I see the scribble. I pick up that damned scrap of paper and stare down at the red writing on it: *Red forest wall three hours.*

There's no name, no further instructions. Hells, I don't even know if it's for me. Maybe Ivy was going to rendezvous with one of her loves. Or maybe it's Vivon, like I want it to be—like I think it is.

I stuff the scrap of paper into my pocket and move for the exit. I put my ear to the wall and listen. It takes a minute to steady myself there, letting my senses reach past the sounds my own body makes. But soon the steadiness of my heartbeat fades into the background. I close my eyes and I'm on-world, on the hunt, listening for prey. The Raiders taught me how to do this, how to survive, how to win. I will win.

When I'm certain no one is walking outside the room, I pull up my hood, slide the door open, and step outside. There's a guard stationed to the right of the door. I jab the taser into his side before he registers my presence and he slumps to the ground.

I hear someone behind me before I see them. I spin from their reach just before their taser zaps the air where I was just standing. My hand hovers over Tinora's gun at my side, but then I catch eyes with the guard. They're scared, terrified even. I stop, surprised by the fear there.

"There's no shame in running," I say. I try to be soft, but my voice still grates hard against my ears.

They look at me, then down the corridor, undecided. They stammer, "I'll lose my job."

I say, "But you'll keep your life. Which is more important?"

In a whisper: "They say you're dangerous."

"I am. If you try to fight me, I will kill you." Then, softer, "But I don't want to."

They don't linger. I'm thankful I don't have to kill them. Fighting an enemy who chooses to battle me is not the same as murdering a kid in the wrong line of work.

The man still on the floor is coming to, so I tase him again before stripping him of his weapons. In addition to his taser, he has a baton and, to my delight, a knife. It isn't as sharp as I'd like, but it'll do. I tuck it into the waistband of my pants and slide the baton up my sleeve as I set off for the red section of the station.

IT TAKES THE BETTER PART OF THREE HOURS TO GET TO RED, BUT MY trek is blessedly uneventful. I see the most guards walking through blue and green, but once I hit gray and then red, they seem to fade into the background as civilians occupy the corridors.

I suppose they don't expect me to be here, this far away from those I know. It's a fair assumption, all things considered. Baz lived in blue, near the green border, and despite my running, I never strayed more than an hour from his home. Now that I think on it, I suppose it was a way of offering myself a bit of safety. I could always go back, if I had no other choice.

There's comfort in that, but sadness, too. I wish I'd realized it before now.

There's a holo at the next intersection flashing my face in shades of blue and white. My hair is still long, so they haven't noticed me and my shaved head yet. Small victory.

A couple stands in front of it, holding hands while discussing the girl on the screen. I hear one of the women say, "What do they expect when they bring those savages up here?" It takes everything in me not to punch the distaste off her face. I want to show her what a savage I am.

Instead, I remind myself of the good people I've met here, though they are few. They aren't all like this woman. I approach the women and with displeasure in my tone I say, "I can't believe they haven't caught that *thing* yet."

The woman nods, but doesn't look at me. "I was just saying the same to my wife."

"The thought of her running loose on the station," I scoff, "it's terrifying. She could be here, right now, and what could we do about it?"

"We'd probably smell her before we saw her. I heard she's been crawling around the waste tunnels," the other woman says.

I purse my lips in distaste. "It probably reminds her of home."

Both women laugh and the first turns to me. She squints like she recognizes me, but can't quite place me. "Are you from around here?"

"No," I say, turning enough to shake her stare. "I'm visiting. I'm supposed to meet my friend at the forest but I fear I've gotten turned around."

"You're not far off," the second woman says. She points down a side corridor and says, "Go two klicks and it'll be on your right. You can't miss it."

I smile as brightly as I can, brighter than a savage Raider has any right to smile. "Thank you so much." I step towards the corridor but slow and call over my shoulder, "Be careful out here. Hard to say what that savage will do next."

SHE WAS RIGHT. I COULDN'T MISS IT IF I TRIED.

One moment I'm trudging through the rounded metal walls, surrounded by pipes of gray and floor of gray and a gray hazy light. Then without warning, without signal or sign, the right side of the corridor opens into a forest. Not a few sporadic trees or a manicured park, like in the center of blue, but a real godsdamned forest.

I walk into the trees, surprised when there is no trail or guidance. This is not a place for people to stroll with ease, but a spot of nature, of home, amidst the monochrome structure outside. I wonder who built it, and why, and if they knew what they were creating when they did. It hits me then, that this beautiful place full of life is probably only here to replenish oxygen. It's as much a utility as the pipes in the halls carrying water and waste.

I prowl through the forest, but there is no need. It is empty, untouched. For a moment, I let my mind return to the ground. I run my fingers over the tree bark, relishing the roughness against my hand. A canopy of green rustles overhead and light shines through, dappling the forest floor with dancing light and shadow.

The ground itself is made of dirt and moss and leaves. The smell of earth and rotting leaves is pungent and sweet. I breathe deep, losing myself in the space around me, forgetting where and who I am.

But the moment is gone when I see a figure ahead. They're walking in a straight line away from me, presumably for the wall where I am to meet them. I trail behind them in silence, all sounds of my steps hidden by the soft ground. Not that I need that. I am a Raider.

We must be nearing the wall, because they stop and turn towards the forest. I duck behind a tree as they turn, hoping I was fast enough not to be seen. I wait, willing myself not to move too soon and expose my hiding place. After a minute has passed, I tip my head around the tree to look for my target, but no one is there.

I stand to survey the area. That's when I feel the taser press against my back. I raise my hands at my side, slowly, waiting for the shock. But it doesn't come. The taser moves away from me and I hear a laugh that I would know anywhere.

I grit my teeth as I turn to see him, his half-smile turning up his mouth as usual. I growl, "Benjy."

"Hey Nova. We need to talk."

CHAPTER
SIXTEEN

I kick the taser from his hand. My movement is so fast, so unexpected, that he yelps as my boot connects with his hand. I smile, unable to help myself. I *want* him to hurt. I want him to bleed.

There's a look of shock that rocks his features, dismissing his stupid grin. His eyes are trained on my right hand. I follow his gaze and surprise myself as well. I don't remember brandishing Tinora's gun at him, but there it is in my hand, my finger on the trigger.

A devilish smile tugs at my lips. "You chose wrong," I say, echoing the words Alexis spoke to him before they led her away.

He sucks in his cheeks, giving his lips a fish-like pucker. With a sound more like a heave than a sigh, he says, "I know."

The admission knocks the smile from my lips. There's no pleasure in shaming him when he agrees with me. I feel anger surge in my blood at his fickleness. "You're a fool."

He nods. "Alexis said the same thing when I told her what I'd done."

The words bite at me and I'm not sure why. I want to end him, forget he ever existed, but something about his statement clicks a missing piece into place. "She knew they were coming."

"For the last few months."

"How?"

He shrugs. "I messed up."

"Yeah, I picked up on that part."

His smile tips up the corner of his lips, but it doesn't stick. "I sold out the trial winners six months ago. I knew it was a mistake before the words were out of my mouth, but I couldn't take them back."

"Why'd you do it?" I ask.

He presses his lips into a tight line. "Does it really matter?"

"It might."

He shakes his head the smallest bit and I know he'll say no more. "I went straight to Alexis after. Told her everything. She was pissed, but we made a plan."

I turn his words over in my head, knowing he could be making this up to gain my trust. But the only way to know for sure is to keep him talking, trip him up. I remember the reactions of Qen and Osric, of Karina and Drev, and ask, "Did everyone know?"

"No, just Alexis." Then as if reading my thoughts he adds, "Guess that makes it pretty hard to know I'm telling the truth."

"One other person knew." We both turn towards the voice. Vivon is standing in the forest, his dark gaze resting on Benjy, a taser aimed at the man's chest.

He blends in well, with his dark green shirt and brown pants. I look back to Benjy in his plain white shirt that stands out stark against the forest backdrop. He may have followed me, may have found me first, but he is not who I was supposed to meet in this place.

"I knew you'd make it here eventually," Benjy says.

"Why are you here?" Vivon asks.

"Come on, Jackson," Benjy says. "We both know why I'm here."

"I don't know why either of you are here. Why don't you enlighten me?"

"Well, Jackson's here because he can't help himself from playing the hero."

"And Benjy's here because he's looking for redemption."

I look between the two men, unsure what history ties them together. Whatever it was is full of malice and mistrust. I venture, "Lovers?"

Jackson pulls a face and says, "You couldn't pay me enough."

Benjy smiles. "He's bitter because I rejected him."

"In your dreams."

"Okay," I say, trying to get things back on track while I process their reactions. "Tell me what you know about the deal Benjy struck."

"His mom was sick on-world. He was trying to get help for her. They told him they'd help her if he gave up the others."

I turn to Benjy, see the clench of his jaw, the crease forming between his brows at the mention of his mother. He grinds out, "They didn't help her."

The words sit in the air between us, immovable. He doesn't have to tell me she's dead; I can see it on his face.

I let my eyes slide back to Jackson. "How do you know about it?"

"I took his statement."

"You promised me," Benjy says, his voice raw.

Jackson's lips pucker in a scowl. "I believed them when they said they would. I swear it."

My hand holding the gun moves from Benjy to Vivon. "You're one of them."

"No," he says, bitterness seething through his tone. "Once, maybe. But not after I saw what they did to him."

Benjy swallows and meets my eyes. "After I betrayed my friends, they sent someone on-world to kill my mother. They made me watch it on the screens, telling me that was the *cure* on-worlders deserve."

"But didn't they realize you'd turn on them after that?" I sputter.

"My little sister is still there," he says. "They said she'd be next if I tried to go back on our deal."

Heat fills my gut and I want to rampage through this whole station, killing the monsters who live here.

"I'm sorry," Jackson says, his voice soft. "I know it doesn't matter, but I am."

"Yeah, you've said that before."

"And I'll keep saying it, because it haunts me. But I don't expect you to forgive the part I played."

"We were friends," Benjy hisses, spittle frothing on the edge of his mouth. "I trusted you. I let you talk me into going to the Règle's people."

"Why are you here now?" I ask, needing an answer from both of them.

They were so caught up in the past, the question seems to catch them both off guard. Jackson regains himself first, saying, "Benjy's right, I'm trying to be the hero. I know I can't fix what happened, but I can look for ways to do good."

"Rebellion in safe doses," Benjy mutters.

"You?" I ask, nodding to him.

"I told you, I messed up." He glances at Jackson before adding, "And I'm looking for redemption."

I chew on their words, their excuses, for a moment before saying, "I don't trust either of you."

"That's fair," Benjy shrugs.

"You need to if you want to survive," Jackson says. "Besides, I've had plenty of chances to screw you over but I've been on your side every time."

"The jailbreak," I say, ticking off my fingers, "and the hallway."

"And the hole in the wall," he says.

"So it was you," I say.

He nods. "You've got luck on your side. If anyone else had checked it, you'd be dead already."

"Dead?" I ask, eyebrows raising.

"You've caused too much trouble, kid. They're done. If they catch you, they'll kill you."

I'm genuinely surprised by the news. I had assumed I'd be taken into custody with the others, maybe sent back to the white room. It made them seem weak in my head, because there was always a way out. But there's no way out of death.

"What are you going to do?" Benjy asks.

It's a good question, but I don't have an answer. Jackson cuts into my thoughts, saying, "She's going to get out of this place."

I stare at him, trying to read his expression. If any part of his story is false and he is loyal to the Règle, I don't want to give anything away. I'm not ready to leave, not without the others, but I won't tell him that. Instead I ask, "How?"

"Your dad's office," he says.

If he knows about Ivy's device and my friends already on-world, he doesn't give any indication. I nod, as if considering his words, though really my mind is racing to process everything I know.

Benjy says, "I heard he was taken in."

I look at him, but find his green eyes staring at Jackson. He's gauging Jackson's reactions, too. For a second I'm thankful he's on my side, until I remember he's not. Or at least, not fully. There's a gray area between us, full of rights and wrongs and in-betweens, and our friendship is somewhere in the fogginess of it all.

"He was," Jackson says. "But his office is intact. They've appointed someone to lead the Chasseur in the interim."

"How are we supposed to bypass them?"

"It doesn't matter," I say, cutting them off before they can start bickering again. "Even if we could get in, I don't know how to use the equipment."

And I don't need it, I think. Ivy's device is suddenly heavy in my boot.

"Do you have a better idea?" Jackson asks.

My thoughts are churning in my mind, but everything keeps coming back to one idea. I nod and say, "Yeah, I do."

I toss my gun on the ground at Jackson's feet, followed by both tasers, the baton, and the knife. His eyes get bigger with each weapon I throw down, as if he's surprised at the treasure I've amassed. I smile at him, hold out my hands, and say, "Arrest me."

CHAPTER
SEVENTEEN

"This is a terrible idea," Jackson said again.

I say nothing. He's repeated that phrase since we left the forest, while we marched through the halls of red, green, and blue, and now as we stand in the processing center. He's said that after each hungry eye has passed over me, after each person has given him a begrudging clap on the back. They want to be him right now.

They should. He gets to live.

A buzzing sound fills the room and the door in front of us slides open. Jackson pushes my back, propelling me forward. I go without resistance. I fought him a bit in the corridor before we got here and I let him drag me in, for appearances, of course. But when the other guards started towards me with their tasers, I dropped the act and feigned a fear of their weapons. I need to be awake for what comes next.

We pass a row of glass boxes. They're so small that a bed won't even fit inside. The occupants are curled up on the floor or standing, glaring out as we pass. One woman takes two steps, turns, takes two steps; she prowls the square like a wild thing, a snarling beast. She has unruly black and silver curls pasted against her forehead above sharp brows and stormcloud eyes. I immediately love her.

When we reach the end of the boxes, I whisper a thank you to whatever gods may be listening. My plan would not work if I ended up in one of them. Jackson doesn't know that part though, because I did not tell him my plan. I didn't tell him much of anything. Though I want to trust him, I don't. I will leave him with his life when I leave here, but nothing will let me trust a guard.

He puts me in a cell only slightly bigger than the glass boxes. I stand at the bars and glare at him, hoping he understands the gratitude I can't express. When he leaves, I throw myself onto the bed in mock frustration. I lie there as the guards form groups to taunt me. This happens several times before they've all had their fill, but eventually the cycle stops.

They bring us soggy nutrition bricks for dinner. Once they've served the entire line and left, I make my way to the edge of my cell and pretend to eat while trying to get the attention of the person next to me. I make noises, hiss and snap and cough at them, but they will not acknowledge me.

"Hey," I say, giving up on being conspicuous.

"Shut your mouth," he says, his voice rumbling like distant thunder. "You're going to get us both in trouble."

"I have a question."

"No one in these cells has the answer. If we did, we wouldn't be here."

"Do you know Alexis the Huntress?" He grunts, and I take it as a signal to keep going. "Has she been here?"

He nods. "This morning."

"Where is she now?"

He shrugs one shoulder. "They took her out a few hours ago, with the other trial winners."

"Out where?"

"How should I know? High security? Death chamber? Once they're gone from these holding cells, I'll never see them again."

"But you're still here."

He smirks. "I'm a nuisance, not worth the resources it takes to guard me. They know I'm contained."

I hesitate. Then, voice going quiet, I ask, "Do you want out of here?"

He looks at me from the side of his eyes, his glance relaying his skepticism. "There's no way out of the Règle's prisons."

"I can get you on-world if you'll help me."

"Bullshit."

"I'm serious. But I'll only do it if you help me."

We sit in silence for several minutes and I think he's done with me. Then from the near-darkness beside me I hear a voice rumble, "What do you need me to do?"

HIS NAME IS HAWKINS. HE REFUSES TO TELL ME ANYTHING FURTHER, no details about why he's here. I find his distrust of me endearing. It makes me trust him more.

In the middle of the night, I crawl into the floor and begin to writhe. I cry out, letting my voice echo through the cells. I don't look around to see if I have anyone's attention. Instead, I squeeze my eyes shut and let my contorting body do all the work.

Hawkins yells, "Medic!" with enough gusto that he genuinely sounds concerned.

I suppress a smile at the growing sound of boots clanging against the metal floor. So far, so good. I scream as a pretend spasm hits me and roll towards the bars between me and Hawkins. There's mumbling at the door, arguing. I catch a few stray words like "vicious" and "psychopath" before someone loses the battle and is forced to open my cage. The door clangs open, I hear the shuffle of boots, and then someone kneels beside me.

Hands go to my face, my neck. A light glows on the other side of my eyelids. A tender voice asks, "Can you hear me, miss? Can you open your eyes?"

No, I think, though of course I can. But I don't want to. Because this is wrong. There should not be kindness in his voice. There should not be compassion if I am to kill him.

I let my eyes turn to slits, but the light he's shining is bright and I can see nothing beyond it. Still, there's a smile in his voice when he says, "Okay, good. Can you tell me where it hurts?"

He moves the light from my eyes and shines it down my body as if searching for an injury. I take the opportunity to look at him, to find his weakness. It takes longer than it should for me to realize I know him. I watch his long limbs as he moves around me, remembering how I felt wrapped between him and Bets.

Damn it. I can't kill him as I planned.

I look past his stubbled head and count the guards behind him. Only two. One is in the cell, barely three feet from me. The other waits on the other side of the bars, hands outstretched as they brandish a weapon at me.

When Bets' roommate comes back to my head and is blocking the others again, I open my eyes and look at him. He still hasn't realized who I am, too determined to figure out what ails me. When his searching eyes finally find mine, I whisper, "Xander."

He jerks back, pulled from his thoughts. He looks at me then, not as a medic but as a man hearing the voice of a lover. He blinks a couple times before muttering, "Holy crap."

"I won't tell if you won't," I say, letting my lips curl into a smile.

"What's going on?" one of the guards asks.

I shake my head. "Just move out of my way. I don't want to hurt you."

He presses his lips into a thin line. "I can't do that."

His hand darts into the air, flying down towards me. I swing my legs out of the way just as a needle lands where my hip was a second before. I scramble away from the medic, surprised by the speed with which he pursues. He lunges towards me with the needle but I dodge him again. He slams against the cell bars and though he turns to attack again, he can't. Hawkins has his hands wrapped around Xander's throat.

I dive for the closest guard. Though they have a taser trained on me, their eyes are wide as if they're shocked to need it. They shouldn't be, if they know me at all, but I'd venture this night crew guard hasn't had to use their weapon in these low security cells before. Hell, maybe they're new. Either way, I use their surprise against them, kicking out before they can register I'm attacking them. I knock the taser from their hand and move in close. I swing my elbow into their face with as much force as I can muster. Their head whips back and they slump down.

They're not dead, but they're stunned enough to let me move to the next guard. She's quicker than the other. She has pulled the cell door closed and backed away from me. Her weapon is aimed at my chest and I can tell she's not afraid to use it. I pull on the cell door but it doesn't budge. She's locked it, though that meant locking the others in with me.

I pick up the discarded taser from the floor and let my fingers trail over it. There has to be a way to use it at a distance. I step back to the cell door and aim it at the guard. She steps back, confirming my assumption. I smile at her, delighted when she takes another step back.

Before I can figure out the taser, I hear a thud behind me and turn towards it. Hawkins is on the ground, Xander's needle jabbed into his hand.

"What did you do to him?" I ask.

Xander rubs at his neck. "He's sedated. But they'll float him once they find out he tried to help you." Xander raises his voice and says, "You hear that? Anyone who tries to help this woman will get floated."

I bare my teeth at him as we square off. He digs in the bag at his hip, pulling out another needle. I ask, "Why are you fighting me?"

"It's my job."

"You're a medic, not a guard."

"I'm both, when I have to be."

"You could stay down and no one would blame you. They know me."

He shakes his head. "There's nothing you can say to convince me."

"What about Bets?" I ask. "She cares about me, and you care about her."

He seems to think about it for a minute before deciding, "She'll get over it. And she'll never have to know I had any part in it."

I sigh. "I want to let you live. For her. But you're making it difficult."

He lunges with the needle, and he nearly nicks me, but he goes wide and I'm able to slip under his arm. I jab the taser against him and watch his eyes roll back as his body convulses. He falls to the floor with a heavy thump. I swipe the needle from his hand and jab it into his leg for good measure. I pull his medic bag from his hip and fasten it to mine. There are two more needles inside.

I turn to the other guard locked in with me. They're up enough to show that they're alive, but instead of attacking while my focus was off them, they've curled into the corner as far from me as they can get. When I take a step towards them, they hold up their hands in surrender.

"How do I add range to this?" I ask, waving their taser at them.

Hands still raised, they say, "Switch on the bottom."

I run my finger along the bottom of the taser and there is a switch. I flip it and turn back to the corridor. I don't know what I expected to find there—obviously the guard wouldn't be standing there doing nothing this whole time—but I'm shocked by what greets me.

The guard is on the floor and blood blooms on the ground beneath her. A slip of a girl stands in the cell behind her, dressed in a dirty shirt that hangs to her thighs, no pants or shoes. She's holding up a sticky red hand, twisting it around to catch the light. She meets my eyes and smiles.

I try to return her smile, but it's more of a grimace. This girl, this *child* who can't be more than twelve, ripped into a guard with her bare hand. I don't know how she did it and I don't want to know. But I owe her.

"Thanks," I say, tipping my head towards the guard.

She smiles again. It's a wolfish thing, more animal than human. When she speaks, her voice is small and dainty. "You're welcome."

I look down at the guard in the corner who chose to live and say, "Keys."

They toss them to me with shaking hands. I'm honestly surprised at the jangling things that land in my palm. You'd think these people would have more advanced imprisonment rather than relying on locks and keys. Then again, Ivy has proven that the electronic systems can be hacked. A physical key has to be obtained. Tried and true, I guess.

I reach through the bars and unlock my cell, closing it behind me as I leave. I step over the body bleeding out and move into Hawkins' cell. I press my fingers against his wrist and feel a pulse. Now I just need to figure out how to take him with me. I'm strong, but he's too large for me to carry. Besides, I'll need my hands free when we find trouble.

"I can carry him."

I look up and find icy blue eyes on me. The man is pressing against the bars with both hands, resting his weight against them. For a second, I'm certain the bars trembled under his force. He is a mountain in human form, bigger than Thoa, bigger than anyone I've ever seen.

"Why?" I ask.

"I'm bored."

A laugh bubbles up and I can't help but smile at him. I nod and walk over to his cell. Hawkins made it sound as if the people in these cells aren't bad enough to warrant stronger security, but I still feel a twinge of panic as I put the key in the lock and release the monster from its cage. He passes by me and I feel a thrill of intimidation run through me just from the sheer size of him. I can't imagine how many guards it took to subdue him.

He comes out of the cell with Hawkins over his shoulder looking more like a sack of flour than a person. The man steps in front of me, his face wearing a question. It takes me a minute to realize he's waiting for me to tell him what's next.

I stammer, "I'm looking for my friends."

"The Huntress," he says. "I heard your plans."

"We all did," a voice says from behind me.

I turn towards the mazulla prisoner. They're perched low on the ground but not sitting, arms wrapped around their legs, chin resting on their knees. I ask, "Why didn't any of you offer help?"

They chuckle. "No one thought you'd get out of the cell."

"But we can help," the mountain says. "Release the lot of us. We'll fight for you."

The idea of having this group at my back is heartening, but terrifying. I glance at the little girl with blood dripping from her arm. I don't know why all these people are here, what they've done, what they might do in the future. If I take them all on-world, what havoc might they wreak?

"She won't," the little girl says. "The big bad Raider is afraid."

"Shut up, Sarah," the mazulla prisoner says.

"Make me, Edi," she taunts, sticking out her tongue.

I press my lips into a grim line and force away my fears like pushing air out of my lungs. I can't be afraid of these people; in many ways, I am one of them. I cross the space and open Edi's cell, then Sarah's. I go cell to cell until there are a dozen prisoners surrounding me.

"What about them?" the mountain asks, pointing to the glass boxes.

"They're the bad ones," Sarah says. "They'll go to high sec soon."

I take a shallow breath at her words. She punched her hand *through* a guard, but seems to be afraid of them.

"Sarah, I told you to shut your mouth," Edi says. "You *know* they're only guilty of trying to survive. They're just surviving in a way that doesn't please the Règle. Don't buy into the bullshit."

I look at the keys in my palm, back at the boxes. The decision is easier than it should be.

I approach the first box and look at the keyhole. It isn't like the others. This slot is thin, too thin for a key. There's a strip of hard plastic attached to the keyring I'm holding and I slide it in, willing to try anything. I refuse to leave anyone at the mercy of the star-people.

It works. The front panel of glass lifts into the air and releases the man within. He pushes past me and heads straight for Sarah. He grabs her and pulls her to his chest, holding her with a fierce protectiveness I've never seen before. She swats at him, but he doesn't let go. Father? Brother?

I release the next prisoner, even though my brain keeps yelling at me that these people are dangerous. But so am I. Now I face the prowling woman. She isn't prowling now. She's as close to the glass as she can get without touching it, staring at me with her intense stormcloud eyes.

Her gaze makes me nervous and I nearly drop the keys. But I don't. I get the box open and she steps out. She takes a deep breath like she's been waiting years to inhale fresh air. Then she puts her hands on my shoulders and presses her forehead to mine.

"Thank you," she says.

The gesture surprises me. Her smile as she pulls away is even more disarming. I finish opening the last three cubes, then turn back to the assembly of criminals. I don't have time to get to know these people, to learn to trust them, so I search through the faces until I find the stoic mountain and I ask, "Where can I find the Huntress?"

CHAPTER
EIGHTEEN

No one knows for sure where they took her and the other trial winners, but the consensus is that they would've been moved to the high security detention center after questioning. If I'd waited, that's where I would've ended up, too.

Little Sarah says she saw them individually taken for questioning, and the prowling woman says they brought back the winners, but not their family and friends.

"They might've sent the family home," Edi says.

The mountain says, "Doubtful. They'll hold them as long as they think they're useful."

"We'll need them all before we get out of here," I say. I look at them and add, "I'm going on-world. I'm willing to take anyone who wants to go."

"How you gonna do that, kid?" someone asks.

I feel Ivy's device pressing against my leg. I'm sure Jackson felt it when he did his mock search when he brought me in, but he left it. "Let me worry about that. For now, I need some volunteers to help me free the winners. I'll need everyone else to clear us a path out of here."

"I've been to high sec before. We can do it with four, I think, if they're tough enough," the prowler says. She points at the mountain and says, "Zeb needs to be one of them."

He nods and hands Hawkins off to two others. He says, "I want Edi with us."

They move to stand with Zeb. Sarah moves to his side as well, but the man from the box pulls her back to him. She shakes off his hand and says, "I want to go with them."

"I don't give a damn," the man says.

"Dad," she whines, "I can handle myself."

"You shouldn't have to," he barks.

She flinches back from him, seeing him as angry instead of protective. I say, "We'll need you with the other group, Sarah. There will be a lot of guards to get past, and they'll need your strength."

I can see the doubt on her face, but she nods and doesn't argue further. Though her father doesn't say anything, I can see the relief on his face. He may not be able to keep her completely out of harm, but at least he'll have her at his side.

In the end, we prep for high security with Zeb, Edi, me, and the prowler, Valeska. Sarah's dad takes control of the other group and starts planning how they're going to find and rescue the trial winners' family and friends, while Valeska fills us in on everything she knows about the high security area.

"We'll go through there," she says, pointing to a door at the end of the hall opposite where they brought me in. "There's a stairwell with a checkpoint at the bottom before you can get into the block. That's the trickiest part because we'll have no cover. Also, I don't know exactly how many will be at the first door."

"We can rush them," Edi says.

Valeska shrugs. "We'll have to unless someone has a better idea." She looks at each of us, but when no one says anything, she goes on. "Once we get past that, there will be a team of guards on the other side of the door. One of them will have access to get us into the regular corridor."

"That doesn't sound too bad," Zeb says.

Valeska nods. "The tricky part is that we'll need to make sure whoever has the access stays alive. After they use their key, they'll still need to verify a pincode to the guard on the other side of the door."

"And we won't know which one it is, so we can't kill any of them," Edi says.

"Exactly. Even after we figure it out, we'll have to keep them alive to get back out," Valeska says.

"Let's say we manage to get in and everything has gone right," I say. "What's after that?"

"If we get in, there will be another team on the other side of the door. Same problem. We'll need them alive to get back out. There will likely be another couple guards walking the corridor. Someone after the second door will have access to open the prisoner's doors, but I have no idea who."

I feel a heaviness settle over us and I want to break it before it becomes too much. I put on my brightest smile and say, "That doesn't sound too bad. Easy even."

Valeska raises one brow as she looks at me. I can tell I'm not fooling her, but instead of calling out my lie she says, "Definitely doable."

I give her a nod, a silent thanks for backing me up. Zeb looks doubtful, but Edi seems excited. I try not to evaluate my own feelings. If I did, I'm not sure I'd have the courage to place one foot in front of the next, much less to storm a high security prison for people I barely know.

"Let's go," I say, before anyone can change their mind. Before I can change mine.

We move towards the end of the corridor, but a half-formed thought pops into my head and I turn back just before going through the door. I catch sight of the guard still locked in my cell and let my lips curl up as the last piece falls into place.

THE GUARD'S UNIFORM IS A LITTLE SHORT AT THE ANKLES AND TIGHT IN the chest, but overall not a bad fit. I release a deep breath as I walk down the steps. I'm too nervous, too unsure. I try to look purposeful but I don't think I'm pulling it off. At least I have backup just above me, hidden on the stairwell switchback.

The first checkpoint comes into view and I furrow my brows as I nod towards those watching my approach. There are only three of them, a woman and two men, and I can feel the tightness in my chest loosen just a bit. The woman's hand has already moved to her taser—no, not a taser, these guards have guns—and she's watching me through narrowed eyes.

"State your business," one of the men says, his words flowing around his yawn.

"One of the prisoners is needed for further interrogation," I say, trying to keep my tone as bored as his.

"Haven't seen an order," the other man says, pulling out a device from his pocket. He punches a couple buttons and shakes his head. "Yeah, still nothing."

"Really?" I ask, stepping closer to him.

I hold out my hand as if to look at the device for myself. He reaches it forward and I grasp his arm and twist it so his body moves in front of me. He gives a yelp of surprise, but moves with ease, as a dancer completing their required steps. I pull his gun from his hip and press it against his temple so that the other guards can see me.

"Put down your guns."

"Screw you," the woman says. "Put yours down."

"I will kill him," I say.

I feel a shiver pass through the man. He knows I'm telling the truth. He whispers, "I don't want to die. Not like this."

The woman grits her teeth and growls, "She won't kill you. You're her only bargaining chip."

I hear a thud and peek out from behind the man. The other guy is on the floor. I didn't see Zeb at work, but I can imagine one hit from his boulder-sized hands would do enough damage to drop him.

Valeska has the woman pinned against the door, hands above her head. She's leaning close to the woman's face, and for a second I think she's going to kiss her. Instead she hauls her head back and slams it into the woman's forehead. Her gun falls from her fingers and she slumps to the floor.

The man in my grip has gone stone still as if hoping to be forgotten. I release my grip on him and say, "Have a seat."

Valeska glances to me. "What are you doing?"

"He's not going anywhere," I say. "If he moves, I'm going to shoot him. He wants to live, so he'll stay right there."

She runs her tongue across her teeth but doesn't say anything. Zeb yells for Edi to come down, not realizing she's already lurking on the steps, and a minute later we're all gathered at the checkpoint.

I point at the guy on the floor and say, "You. Get me in there."

He shakes his head, but it's not convincing. He's already given himself away, telling me he doesn't want to die, and that's a weakness I can use.

I stare at the weapon in my hand. It isn't like other guns I've seen. There's no place to insert bullets, no trigger to pull. The barrel is sleek and cylindrical, coming to a narrow point with a tiny hole at the end. I point it at the wall a few feet from the man and press the button where the trigger should be. A thin red light blasts out of it, putting a hole in the wall.

Surprise registers on my face, delight even. No recoil, no smoke or scent, and the sound was so minimal, it's difficult to believe it blew a hole in the wall. But it did. A big one.

A smile spreads across my face as my eyes slide to the guard. "I'll count to three." His eyes go wide but he doesn't say anything. I point his own gun at his leg and say, "One."

"I don't know," he says, breathless.

I aim at his arm and say, "Two."

"She's the one who goes in," he whines, holding up his hands. "I've never been past the checkpoint."

I move the barrel to one of his upheld hands and say, "Three."

He must see my finger lingering over the button and realize I'm really about to blast his hand off because he drops into a ball and bellows, "Wait!"

I keep my hand steady, though I'm itching to press the button. I've got nothing against this man, but my blood is singing in my ears, my Raider heart begging for a fight.

Valeska says, "I'd figure it out if I were you. She will shoot you."

He nods. "I believe you."

"Then why are you still wallowing on the floor?" she asks. "Get your ass up and get us into the next section."

He scurries onto his feet and moves to the door, hands raised the whole time. He bends towards the woman on the ground but thinks better of it, looking from Valeska to me and back again. "I need her badge. Can I go through her pockets?"

I nod and he starts searching her pockets. He pulls a small red triangle from her pocket and puts it into a slot in the door that I wouldn't have noticed without him pointing it out. His fingers are shaking.

"You know the code?" Valeska asks.

He shakes his head. "Only the card at this point, but the next one requires a passcode as well."

"How many are beyond these doors?" I ask.

He nearly smiles at the question, seemingly relieved that he can answer me. "A quad at each point."

I nod. I point the blaster at the door as it starts to slide open. Remembering that we need these guards alive, I put away the gun and pull out my taser. "Get ready."

"Can I go?" the guard asks.

I know what he means, but I can't let him leave. "Sure. You can go first."

His face rises and falls, a tide of emotion and my words are his moon. He swallows, turns to face the door, and steps through.

The next few minutes are an exercise in chaos. There are not four guards inside, there are eight. I throw myself in after the guard, who has fallen into the corner of the room to get out of the way. I swing my taser hand into the chest of the closest guard and press into the fray. The guards are slow, shocked, and though they are clearly better fitted and equipped than the guards upstairs, they are not prepared for us.

I jab my thumb into the eye of the second guard I reach, duck away from his wild punches. I drop in front of him and reach forward with the taser, hitting him right on his soft bits. Wild pain smears across his face, painting it red and blotchy, before he plummets to the ground like a sinking stone.

As I rise, I see a fist coming towards me but can't dodge it. I turn my head enough to avoid a direct hit, but the punch is hard enough that I feel my nose crack under their knuckles. I slip under their arm, still held up from their valiant nose-breaking victory. I hammer against their ribs in quick succession, my grin bloody as I'm rewarded with breaks of my own.

They've pulled back now and moved into a fighting stance. We dance around each other in the midst of the other fighting, both of us sporting wolfish grins. I take in the gray at his temples, the wrinkles at the corners of his eyes. He's not new, not afraid; no, this man is hardened, a force to be reckoned with. Even as I think this, I'm certain he can win this fight.

But then his body stutters, shakes, and falls to the floor.

I look up to see Edi holding a taser. I say, "That was my fight."

"You weren't fighting. You were just grinning like you wanted to screw him."

I scoff. "He is a warrior, a fine specimen. I wanted the challenge, the grudging respect from a fellow brawler."

They roll their eyes, ignore everything I said. "We don't have time for you to screw him, Nova."

I drop my fists and look around the room. The other guards are subdued and everyone is waiting for me. I shrug and mumble, "I'm not saying I wouldn't."

Edi smiles and I do, too.

Valeska has found a locker in the corner of the room full of batons and security cuffs. She passes us each a baton as we use the cuffs to secure the guards. She looks around when we're done, her eyes finding the guard from the first checkpoint. She hauls him up and says, "You said a quad. That's four, asswipe."

"Sh-shift change?" he asks.

Valeska and I are both staring death glares at him, but Zeb starts laughing. Valeska asks him, "What's so funny?"

"Nothing," he says, though he's still chuckling. "It just seems fitting that we'd show up in the middle of a shift change."

"That's our lucky break. There should be two with a code," Valeska says as she pushes the guard back to the floor and meets Zeb's laugh with one of her own. After a moment of easiness, we turn back to the task at hand. Valeska looks around the room and asks, "Okay, who has the code?"

No one moves. No one speaks.

Valeska pulls out the gun she'd taken from the woman at the first checkpoint and spins around, pointing it at someone random. She stares into the man's eyes and asks, "Who has the code?"

Again, no one says a word. Valeska pushes the button. The red line shoots straight through the guy's chest, leaving a smoking hole and the stench of burnt flesh. She spins again, her aim on someone else. "We can keep doing this. I know there are two of you in this room. What are the chances I'll kill you both?"

I say, "Or you can tell us who has the code and live."

"Kill each of us," a gruff voice says, "but you're not getting into high sec."

Valeska spins to the voice. She points her gun at him and smiles. "Nova, it's your boyfriend. He's got it."

The older man's eyes shift to me, but there's no denial on his lips. Zeb bends over and lifts him to his feet. I step in front of him and say, "Look, we both know you don't want these men to die. Just give us the code and we'll be out of your hair."

"Screw. You."

I smile up at him, unable to resist his charm. "I'm flattered, but I don't have time right now. I'm trying to rescue some people illegally imprisoned."

"Enemies of the Règle are in these cells. Enemies of the Règle will remain."

I shake my head. "Don't be like this. Save yourself and all these people you're responsible for."

"I will not break my oath. Kill us all. Paint this place in my blood. I serve the Règle now and always. We all do."

I see his eyes flick to the ground, so briefly I almost don't notice, before Edi steps forward with her taser and says, "Let's get this done."

She jabs it into his chest. The man falls back, shaking against those still seated. Valeska sighs and says, "Look, I don't really want to keep killing you, but this old asshole isn't giving me much choice."

I point at the woman on the ground, wedged between the dead guard and the one from the first checkpoint. "You have the other key and code."

Her eyes go wide. "How…"

"Look," I say, "we're not here to hurt you. We want to get our friends and get out."

"But what does that mean for us later?" she asks, and I can see her brain spinning through scenarios.

"Nothing. We're leaving the station," Valeska says.

I want to smack her for giving out that secret, but at this point I don't know that it really is a secret anymore. By now, they must've worked out what happened to Ivy and the others.

"Impossible," the girl says.

"It's really not," I say. "You let us get our friends and we'll be out of your hair forever. The Règle will be grateful not to have to deal with us anymore."

"You'll probably get a promotion," Zeb says.

She looks around the room, at us, at her comrades, and the dead man beside her. But her eyes skip over my sexy tough guy and I know she's ours. "I want your word you won't kill anyone else."

"I give it," I say. "And I want your word you'll let us pass when we're finished."

Now her eyes do flick to him, but she returns her gaze to me and says, "Agreed."

I help her to her feet, confirm she's disarmed, and uncuff her hands. She pulls a piece of plastic from her pocket, a violet disc, and slides it into the door. She punches in a code before pressing a button on the speaker beside the door. When it crackles to life she says, "Captain Alik Rolfrun, second shift, requesting entry."

"*Passcode.*"

There is no question in his voice. It is a demand. Captain Alik Rolfrun replies posthaste. "4qr759hrk12p-yu7f."

"*Confirmed.*"

The door slides open and we're met with four blasters aimed at our heads.

CHAPTER
NINETEEN

My eyes glide to the Captain. She's smiling, clearly satisfied with herself. I say, "Guess your word wasn't worth much."

"I gave my word to the Règle long before today. Anything else I say must be in service to him or it is void as soon as it crosses my lips."

"Soooo, you're a liar," Valeska says.

The Captain grits her teeth together. "I will not have my honor questioned by the likes of you." She steps past us to meet the guards in the other room. "Take them into custody. And be sure to check them for weapons."

They pull us into the next room, beyond the second checkpoint, and close the door. The room is larger than the last, but not by much. There are windows and a door at the front of the room, looking out onto a darkened cellblock. Two guards keep their guns trained on us while the other two break away to tie our hands and pat us down. None of us struggle or attempt to fight, though I can see how difficult it is in the set of Zeb's shoulders, in the twitch of Edi's jaw. Valeska doesn't try to hide it, simply bares her teeth at them.

"I was afraid you wouldn't recognize the code," I hear the Captain say, making small talk with one of the armed guards.

His lip curls in obvious disgust. "Why wouldn't we?"

Her smile falters and she seems to lose her confidence for a moment. I watch as she glances at him, trying to think of what to say next, and that's when I realize that she has a *thing* for him. This was never only about her loyalty to the Règle, it was about impressing this guy as well.

There's something strangely relaxing about knowing you can't save yourself, and for a moment I am lost in that feeling, lost in an awkward moment between two people I don't know.

She has good taste, if I'm being honest. His skin is brown, smooth aside from the dark stubble on his head. Tattoos scroll up thick arms and disappear under the sleeves of his uniform before they tell his full story.

I feel a twinge in my gut for what I'm about to do, but I need the Captain gone and this man is a weakness I can exploit. I meet his brown eyes that glint gold when the light catches them and I give him a conspiratorial smile. "You know she wants to sleep with you, right?"

He doesn't spare her a glance, though he smirks at me, when he says, "Yeah, I know."

Asshole, I think, but I'm not sure if I mean him or me.

The woman's face is instantly crimson and she looks like she wants to crawl into a service vent and die. Lousy move on my part, but the results are immediate. She turns on her heel and presses her card into the wall slot, giving a code through the speaker.

I jolt as hands move down my back. I'd nearly forgotten about the pat down. Still, I ignore the guard touching me and manage a smile at the Captain's back as she leaves, thankful to have one less set of eyes on me. Before the relief can set in, the guard patting me down runs his hand along my boot for a second pass, realizing there's something hidden there.

"Gun at the ready," he says. "Got something."

When he pulls Ivy's device from where it's been pressed against my leg, I feel a strange sense of relief. I'm glad this is over.

The guard stands in front of me, finger roaming over the metal. "What is th—"

Pop!

The device falls to the ground as the guard disappears to the world below us. Confusion settles thick between them and my crew, everyone but me trying to figure out what just happened. I waste no time, diving for the tool while the rest try to gather themselves.

My hands are bound in front of my body, but that doesn't stop me from grabbing the device and rolling to a stop in front of the closest guard. I flick the device onto his boot and press the button, sending him planet-side.

"Stop!" one of the guards yells.

I freeze, glancing up to see the non-hot guard with a blaster pointed between my eyes. I'm pinned down, and my crew seems to just now be realizing that a.) the two guards are gone because of me, and b.) we've just missed our only chance to escape. Valeska's arm twitches towards the guard, but the Captain's hot-guard points his gun at her.

"Put it down," hot-guard says. He's looking at Valeska, but I think he must be talking to me. I move as slow as possible to put the device on the ground, but even as my fingers let it go, he repeats, "I said to put it down."

"She did," the other guard says.

"I wasn't talking to her."

The second guard spins his gun on hot-guard as he realizes what was said, but it's too late. A red energy bolt passes through his forehead, splattering viscera over the floor, the wall, and Valeska.

Hot-guard holsters his weapon and heaves a sigh. "Well, that was intense."

I close my dropped jaw as he steps towards me and helps me to my feet. I mutter, "Thanks?"

"Yeah, no problem. Honestly, thank you. I didn't want to shoot *all* of them so you really helped me out."

"But you wanted to shoot some of them?" Zeb asks.

It seems we're all a bit surprised by this turn of events and unsure how to proceed. But hot-guard doesn't miss a beat. "I mean, I guess? Not really? I'm not sure how to answer that. That guy was a bit of a dick, but I hadn't intended to kill him."

Nothing he's saying is clearing up the confusion, so instead of trying to figure it out, I say, "Well, thanks for the help. How about you untie us and I'll take your gun."

He shoots me a wicked grin, pulls a knife from his pocket and slices the plastic binding my wrists. He flips his gun in his hand and gives it to me grip first. "Here you go."

I take his weapon while he moves to untie the others. After I put Ivy's device back in my boot, I consider pointing the gun at him, but the action seems fruitless considering how much he's already done for us.

"What's your name?" I ask.

"You can call me your Hiro."

I frown. "I'm never calling you my hero."

He flashes a grin and says, "But Hiro is literally my name."

I feel my brows furrowing, but I don't say anything else. I feel like Hiro gains ground every time I speak and I don't want to give him anything else until I know what his endgame is.

When everyone is free, I ask, "Where are the trial winners?"

Hiro holds up his hands as he moves towards the console in the corner. He says, "I'm gonna turn on some lights."

As the lights come on through high sec, I see eager faces staring back at us. They must've heard the commotion and, though we couldn't see them sitting in the dark, I'm sure they saw us in this well-lit box.

"I have the key," hot-guard says. "Just show me which ones to open."

"All of them," I say.

Zeb turns on me. "Nova, you can't do that here."

"Why not?"

"These aren't just petty criminals and people who pissed off the Règle," Edi says. "There are some bad people here."

"Who better to sew chaos?" Valeska asks. I meet her gaze and see something dark there, something frightening. "They'll be so busy trying to capture the killers that they'll let us slip by."

"That is a terrible idea."

I turn towards the voice of my father. The last time I saw him, I punched him in the face. Now though, his face is like a beacon in the dark. We step towards each other at the same time, wrapping each other in an embrace. It doesn't last long, but it's enough to buoy me and let me know I'm on the right path.

As soon as our hug is over, Ledwin Kennedy goes straight into serious talk. "You can't let all these people out. No matter what the Règle has done, there are innocent people on this station and you'd be subjecting them to torture."

"The Règle already tortures her citizens. You should know, since you've been helping her for years," Valeska spits.

I grind my teeth at her words and find myself speaking before I realize I'm doing it. "He may have led the Chasseur, but it wasn't like he had a choice. He was appointed to the job. And he's been working from the inside to prepare for the Règle's demise."

Ledwin puts his hand on my shoulder to still me, but I can see the pride on his face. He's happy with my words. He says, "I remember you. You tried to go on-world with a trial winner, what, six years ago?"

She nods. "Your people shot him in the back. We'd been on-world less than a minute."

"I'm sorry," he says. I know he's telling the truth, that he really does regret what happened to him, but Valeska pays him no mind.

"Save it for someone who cares."

"You won't find someone who cares more than me. I know it may not make sense to you, but every deed I've done for the Règle has been a tragedy in one way or another. For someone here, or on-world. But that doesn't mean we should punish those who had nothing to do with Marc's death."

She looks up at the mention of his name. "You..." she shakes her head like she's trying to get something out.

"I remember," Ledwin says. "You know, they took my wife from me, too. And my daughter." He points at me. "For years I thought she was dead. When we found her, I petitioned the Règle to go to her. I was refused. I had to watch her toiling below, growing up without her parents, because the Règle was petty and didn't want me distracted from my duty."

I blink at the words and stare between them in stunned silence. This is a side of the story I haven't heard. Maybe because I wasn't ready to hear it before. I was too busy judging my father for leaving, for not finding me sooner, not realizing what it had cost him.

After a moment Valeska says, "I'm here because of Nova's mercy. I won't go against her decision and because of her, I will still my hand against you. But I do not forgive you, no matter what you say."

"You're right," Ledwin says. "The choice is Nova's."

All eyes turn to me and I feel the weight of their gazes. Both decisions are wrong, so I make the one that feels less bad. "We'll free those we came to free, but the others will stay."

"Alrighty," Hiro says as he moves to Osric's cell.

Ledwin asks, "How did you know Hiro was on our side?"

"Our side?" I ask.

He smiles. "You didn't know, did you?"

I shrug. "Just lucky, I guess."

"He's a good guy," Ledwin says. "Oddball, but good."

"How do you know him?" I ask.

"I trained him as one of the Chasseur. He never had the stomach for traveling on-world, so he left a couple years ago to work as a guard."

There's a group gathered around us now and I meet the eyes of each of the trial winners. But one set of eyes is missing. My eyes flick to the other cells, but I don't see her. My insides are quaking as I ask, "Where's the Huntress?"

"She should be in the upper cells," Grieva says.

I shake my head. "That's where I was. She's not there."

"With the kids?" Osric asks, though his tone suggests he isn't convinced, and neither are the rest of us, but it's the only hope we have right now.

"I sent some others to look for any family still being held. She's probably with them."

"What about Drev and Karina?" Qen asks.

I can see the unspoken question on their face, but they dare not ask about Benjy. "They're on-world. We'll be with them soon. Benjy is still here, still free."

"To hell with Benjy," Qen says, the words falling from their lips like bricks.

"There's more to his story than you know. Yeah, what he did was awful, but don't write him off just yet."

"I'm gonna kill him," Qen mutters.

"No, you're not," Osric says. There's something unusually still about him, contradicting his normal twitchy behavior. "Nova says there's more to it than we know. I trust her judgement."

"I don't," Qen says.

"You should. She's here, saving your ass, when she doesn't have to be," Osric says.

With that, they all fall silent. I give an appreciative nod to Osric, but I don't bother stretching out the moment of our bonding. Instead, I turn back to Hiro and say, "Time to use your key and get us out of here."

"About that," he says, rubbing the back of his head. "I don't have the code for the door."

"What? But you had the cell key," I say.

He nods. "Yeah, but we all do."

"Who had the code?" I ask.

"Uh, the guy I blasted."

I press my fingertips between my eyes. "You shot the only person who could get us out of here?"

"In my defense," he says, "I had to get your attention somehow or you were going to kill me."

From behind me, Zeb says, "Fair point."

I turn and give him my most hate-filled glare, but he still chuckles after I turn back to Hiro. I take a deep breath and shake my hands at my side as if I can free an idea with movement. I look at Hiro, silently and possibly not-silently cursing him while my mind races for a solution. He's standing there looking sheepish, massive arms folded across his chest, tattoos bulging as he clenches and unclenches his fists.

"Holy shit," I say, a smile spreading across my face.

His brows go up and he asks, "Got something?"

I shake my head. "Not me, but you do."

"I said I don't have the access."

"Forget the access," I say. "You've got something way more in demand." I let my eyes drift down his body until they're firmly planted on his pants. And honestly, I'm not mad about having to look there to get my point across.

He gets my meaning and tips his head back. "Oh, you're kidding me."

I laugh. "She wants you. And we're going to use that against her. Let's go, you sexy sonuvabitch."

CHAPTER
TWENTY

Hiro waits for us all to hide before he presses the button by the door and says, "Hey guys, I need to talk to Alik."

There's a pause. Then a feminine voice says, "State your position and code."

"Come off it, Alik," Hiro says. "You know it's Hiro and you know I don't keep a code."

"This line must be kept clear for official business, Sergeant. Unless this is an emergency—"

"Fine, screw it," he says, cutting her off. "I just wanted to tell you I'm sorry. That I thought about what happened and I wanted to apologize to you in person."

There's another pause before her voice comes back, softer, "Really?"

I swear I can almost hear her blushing through the speaker. But Hiro doesn't miss a beat, even making his voice crack when he says, "Yeah, really." He pauses now, only for a few seconds, then says, "I thought maybe we could talk. You know, about where to go from here."

The door hisses open almost instantly and Captain Alik Rolfrun steps through the door. It closes behind her but not before I hear one of the other guards say, "Go get your man, Cap," while another calls, "Don't screw her over, dick." These people are her friends, rooting for her, proving she isn't entirely without merit. She has a life, hopes, dreams, loves— we're two sides to the same coin, warring to see which lands face up.

She looks around and asks, "Where are the others?"

"I asked for some privacy," Hiro says. From the edge of the glass windows leading to the cells, I watch him reach for her hand. Her whole body practically melts against him. He slides his hands to her hips and presses her against the control panel so her back is to the windows.

She's giggling while he whispers something to her and I take the chance to move towards the door. As I start to creep it open, she twitches her head towards the door and I'm sure I'm caught. But then his lips are on hers and the world around her is forgotten. I press the door open and shove a blaster against her back.

The Captain's body tenses at the metal against her. Hiro pulls from her arms and gives an embarrassed shrug. She doesn't even acknowledge me, instead staring daggers at him. She asks, "Again?"

"Sorry," he says, though his smile says he's not even remotely.

As I disarm her, I can't help but ask, "What do you mean 'again?'"

"This is the third time we've kissed," she says. "And it's the third damn time he's ditched me and left with another woman."

"I have a type," he says, but doesn't explain further.

"You're an asshole," she says.

"Sounds like it," I agree.

He smiles back and it's a little scary how perfect he looks when he does it. Part of me wants to smack the Captain for falling for his bullshit three different times, but the rest of me understands how it happened.

I look at her and say, "You're going to give us your key and code—the *real* code—and we're going to leave. Do it right this time and no one has to get hurt."

She meets my gaze and nods once. No fuss. I'm fairly certain she's going to betray us again, but at least there's no pretending between us this time. She withdraws her key and passes it to me.

I tell Hiro, "Get her something to write with." He scrambles around for a minute before producing a nub of pencil and scrap paper. "Write it down."

She complies wordlessly. I take the paper and look at it, expecting a trick or snarky message. Instead it's a code like what she spoke before. I pass it to Hiro and ask, "Does this look right?"

He takes a few seconds to look it over and says, "This is it."

"You're sure?" I ask.

"It's right," she says. "There are three men on the other side of that door and I don't want a single one hurt."

"What about the first checkpoint?" I ask.

"They're replaced by now, probably reinforced. I don't know for sure. I haven't left my station. But if things go well, your ass will get blasted when you go through that door."

I nod, appreciating her candor even if she's trying to piss me off. I call out for the others to get ready, then step up to the speaker. I try to soften my voice to match hers and say, "Captain Alik Rolfrun, second shift, requesting entry."

"*Passcode.*"

I look at the paper in my hand and say, "7tg26/gidhrk-01a-5."

"*Confirmed.*"

And the door slides open.

MY ASS DOES *NOT* GET BLASTED WHEN I GO THROUGH THE FIRST DOOR. The guys inside are lax, despite what happened earlier, and I can't help but wonder what kind of life these people are used to that they can fall so easily into a false sense of security.

I elbow the first guard in the nose and his heard jerks back. Hiro slides in behind me and cuffs him while he's distracted and I move to the next guard. He had the sense to pull his gun, or try to pull it, at least. I spin and kick the hand going for his weapon. My foot lands hard against him and I'm certain I broke at least one of his fingers.

Before I can hit him again, Valeska pushes the Captain into the room with a gun pressed to her temple. Valeska says, "I'd suggest you drop your weapons and calm your tits."

"She will kill me," Captain Alik says. She has no malice in her tone, no question, no fear; in fact, her voice is strangely even. "Please, put down your weapons. I have their assurances that we will be spared as long as we cooperate."

The first guard is held by Hiro, and though the second is still at her words, I move to tie him up as well. The third guard, the one I hadn't reached yet, has his weapon in his shaking hand. I can tell by the expression on his face that he doesn't plan to give up his gun without a fight. He says, "These people killed Dench, but you're making deals with them? You're supposed to be our leader."

Alik clenches her jaw before growling out, "I know. I hate every second of this. But I didn't have a choice."

"There's always a choice," he spits.

"Yeah, Iggy, a choice between bad and worse. At least this let me keep you safe." His hand is still shaking even as his finger flickers over the button on the gun. Alik straightens her back and shoulders, stepping into a stance of authority despite being our prisoner. She says, "Put down your weapon, soldier. That's a direct order."

His eyes meet hers and for a second I think he might shoot her rather than take her order. But the moment passes and Iggy puts down his gun. There's a collective releasing of breath in the room and I move to tie Iggy's hands. We move him and the other two guards through the next room and into an empty cell before piling into the cramped space of the second checkpoint.

I look from face to face, running through the possibilities of what waits for us on the other side of the door. Valeska, Zeb, Edi, Qen, Grieva, Osric, and my father—they're all staring at me as if I hold the key to making it out of here. I don't know how to tell them I don't have a clue what comes next.

I hear a throat clear and turn my head to Hiro staring, head bent like he's embarrassed. I sigh, noticing again how calculated he is in everything he does, and how disarming it is. "What, Hiro?"

"You know there's a camera outside the door, right? So we can see what we're up against."

I rub a hand over the stubble on my head. "Seriously? You're just now telling us?"

He shrugs, looking chagrined. "There's a lot going on. Slipped my mind."

"Show me," I say, walking to the console.

Hiro sits in front of the console and presses some buttons. A screen comes to life and I see a handful of guards stationed outside the room. They're facing away from us towards the stairs, weapons drawn.

"There's only three," I say.

Edi is standing beside me now, though I didn't notice them approach. "The same three as before."

I look over my shoulder to the Captain. "You said they'd be reinforced by now."

"They should be," she says, brows furrowed.

"Unless they can't get through," Edi says, a smile blossoming on their face. "The other group must be giving them hell."

Or pinned down, I think, though I don't voice the fear. Better they think the others are succeeding.

"We need to get upstairs," I say. I turn to the Captain to ask for the code, but remember the first guard had only needed the key for this one. I say, "Here we go," and put the violet disc in the door.

It hisses open. The first to turn and see our motley crew is the scared guy from before. His gun is on the floor and hands in the air before the door is fully open. We rush the other two and take their weapons—again. We tie them up and put them and Captain Alik into another empty cell.

As we're leaving, Hiro stops in front of Alik and gives her a grin. "Sorry about this, Turtle."

"I hate it when you call me that."

"I know," he smiles. "More proof that we were never meant to be."

"Go to hell," she hisses.

He nods. "I might. But wherever I end up, it'll still be better than this. See ya, kid."

I'm curious about his words, the familiarity between them. I'd thought they were a casual almost-thing, but now I'm not so sure. In the end I guess it doesn't matter.

Finally, we're on our way out of high sec. At the door to the top level of cells, I pause and press my ear to the door. There aren't any sounds coming through, but I don't know if that's because the cells are empty or because the door is soundproofed.

We clear from the door and whip it open. There's no rushing force, no shots fired. I peek around the edge of the door and a relieved laugh escapes me. Sarah is standing in the middle of the corridor, a blaster in each hand aimed at our door.

"Sarah," I yell, "it's Nova. We're all good and coming up."

She spins around to face the other door now, the incoming door. As we get closer she says, "Took you long enough."

"We weren't gone long," Edi says.

"Felt like it," Sarah shrugs.

I look at the cells around her. Several contain unconscious guards. In one cell is the shift-change guards from the second checkpoint. I smile at the rigid silver fox I'd fought below. I feel his eyes burning into me as I pass and I give a little shimmy as I walk forward to meet Sarah. I ask her, "What happened here?"

"Dad keeps bringing them," she says. "I'm in charge of keeping them secure."

Zeb says, "That's an important job. I'm glad he put someone here who could handle it."

She beams up at him and I can already see her crush taking form. I interrupt her admiration of the mountain to ask, "Where are they now?"

"After he brought the last group he said they were going to look for the families. That was just a few minutes ago."

I nod as I turn back to the trial winners. "Let's see if we can help them. Hiro?"

"Yeah, boss?"

I cringe at the moniker. The last thing I want is to be in charge, yet that role keeps falling to me. "Where would they keep the families of the trial winners?"

He strolls up beside me like we're not in the middle of a jailbreak. "Probably in the rooms across the corridors. They're usually for witnesses to relax before they're statements are processed."

"Surely they wouldn't take Alexis there. She's tough, dangerous," I say.

"She's an old woman," he shrugs.

I'm thrown off by the statement. I'd registered her age just like I'd registered her eye color or height. It's just part of her. But it never diminished her in my eyes. I look at her and see strength. I see the warrior within. It's strange to know that everyone else doesn't see her the same way.

We pass through the empty corridors of the prison. It's disconcerting to see the place void of life. I've seen deserted places before, remnants of the world before the cataclysm, things left behind by whoever lived long ago; still, this is different. Maybe it's because I saw it bustling when they brought me in, and now there is nothing but bloody footprints guiding us out.

We make it all the way through the station and near the front before we see anyone. There, slumped against the wall, is a guard. His eyes are glassy, but he hasn't gone yet. It seems cruel to leave

him like this, and I pause to put him out of his misery, but Hiro
stills my hand.

"He may yet live," he whispers.

I look from Hiro to the guard and back. "He's a dead man. It's a
mercy."

"If the doctors get to him while he still has breath, they can save
him." I start to protest again, but he shakes his head. "They can do
wonders. Leave him. Let the stars decide his fate."

Hiro keeps walking and I follow, but there's an uneasiness in
me as I leave the dying guard. As we move into the corridor, I feel
something brush against my arm and realize Sarah is with us,
nearly clinging to me. "You're supposed to be guarding the cells."

She rolls her eyes. "They'll be fine. I wanted to see some action."

Hiro opens the door to the apartment and closes it immediately.
He turns back towards us, face ashen. When his eyes meet mine, I
can see that whatever is in the room is too much for him to charm
away.

"What is it?" I ask, as gently as I can.

He shakes his head. "Don't open the door, Nova. Just, don't."

I squeeze his arm as I pass. He steps aside, not trying to stop
me. I open the door and wish I hadn't. My stomach lurches and if
I'd eaten recently, it would be on my shoes right now. There are
bodies. Everywhere. Splatters of blood paint the walls, the floor. It
isn't the precise lines I've seen from blade slashes; no, this looks
like someone has taken buckets of blood and tossed them against
the walls.

I stand there blocking the door, searching the faces among them,
but I don't recognize anyone. I feel a press against my side as Sarah
slips by and dimly, barely louder than the blood pumping through
my ears, I hear her screaming. She runs in and falls beside a body,
throwing herself onto the bloody carcass.

Bile burns my throat and I realize it isn't the families, it's the
prisoners. The people I freed. Those who are here because I told
them to clear the way. More blood on my hands.

Someone pushes me aside then, shifts past me. Zeb. He grabs Sarah and pulls her away from the body. She struggles against him, beating him with her fists, but still he holds her against his chest and carries her from the room.

Hiro closes the door behind me and wraps an arm over my shoulder. I stare at him for a long moment, the action not registering in my head while he leads me away from the door. He passes me off to my father, who wraps his arms around me, but I can't seem to return the gesture. My arms don't want to move.

"There's one more room," Hiro says.

I shake my head against my father's neck. I don't want them to open the door. I don't want to see what's there, what I'm certain we'll see when he does.

But he opens it anyway.

Over Ledwin's shoulder, I see Osric fall to his knees. Grieva's hand goes to her mouth as if to cover the wail that comes out, high and reedy. I pull away from Ledwin and move to the door. Though I have no desire to see what they've done to her, I must.

I step into the room where Alexis the Huntress—the mighty warrior of on-world, trial winner, savior, friend, mother—is pinned to the wall in pieces. It looks as though they hung her there, arms and legs sprawled, and tore her apart. There are gouge marks in the walls behind her from whatever they did to cut her apart.

When my eyes find her face, I also find my resolve. She isn't broken, not there. Her face looks peaceful. She could be sleeping.

I stare at that face for a moment, letting the rest of the scene fall away. They've tried to break her for fifty years, but even in death she defies them. With this act, they hope to break the rest of us, too. But I can't let them. The longer I look at her, the more certain I am, that this will not be our end.

There's a sharp intake of breath behind me and I turn to see Benjy in the doorframe. The look on his face is full of horror and I can see the pain burrowing into his heart. I have no doubt he will blame himself for this.

Qen sees him now and, as if in slow motion, I watch them run at Benjy. Their teeth are bared as a vicious growl escapes them. Benjy doesn't move, doesn't block, just takes the full force of their attack. They hit the floor in a heap, rolling until Qen is on top of Benjy, slashing at his face with their hands.

I watch it happen, my body in a strange daze. No one moves to separate them for a long moment, too long, until finally my brain snaps back and I rush to pull Qen off of him. Despite their slight stature, Qen is fierce and I'm unable to move them. Another pair of hands joins my efforts and together we haul them off Benjy.

When I look up, I see it was Jackson who helped me. He's shed the guard uniform he wore when he dropped me off, but everything about him reads as a soldier. I'm amazed he made it this far into our midst without being shot, but then, we're not operating at full capacity right now. Most of us are shattered.

"What are you doing here?" I growl. My anger with the Règle and her forces outweighs the help he's given me.

"I've been helping since I brought you in," he says, hurt registering on his face. "Benjy and I took your computer guy to the control center. We've been keeping the footage from the Règle so she wouldn't send more forces."

I grab him by the front of the shirt and drag him to the room where Alexis is. I point at the wall and say, "They did this *without* reinforcements? What kind of monsters can do this to other people?"

Ledwin approaches, putting a hand on my shoulder. "We'll have time to mourn later. Right now, we need to get the living out of here. What's your plan?"

"We're going on-world."

I pull Ivy's device from my boot and he looks at me like I've sprouted a second head. "What good will that do? The Règle will just track us down and kill us there."

"Ivy has a way to remove the tracking devices."

"Ivy is there? You sent my daughter there?"

I flinch from the accusation. "It was her idea. She knows what she's doing." As an afterthought I add, "And in case you've forgotten, one of your daughters lived there for a dozen years, without you, and she did fine."

He presses his lips together for a second before saying, "I'm sorry. I know. It's just, she's not like you."

"She's tough," I say. "Besides, it's our only option. We need to regroup and figure out what to do next. If we stay here, we're dead."

My father points to where Zeb cradles Sarah. "Start with them."

I do. Soon I've sent Zeb, Sarah, Edi, and Valeska on-world. I turn to send the next person and realize it's Hawkins, the first prisoner who agreed to help me, the one the medic needled. He's awake, though there are deep purple bruises under his eyes. I say, "I thought you were dead."

There are tears in his eyes when he says, "I would be, if I hadn't gone with your friends."

Friends? I think, but then I see him nod towards Jackson and Benjy. Jackson said they'd taken our tech guy to mess with the cameras.

"I'm glad you made it," I say. "Now it's time to make good on my promise. You ready?"

He nods and I press the device against his hand. With a slight *pop*, Hawkins is on-world.

"Me next," Hiro says.

I turn and eye him, unsure. The guy helped us, saved us, but he's one of the star-people. One of the guards. I don't know that any amount of help will ever shake the mistrust I feel when I look at him.

He must read the doubt on my face because he spreads his arms wide and smiles just as broad. "Come on, you owe me."

"Are you sure about this?"

"I can't stay here. Not after what I've done."

"It's different down there. It isn't like here."

He nods. "I don't belong here, Nova. I never have. I might not belong there either, but I need to know for sure."

I step close to him, so close I can feel the heat from his skin. I whisper, "If you betray us—"

"You'll murder me, right?" he smiles. "Counting on it, love."

I press the device against him and watch him disappear. I move to my father next. He argues with me, wanting to wait until I go, but I finally convince him they'll need someone thinking clearly on the ground. I don't tell him that I'm not going.

I've known for a while now. The problem is with the device. We can use it, but it doesn't travel with us. At least, I don't think so. If I disappear, the device will fall to the ground wherever I am. Anyone can pick it up, use it, trace us. I can't risk it. So I'm going to send them all down, destroy the device, and figure it out from there.

"Time to go," I say, stepping towards the trial winners. They've left the room holding Alexis, but the sight seems to have left them a shade duller than they were before, like someone drained away their colors.

I send Qen first, despite the fight they put up. Grieva and Osric go without protest, leaving me with Jackson and Benjy. I look to Jackson, and no matter how I feel about the guards, Hiro was right. They wouldn't be safe if they stayed after helping us. I ask, "You ready?"

"What? No," he says, eyes widening.

"They'll kill you."

"They don't know it was me," he says.

"Jackson," I say, shaking my head, "They'll know."

"I'm sorry—" he says, but I cut him off when I press the device to his neck and he disappears.

"Just us then," Benjy says. When I nod, he asks, "Do the others know?"

"Know what?"

"That you're not going?"

I stumble for words for a moment, unsure what to say. I don't know how he knows. I search his face, marred with thick red scratches still bleeding after Qen's attack. There's a tenderness there that wasn't there before.

"They're not all dead, you know. The families are somewhere, hiding. Whoever stays can still do some good."

Whoever stays...

His strike lands while the words are still sinking in. I stumble back, fighting for breath after he punched my throat. I dodge his next jab before a coughing fit hits me. I swing wildly, flailing with the device as I try to send him on-world.

He sweeps past me—he's astonishingly fast!—and pins one arm behind my back. I try to spin away from him but he twists my hand until I release the device. He whispers, "I'll save them," before pressing cold metal against my neck.

A horrible suction twists at my gut and I feel like I'm being ripped apart. I open my mouth to scream but nothing comes out.

And then it's over.

I'm lying on cold earth. The sky above is bright and full of warm sunlight. My eyes blink back tears at the brightness I haven't seen for the last year. I feel air on my cheek, real wind, not the forced air of the station. Now the tears are coming in earnest and I stop pretending it's because of the brightness.

I'm home.

CHAPTER
TWENTY-ONE

The next time I open my eyes, I'm lying on a bed. It's the softest thing I've ever felt and I don't want to move. So I don't. Instead I stare at the gray ceiling above me, the knotty wood forming tiny faces. There's a squeak as the door opens and I clutch the blankets covering me, wishing whoever it is would go away and let me stay here alone forever.

But then Ivy sits on the edge of the bed and I've never been so happy to see another person. I wrap my arms around her waist and pull her into the bed with me. She laughs and fights me for a minute, but then she gives into my hug and lets me give her the love I've been storing up.

We lie there for several minutes before she breaks the moment's sweetness, saying, "They're all waiting for you."

I sigh. "Can't they wait a little longer?"

"I've been making them wait," she says. "For nearly two days. I told them you needed to rest."

"Two days?" I ask.

She shrugs as she sits up. "Do you remember the last time you slept?"

I shake my head. "Honestly, no."

"When did you eat?" At her words, my stomach lets out a violent rumble. She says, "That's what I figured. Abigail is making breakfast. Get dressed and come downstairs. You need to eat and they need to see that you're still alive."

I USE THE BASIN IN THE CORNER OF THE ROOM TO WASH AWAY SOME OF the blood I've been wearing for the last few days. Beside the basin is a full set of killing leathers and a copper-colored covering.

Rego has been here. Rego has left me this gift.

The thought of seeing him buoys me, clears away the haze. I dress in Raider garb and find my way downstairs. Halfway down, the smell of bacon hits me and I have to wipe the drool from the corner of my lips.

Abigail is in the kitchen, fighting away Wolfie's grabby hands with a spatula. When she looks up and sees me, a smile lights up her face. Wolfie grabs a piece of bacon while she's distracted, sending a smile over his face as well.

She waves me to the table and I realize it's full of faces I know. Osric, Zeb, Sarah, and Krew's sister, Zazira, sit across from Baz, Aunt Rachel's girlfriend, Permilla, Rego, and his husband Jasper's daughter, Edith-Ann Roody. The sight of the little girl is a surprising anchor. I only knew her a short while, as the girl who kept the stolen children in order before I knew she was Jasper's daughter, but for some reason it is her presence that makes me realize I am really on-world.

I watch her pass something across the table to Sarah and it strikes me that the two girls are of similar age. They've both been hurt, broken in ways that children shouldn't be. I want to scoop them up and rescue them from the world, but where could I take them that would spare their young hearts? We are all children of brokenness, here and above.

"Little Star," Rego says, standing.

My eyes move to him, taking him in. He's put on weight since I last saw him, rounding out his too-thin cheeks and giving him a little belly. His face has more laugh lines, his smile comes easier to his face. This last year has been good to him.

"Hello, Rego," I say.

He moves towards me, his movements slow and steady, like he's approaching a wild thing. And maybe he is. But even wild things know love.

I close the distance between us and wrap my arms around his neck. He burrows his cheek against my shaved head, nuzzling me like he's always done. Encapsulated in his arms I feel solid again, like the last year was a bad dream and I've finally awoken. This is the safest I've felt in a long time and I don't want to leave this feeling again, so when Rego releases me, it is too soon. Anything less than forever is too soon.

He leads me to the table and makes room for me to sit between him and Permilla. As I join them, Abby brings me a plate and drink, accompanied by her warm smile. The food is steaming, sending delicious tendrils floating towards my nose, making my mouth water. I dig into the eggs, bacon, and shredded potatoes. Rego slides a saucer towards me and tells me to put the contents on my potatoes. The red sauce is sweet and tomatoey, like nothing I've tried before.

"It's good," I say around a mouthful of the stuff. "What is it?"

"Ketchup," he says, smiling.

"It's an old family recipe," Abigail adds. "Passed down for generations."

When my potatoes are gone, I put the ketchup on my eggs. Across the table, Hiro makes a gagging face as if I've committed a cardinal sin. I take a big bite and give a toothy grin, hoping to gross him out.

He rolls his eyes but smiles. He says, "Glad to have you back among the living."

"Took you long enough to get here," Baz says from the other

side of Permilla. "You gave the others scare. Not me, of course. I knew you'd be fine."

"Of course," I agree.

But I see the relief on his face, the smile in his eyes. Somewhere along the way, Baz and I became friends. I haven't forgiven him for his part in the trials, but I have come to accept it and move past it.

"Where are the others?" I ask.

"The barn," Osric says. "I'll take you when you're finished eating."

I grab a biscuit from the middle of the table, split it open, and put my bacon in the middle. I take one huge bite and stand, saying, "I'm done."

Rego grabs my wrist and draws my attention to him. "You don't have to lead this time, Nova. After all you've done, you're allowed to rest. Let the others carry the load."

I nod, but his words do little to discourage me. Maybe the girl he knew could have done what he asks, but I don't know if I can. I don't think I want to.

I step onto the porch and breathe deep. The air is fresh and clean, not the filtered stuff the star-people have. Their air is a poor imitation, as if someone who'd never breathed created it based on what they thought it should be.

In the distant fields, a group of kids are chasing one another. I don't know the details of the trip to save the children, haven't had a chance to ask, but this seems like a good sign.

Osric and I walk to the barn in silence. It isn't far, and I don't know why he wanted to escort me since I've been to the farm before. Just before we reach the doors, he stops and says, "I need to thank you."

I stop and turn to him, looking into his one brown eye. "There's no need."

"You don't understand what you've done," he says. "Alexis thought," his voice cracks and he clears his throat as if to tear the thought of her from his mind, "Alexis *knew* you would be the one to change things. I don't know how she knew, but she was strong in her conviction. I've been at her side nearly thirty years, but I've never seen her as certain of anything as she was of you. The fact that she's gone doesn't change that. I placed my trust in her all those years, and now I'm placing it in you."

Osric's words knock my breath away. I don't know what Alexis saw in me, or what she said to this man to make him believe in me now. I open my mouth to protest, but I don't have the words. He squeezes my shoulder and walks into the barn, sparing me from the mediocre response I'm brewing.

I stagger after him into the barn. It's different from the last time I was here. There are globes of light floating in the rafters—clearly Ivy's handiwork—lighting up the assembly. Nearly everyone I know is here, seated on seats, hay bales, blankets or standing against the support beams positioned around the barn. The place is packed.

My father and his wife stand in the middle of the room and I can tell by his expression that he's rattled. I follow his gaze to the woman standing against a pole, casual as can be in her slacks and suspenders, her thick-soled boots: Aunt Rachel. I focus on the words between them, realizing they're arguing and neither are holding back.

"I don't give two shits about the plight of the wannabe-gods above," Rachel says, crossing her arms over her chest.

"You should," Ledwin says. "There are good people up there. They're just trying to live their lives."

"Good people don't do the sorts of things you've told us about. They wouldn't be watching us for entertainment, they wouldn't be killing us for their games."

Ledwin nods. "There are bad things there, just like here. And it's not okay. But it's what they know. They've never been shown another way."

"It's not our job to teach them how to be human," Rachel says.

"You're both right," I say, stepping into the barn and making my way through the crowd. I feel the eyes turning, taking me in, but I refuse to meet their gazes. I need to get this out before I get lost in the relief of being returned to those I love. "I've lived in both places. I've hated and loved things about both. Neither are perfect, neither deserve the hands we've been dealt. Ideally, we could work with the star-people to build a better life for all of us."

Rachel scoffs. "Sounds like you've spent too much time in Ledwin's shadow, learning to parrot his words."

"I've barely seen my father this past year. I spent most of my time locked up or running, trying not to be caught again."

"Still," Rachel says, stepping towards me. Whatever hatred rests between her and my father seems to be turning its head on me. "You're not the same girl who left for the trials."

"I'd be dead if I was," I say. "That girl was naive, seeing black and white without realizing there's a lot more gray than anyone wants to admit."

"If you were locked up, how do you know there are good people there?" Coco asks.

I turn to meet her eyes, green and bright and perfect. I can't help but smile at her, despite the seriousness of the situation, and I'm delighted when she smiles back. She's sitting on a blanket towards the back, propped back on her elbows. Her hair is silver with a lilac tint at the ends, her skin still rich brown and radiant as the day I first saw her in the market on Aeroport. I don't know how she manages to look like an oasis, but I stare at her and my insides ache to escape this desert and drown in her beauty.

"When I was imprisoned, they would beat me, shock me, tell me the people I loved were all dead. They isolated me for months, made me question my sanity."

"That's not a glowing recommendation," she says.

I nod. "There were some really terrible people up there. But the same can be said for here. Weren't you rescuing kidnapped children last we spoke?"

"Fair point. But there were a bunch of us trying to make it right."

I point to Jackson at the edge of the room. "That man is the guard who helped me escape." I look around until I find Okada and Krew. "They gave me a place to stay, helped disguise me and kept me safe." I point to the huddle of trial winners—Karina, Drev, Qen, Osric, and Grieva—on a blanket near Coco. "They were forming a rebellion long before I came along. One of them sent me on-world, sacrificing himself to keep the rebellion going above. Another died in prison, but she died believing we could win."

"So there's a handful of decent people and they're all here," Rachel cuts in. "Leave the rest to their own devices."

I shake my head. "There are more who could be good, if they knew it was an option."

"Like me."

I spin to see Nigel Weatherfield, Mayor of Gearhaven sitting on a seat next to Thoa. *Thoa. Holy hells he looks good, like his return has cured his ills.* I shake my head as I do my best to ignore Thoa, unable to focus on that situation right now. Besides, I can't hide my surprise to see Nigel, even as he rises and moves forward. The last time I saw him, I thought Herol would've killed him for his role smuggling children.

His smile is tentative, unsure. Unlike the man I knew, so full of himself. He turns to the crowd and says, "Some of you know me, what I've done, and what I'm still doing to fix it. Some of you don't. Either way, it doesn't change what I know about myself: I am not a good man. I may never be. I've done terrible things, things I regret but can't take back. But I try. Every damn day, I try. And I keep trying, making the choice each morning to be better. Not perfect, not even good, just better. Sometimes people need to be shown there is another way and given the chance to make the choice for themselves."

When he's finished, he holds his hand out to me. After a breath, I take it and he gives me a warm smile. I'm dumbfounded. I watch

Nigel move back to his seat, smiling when Thoa claps him on the back. This can't be real life. That snake has somehow shed his skin. I don't know what he's done this past year to try to make things right, but from the heads nodding around the room, it's clear he's been doing something.

Still, I don't trust him and I like him even less. But he's made my point, so I clear my throat and say, "Yes, like Nigel said, everyone deserves the chance to be better. Who are we to deny them that?"

Rachel straightens from her position, no longer looking casual. Now, she looks dangerous. "Say we agreed and went along with you, what's the plan? How are you going to free the star-people from the hold their government has on them? How are you going to make sure it doesn't happen again?"

When I look into her eyes, so much like mine, I see the trap. It isn't trickery with words or angry rebuttal or anything else; it's hope. Aunt Rachel *wants* this as much as I do, she wants to be wrong and for things to work out between us and the people orbiting on the space station. But she's no fool. She's practical and intelligent and she knows there is no plan that can turn this dream into reality.

I open my mouth to speak, but a soft voice from the edge of the room cuts me off. Ivy is there, smiling from ear to ear. She says, "Don't worry, I've got that part covered. All we need now are some Raiders."

CHAPTER
TWENTY-TWO

I think about Ivy's plan all afternoon and into the evening. I dwell on it through dinner, ignoring the lively conversations around me, and it haunts me as everyone piles around the bonfire to share stories and songs and solace. It is good, of this I am sure, but somehow I know it will not work.

There are many moving parts, each reliant on things we can't control. Her plan will work *if* the Raiders agree to fight with us, *if* we can get word to Benjy, *if* he can raise his own army, *if* we can get back to the space station, *if* we maintain the element of surprise, *if*, *if*, *if*.

But I don't share my fears. Her plan is the only thing giving us hope, and we need to hang onto that if we want a chance at this. Besides, I've got nothing better to offer.

In addition to the many *if*s of her plan, there's a technical element that I don't fully understand. Ivy takes to machines the way I do to the blade. She inhabits them, her whole world revolving around what she can make and change and invent. She tried to explain the details to us all, but our father cut her off after only a minute or so, asking her to move past the specifics. Afterwards, I saw her meeting with Hawkins, Krew, and Drev—those among us who can keep up with her technical jargon.

I excuse myself from the bonfire, though no one is paying attention to me. It's nice to be able to walk away and find some silence. It's been a long time since I've had the luxury.

But maybe Rego is right. There are capable people here who can manage things, make plans, and lead this group. Maybe it's okay to let them.

I wander through the meadow, passing a group of the domesticated animals that Coco's family rides. I watch them for a long time before I remember their name in the old tongue: horse. They are lovely creatures, majestic, and I wonder how they came to be here when so many other things perished with the cataclysm.

In the distance, a beam of light catches my eye. Shining up into the sky is a tower of red, letting the City of Trials know there has been no winner in the tower battle tonight. Vaguely I wonder who is hosting the show since Baz is here with us. But the thought is almost instantly replaced with the realization that the star-people have weeded out another thirty or so of our strongest, and they'll keep doing it, hoping we can never build up enough strength to be more than what we are.

There's a rustling behind me and I turn to see Thoa approaching. I raise a hand in greeting, give a small smile, though part of me is saddened to lose my alone time. The other part of me is doing silent somersaults, delighted for a chance to talk to him. It has been so long since we've talked, really talked, and I don't know what to expect. The writhing pit in my stomach has me convinced that whatever it is, it won't be good.

He stops beside me and stares at the lit column in the distance. After a moment, he says, "It was green when we won."

I look at him, surprised by this. I don't know what I expected him to say, but it wasn't this. All I can manage is, "Yeah. I'm surprised you remember."

"I don't," he admits. "When Jane and I were watching the trials one night, I asked about the light. She told me it changes when someone wins."

Jane. Damn it. I forgot about her.

"Where is Jane?" I ask.

"The red-haired pirate has her in custody on her ship."

"Rachel?" I ask with a laugh.

He nods, but doesn't smile, just keeps looking at the light. "I didn't love her, you know. I always felt like something was wrong."

"But you didn't question it further?"

He shrugs. "What was the point? There wasn't anything else for me up there."

"There could have been."

He shakes his head. "I wanted to forget it all, Nova."

He used my name. I wasn't sure he remembered it.

"Why didn't you?"

"I couldn't, not really. They took a lot of it, things I may never get back, but not all. It came back in my dreams, in flashes of color, when I saw your face. Gods help me, your face changed everything."

I dare a glance at him and he's staring at me with an intensity I haven't seen these long months away from him. But as I look back, taking in his eyes, his scars, the planes of his face, I realize it isn't the same as it was before. His look is intense, but it isn't full of the love that it once had. Curiosity, maybe even admiration, but Thoa is not in love with me anymore.

I reach forward and push a strand of his dark hair from his eyes. He still stares at me, but he doesn't move. As my hand trails from his hair to rest against his chest, he doesn't move. I can't even feel him breathing. Then again, I'm not sure I am either.

I step closer, pressing myself against his firm body. I push myself onto my tiptoes, stretching so the tips of our noses are touching.

"Nova," he breathes.

I press my lips against his before he can say more. Whether he was going to stop me or beg me to kiss him, I do not know. But now my lips are on his and he has not pulled away. He wraps an arm around my waist and kisses me deeper. The moment stretches, but all else fades except the softness of his lips, the firmness of his chest against me, the salty taste of his kiss.

When he pulls away, I gasp for breath. One arm still wrapped around me, he uses his free hand to wipe my tears. He asks, "Why are you crying?"

"I don't know," I say, shaking my head. But I do. I do. It takes me a moment to work up the courage to ask, "Did that mean anything to you?"

I feel his arm around my slacken. He whispers, "I'm sorry."

I nod, knowing if I try to speak my tears will fall in earnest.

"It was nice," he continues. "I think you're a wonderful woman, fierce and smart. It's just—"

"You don't remember loving me."

He shakes his head and I feel the part of my heart where Thoa lived going dark. I will never give that part of my heart to another. I will never fill it with anything else. It only ever belonged to him. It will always only belong to him.

"Why did you follow me out here?" I ask.

He looks away from me, shuffles his feet in the grass. "I wanted to talk to you about the Raiders. About going to get them."

"What about it?"

"Rego said something about it, about us going to find them, and, well, I wanted to be the one to tell you that I'm not going."

"What? You have to. We need the Raiders on our side."

He nods. "And you'll get them, just, without me."

"You're Thoa the Bonecutter. They'll listen to you. You were the best warrior among the Raiders."

He shakes his head. "*You* were the best among them. They just didn't know it."

Something about his words makes me think he remembers

being a Raider, remembers what it was like for us. I begin, "How do you—"

"I told you," he says, cutting me off, "I remember some things. Other things, I've heard these last few days. Rego likes to tell stories about you. He loves you, you know."

"He has been like a father to me."

"He seems like a good man. The Raiders will listen to him, too."

I don't know when I held my hands out to him, but now that he's looking down at them, all I can think of is the night he held his to me at the solstice marriage fire. The night I turned my back to him, just as he turns his to me now.

He takes a few steps away and I call after him, "What will you do instead?"

I can't see his features in the darkness, but I can hear the smile in his voice when he says, "I honestly don't know. But whatever I do, I'll know I'm doing it for me."

He walks into the darkness, leaving me staring into the night after the ghost of the man I once loved.

CHAPTER
TWENTY-THREE

We load Rachel's ship with supplies for a month, not knowing how long it will take to find the Raiders. Rego and I agree that at this time of year they're likely to be going north. The ice has melted and the streams are fresh and sweet, life returning to the land once more. Chief Eija loves the spring more than any other time, often wanting to turn north before the snow is fully melted, as if the Raiders return will herald the changing of the seasons.

Going back to my people is exciting, but I worry that going back to them on an airship is a bad decision. It makes sense in that it will be easier to find them, faster for traveling, but I feel as if I'm betraying them by doing things the easy way. Raider life is hard; of course, it has to be if it's going to breed strong people.

I lived with the Raiders for twelve years, and in that time, I had never seen an airship. We traveled with the seasons, following our circular route year after year. We visited cities, albeit few and far between, but never once did we encounter one of the flying contraptions. Taking one to the Raider's doorstep doesn't sit well with me.

I tell these reasons to myself each time I feel uneasy, but at the back of my mind I know it is only a portion of the reason for not wanting to take Rachel's ship. The other reason, the bigger reason, is that the last time I saw Chief Eija she was saying goodbye to her wife, Nukiki, just before we left to take Krew to the City of Trials. When Rachel's crew found us, they killed Nukiki, and we were forced to leave her body behind when they took us onboard. I am returning with the airship, captain, and crew who killed Eija's wife.

But I can't say it aloud, can barely stand to think of it. So I focus on the other reasons, the part that's easier to bear. When I try to discuss it with the others, I am overruled. I understand their position and I don't try to fight them on it. Rego agrees with me, understands my concerns, and probably has Nukiki on his mind as well, but in the end even Rego thinks we should take Rachel's ship.

So we do.

Two days after the meeting in the barn, we're ready to set out. Ivy gives me a handful of things like buttons and tells me to distribute them amongst those on the airship. They will disable cameras and keep the star-people from seeing what we're doing. Their radius is only a dozen feet, but if we spread them out it should hide us well enough. It isn't much, she tells me, but it's the best she can do.

Rego and I join Rachel and her crew at the ship, but we are not the only ones ready to board. We asked for volunteers to accompany us, to show the Raiders something they would understand—a show of force—and we were not disappointed with volunteers. We are joined by Drev and Karina, of the trial winners; Valeska, Zeb, and Sarah, of the prisoners; and hot-guard Hiro.

Before we leave, Krew catches me by the hand and pulls me around the side of the house. It's been awhile since we've spoken more than a few words to each other, since we've had the opportunity to talk with all the trouble we've been dealing with, and I can feel the wall being built between us.

It takes a minute of awkward small talk before he gets to the crux of what he wants to say to me. "I couldn't volunteer, you know that."

I nod. The Raiders would never understand why we'd brought him back when two of our people didn't return. Plus, he's one of the few who can make sense of Ivy's mad plan. She needs him more than I do. Still, the last time we were here at the farm, things were different between us, intimate. We'd taken comfort in each other. And he did volunteer then, to go rescue Thoa.

I'm certain he must be thinking the same things, but then he says, "Yosh needs me to be here. He needs to know I'm choosing him and not running off with you again."

The words are a dagger in my heart. Thoa walked away from me last night and now Krew makes it plain he's choosing Okada over me. I mean, I knew Krew loved him, knew that whatever we had before was different, morphed into something resembling friendship, but to hear the words from his lips...

Damn, it hurts.

I try to shift my face into something that hides my pain and shows I understand. I force myself to meet his eyes, that heavy black gaze that seems to drain away all the color from the world. "Of course. You're needed here."

He nods and leans forward, wrapping his arms around me in an awkward embrace. When he pulls away, I give him the best smile I can muster and let him wander off before I let myself crumple against the side of the building. I know I don't have time to linger—the airship will be taking off in a few minutes—but if I don't take a minute to catch my breath, I know I'll be overwhelmed.

"There you are," Coco says, coming around the corner. She catches sight of my face and adds, "Yikes. You look rough."

I laugh, thankful that she doesn't ask what's wrong. "I'm dealing."

She nods, accepts my words as truth. I know that I could talk to her if I wanted to, but unless I offer, she won't pry.

"I never got to thank you for saving Wolfie. He told me what happened."

I sigh. "That seems like a lifetime ago."

"I know you've been through a lot, probably more than I can guess. Still, there has been good to come from it, too. I'll never forget that it was you who brought my brother back to me. Every day I have with him is a gift you've given me. So, I have something for you," she says. She pulls out a dagger, flips it in the air, and catches it by the blade, handing me the hilt. "It's nothing fancy, but it reminds me of you."

It's plain, simply designed, but wicked sharp. I smile and say, "It's perfect."

Coco's brown cheeks seem to color the slightest bit. She leans forward and brushes a kiss onto my cheek. "I'm glad you're home. Maybe next time I see you, I can give you a proper welcome before we have to save the world."

Before I can utter a word, she flashes a smile and heads off, running off to handle other business. Heat burns through me, chasing away everything else that had held me captive only moments ago. I walk back around the building, watching her jog away, and feel color sweeping up my neck. Good gods above, I hate seeing her go but I love watching her leave.

As we fly across the land, I watch them move around the ship and vaguely wonder if any of them would be accepted as a Raider, if I will at long last become a life-bringer.

It seems like a strange thing, now, the desire to bring someone into that life. Why would I want to subject someone else to the suffering I endured? Yes, the Raiders made me strong and I love them for it, but there was plenty of hurt and brokenness in my life with them as well. After a dozen years, I was still fighting for my place among them, struggling to gain their approval.

I catch sight of Sarah as she passes, walking aimlessly across the deck. She grieves the loss of her father, clings to Zeb simply to remain upright, but now she is alone, looking like the lost child she is. As I watch her, I feel an uneasiness in my gut, and all I can think of is wanting to protect her. I would pick her up and ferry her away, hide her from the star-people, the Raiders, and everyone in between. Let her become her own person, in her own time, with her own pains, not reliant on the offenses of others and how she should respond to them.

But I can't protect her any more than Rachel could protect me. She tried. I was eight, she was fourteen, when we wandered the land together, lost children of a dead and dying world. I didn't understand what was happening, why we couldn't go home. Poor Rachel had to carry all that grief and responsibility on her own. She carries it still, though I'm not sure she realizes it.

I feel a nudge in my ribs and look over to see Hiro sidled up beside me. I roll my eyes, now a habit every time he's near. There's a strange joy in the man, infectious in the way it buoys those around him. It's unexpected, not something I picked up on when first meeting him. It's easy to see what drew Captain Alik to him, even though I'm not attracted to him myself.

"This is exciting, huh?" he asks, face alight.

"Is it?" I ask, though I feel a similar smile crossing my face.

"Well yeah, Squirrel, it is."

"Squirrel?" I ask, brows raised.

A slight pink tints his cheeks and he says, "Trying out something new. Does it annoy you?"

"A bit," I say.

His grin turns from excited to devilish as he says, "Perfect."

I shake my head. "You're a strange one, Hiro."

"You say that, but you can't deny my charm. We're basically best friends."

"Are we? I had no idea."

He points across the deck to where Karina stares darkly at the sky beyond. "Do you think I could get away with calling *her* Squirrel?" I laugh and he continues, "I get that this is heavy and serious and stuff, but that doesn't mean every second needs to be spent brooding. It's okay to smile sometimes. You get that."

I nod, though I'm not certain I do. I've spent my fair share of time brooding and being serious. Maybe Hiro sees something in me that I don't. Maybe that's part of being best friends.

"If I'm Squirrel, what does that make you?"

"Moose, obviously."

I squint at him. "How is that an obvious combination?"

"It's an old joke," he says. "From before the world ended."

"How do you know about it then? And aren't jokes supposed to be funny?"

"The station has archives, Squirrel. There's tons of histories up there, including old entertainment. Most people don't bother with it, but I always loved learning about the old world."

I remember Baz talking about the archives and how his parents used it to choose traditional names for their children, but I had no idea what else was there. Now I can't help but wonder what knowledge is stored there, unused, and how it's wasted on the star-people.

"I'm not calling you Moose," I say.

He laughs. "You said the same thing about calling me Hiro, but here we are."

THE DAYS PASS IN COMPANIONABLE EASE. HIRO AND I SIT TOGETHER ON deck or below, sharing stories, practicing weaponry, or talking through details of Ivy's plan. He has noticed the same *ifs* I have and has his own worries. We're careful not to mention them to the others for fear it will discourage them, but it's nice to have someone to talk to about it.

Mostly though, we spend our time trying to make the other laugh. Hiro's smiles come easy, but his laugh is another matter entirely. He does not waste it on trivial things, but saves it so that when the sound fills the air, it is wholly pure and unexpectedly delightful.

By the fifth day of our search, we've scoured the grounds where the Raiders should be but have found them empty. Rachel calls me and Rego to her cabin and asks where we should check next, but neither of us are sure.

"Eija could've led them north sooner," Rego says, now speaking the old tongue as proficient as I do. "It is her way."

I nod, but I'm not convinced. "Aye, it is. But it's just as likely that they haven't yet come north. They have lingered in the south before."

"When the winters stretch their icy fingers into spring. That has not happened this year."

Rachel says, "I'll turn whichever way you want me to, but I'd like you to decide together."

I bite my lip, weighing the decision as I look out Rachel's window. While I think, we pass over a herd of grazing whitetails. I point them out to Rego. He puts his fingers to his lips and lets out a loud, sharp whistle like the Raiders do when hunting. The animals turn at the sound, but continue their grazing.

I say, "The animals are undisturbed, unhunted. Surely no Raider has passed this way."

He nods, accepting this proof. "Then we go south."

WE GO SOUTH, BUT STILL THERE ARE NO RAIDERS. I WATCH FROM THE bow of the ship, noting hills and plains and rivers I've seen a dozen times in a dozen ways, changing as easily as the seasons. We pass a forest I recognize, a forest I stood inside when Thoa told me how he became the Bonecutter. Just past it is the field where Nukiki died. I close my eyes as we pass, unwilling to see the place where she fell for fear the place is still stained red.

Two days into our southern journey, I walk the bowels of the ship, looking for...something. I don't know what exactly, but I know I've forgotten something important. I slip between the supplies that dwindle with each day we don't find the Raiders. There's still plenty of food, and we can refresh our water if need be, though we've got several casks of wine to make do in the meantime.

I pull my dagger from my hip, relishing the feel of it in my palm. It was a gift from Coco, and after so long without a blade, this is a treasure that makes me feel complete like nothing else could. I feel a smile creeping onto my face at the thought of my friend. She is one of the few people who truly understands me, despite knowing me for such a short period of time. With Krew occupied helping Ivy and Thoa off doing stars-knows-what, it's nice to know there's still someone around to care about me.

I think of how she pulled me aside before we left, the way her tanned cheeks seemed to color the slightest bit. She kissed my cheek then, told me how delighted she is to have me home, before running off to other business. I can't deny the heat that coursed through me then, the color sweeping up my neck as I watched her jog away. Good gods above, I love watching her leave.

When I last saw her, more than a year ago, I'd never known a lover. Mentally I understood what it meant to have one, to share myself with another, but the bodily practice of it is something else entirely. And though I haven't had much practice since, I've experienced enough to understand when my body is calling out to share another's.

While I'm thinking about Coco, warmth spreading unbidden through my body, I come across a door with a strange lock. It's iron, I think, heavy, with the largest keyhole I've ever seen. The key that fits it must be the size of my finger. I lose all thoughts of anything else, curiosity crawling through me as I consider what Rachel could have locked up down here.

An intake of breath behind me and I turn to find my aunt, surprise drawn across her face in raised brows and an open mouth. "Nova," she breathes, "what are you doing down here?"

"Nosing around," I say, trying to give nothing away.

She smiles. "Yeah. You always did like to do that."

I don't return her smile. "What's behind the door, Rachel?"

"It's nothing to worry about."

"You're not a good liar."

She pulls a face. "I'm a fantastic liar, thank you very much. You're just better at reading people than you should be."

I fold my arms and block the door. "Tell me."

"It will only make you angry." I raise my brows but don't move until she sighs and pushes past me, saying, "Fine. But remember, I tried to protect you from this."

She pulls out a massive key that is indeed as large as my finger, as long as my hand even. The lock clicks open and she pulls it from the door, placing it on the floor before pulling open the heavy door. I take a deep breath and follow after her.

There, reclining on a small green duvan with a thick book in hand, is Tinora/Jane.

A string of curses falls from my lips, but the woman doesn't spare me a glance. She holds up a finger while appearing to mouth words from her book. I take a step forward but Rachel pushes me back, waiting with patience I can't comprehend. After a moment, Tinora folds over the corner of a page and closes the book, turning her gaze to me.

"Hello, Captain," she says. "Lovely to see you, as always."

"Jane," Rachel says, nodding her way.

"What is she doing here?" I hiss.

"I believe I'm her sexy prisoner."

Rachel chuckles, stymies it when she sees my expression. I'm certain if I rolled my eyes any harder they'd fall from my face. Still, aside from rushing her, there's not much more I could do. Then I realize I have Coco's knife at my belt and rushing her is an option. Tinora is weaponless here, powerless, and the sweet song of revenge sings at the tip of my blade.

I take a single step towards her before Rachel moves in front of me. "What are you doing?"

I pull my knife and say, "Something I've wanted to do for a long time."

"What about all that horseshit about people deserving the chance to change?"

"Not her," I growl.

"Why? She's no worse than the rest of us. No worse than Nigel, yet we've allowed him the time and opportunity to change."

I still haven't taken my eyes from Tinora and the blade is now heavy in my hand, begging for its chance to slice. Rachel grabs my shoulders and with a shake, directs my gaze to hers. I glare at her and say, "You don't know what she did."

"I do. I've heard her story. That's why she's locked up in here. But that doesn't give you the right to kill her."

I shove at Rachel's hands. "You have no say in this. She deserves death and I shall deal it."

Rachel's face hardens. "The hell you will. This is my ship and she is my prisoner. You even try to harm her without my consent and I'll toss you overboard."

I step back at her words. "You wouldn't."

"Try me. It will be a cold day in hell before I let my ship fall to mutiny."

The woman before me is not my aunt Rachel, but Captain MacGale of *The Disorderly Glory*. I furrow my brows, try to bite back my anger before it extends to Rachel. With as much calm as I can muster, I ask, "You would protect her life over mine?"

Rachel puts her hands on her hips. "Don't you get it, kid? I *am* trying to protect yours. Revenge is a bitter dish, poisoned. Better to let it go."

Let it go, I think, a laugh dying in my throat. "I am not the sort to 'let it go.' But for your sake and the respect I have for your command, I will not raise my blade to that woman until we are off your ship."

"And after that?" she asks.

I let my eyes find Tinora's again. "I'll wash my hands in her blood."

SMOKE CURLS AT THE EDGE OF THE WORLD. I JOIN REGO AND RACHEL at the bow, staring into the distance.

"Could be them," Rego says, rubbing at the white beard he's grown while I was gone.

"It's too far south," I say. "We don't go to the sea's edge."

"We don't, aye, but perhaps they do."

Rego's words sting and I ask, "Are we no longer counted among them? Have we lost what made us Raiders?"

He shakes his head. "Forgive me, Little Star. I would not diminish your place among them. But me? I'm an old man whose heart is waiting on a farm far from here. I gave up the Raider life the moment Jasper stepped back into mine."

I nod once, accepting his answer even if I don't understand it. Though I haven't lived as a Raider this last year, I still know that's who I am at my core. I switch my thoughts back to the smoke in the too-far south. "When is the last time the Raiders changed their path?"

Rego shakes his head as he shrugs. "The pattern changes slightly over time, but nothing drastic. Sometimes a new chief will make alterations, but..."

Our eyes meet with the realization of what this could mean. I whisper, "If something happened to Eija—"

"Papa-du would lead until another chief could be chosen," Rego finishes. "Unless he couldn't."

I look at Rachel who seems to be following our conversation as best she can. I nod towards the gray tendrils and say, "Make for the smoke."

A few yells to her crew and the ship is turned to face the curling finger that beckons us closer. On foot, it would take us days to track the fire that hisses into the sky, but on Rachel's ship we near it in a matter of hours. I ask Rachel to put us down when I estimate the walk is under an hour. I'm certain the lookouts would've seen our descent, but at least this way we can approach them on even ground.

We disembark the ship as the sun sets, leaving only Rachel and her crew aboard. She was not happy to be left behind, but I cannot take them into the Raider's home knowing that it was her people who killed Nukiki. I instruct them to take flight if anyone tries to board and she seems to understand my cautiousness—if Raiders could take her ship, they would, dragging it home like one of their skiffs. It's what I would do.

The trek towards the smoke is a quiet one. Moods are sour after so many days of brooding, too much time aboard the *The Disorderly Glory* to think about the wrongs done to us, the wrongs we have done, and not enough to do to fill the time. Even with Hiro's constant barrage of gleeful comments and excitement for the unknown world he's experiencing, I haven't been able to recapture the spark of joy I was guarding before I saw Tinora below deck. Another thing she has taken from me.

We approach a rise and I feel a prickle at the back of my neck. I stop, motioning the others to do the same. I sniff the faint breeze, letting the scents filter through my head: grass, dirt, leather, sweat.

"Fatboy," I call, the Raider words feeling strange on my tongue. "It is Nova, returned from the City of Trials. I bring life."

Rego shoots me a sidelong glance, unhappy with my choice of words. He growls, "They have not chosen that life."

"Neither did I," I say. "Since when do we give them a choice?"

A head peeks up from the grass. Shaggy black hair plastered on a wet forehead, small black eyes over a sharp nose, a smile like a knife's edge. I hadn't seen him there. He's gotten better at hiding, or I've gotten worse at reading the land.

Fatboy grins, hailing me with one hand in the air. "Little Star. How did you know I was here?"

I return his grin. "Smelled you."

He laughs heartily as he looks over those with me. "Fine hunting you've done." His eyes linger a little too long on Karina and she snarls at him. He laughs again and says, "Fine, indeed."

"We would see the chief," Rego says.

Fatboy whips his head back as if noticing Rego for the first time. His eyes linger on him even longer than they did on Karina and I wonder what he's seeing. A moment later he nods and turns his back to us, heading off through the wisps of grass that shouldn't be able to hide a man of his girth, but do when he wants them to.

We trail behind him for no longer than ten minutes. I want to ask why he's hunting so close to the tent grounds, but hold my tongue. I do not hunt for the Raiders any longer, do not know what has changed these many months.

At the edge of the tents I expect to see lookouts, but my eyes find none. I do not hear the sound of Raiders coming to life, waking from their daytime slumber. We pass one fire nearing its death, the fire that brought us here, but there are no meats spitting upon it, no incense burned in celebration. It smells of nothing more than smoke.

There are no children running through the camp as Fatboy leads us to the tent in the middle of the others. I think he is taking us to the meeting tent so that we may rest while we wait for the chief to join us, but as we step inside, my eyes are met with glowing lamps surrounding a large bed, plush animal furs lining the floor, colorful pillows strewn about the place.

"What is this?" Rego asks.

"Chief's tent," Fatboy says. I meet his eyes, but can't read what's behind them.

"Since when does Eija use a tent such as this?" I ask, unable to keep the disgust from my voice.

"Guard your tongue, Little Star. Eija is no longer chief and the new one is not as accepting of your antics."

"Ukaru," I say, trying to keep my tone neutral as I turn to the man entering the tent. I've known him for many years, but I cannot call up a smile with which to greet him. The last time we stood before each other, it was on opposite sides of the decision about Krew. I wanted to keep him as a Raider, but Ukaru incensed the others to side against me. If it were not for him, perhaps Krew would've stayed, Thoa would still be here, we wouldn't have faced the trials or the torment the space station brought.

But I wouldn't have found my family, found myself.

"You disrespect me," he spits.

I grit my teeth but manage, "Apologies, Ukaru-du."

"*Chief* Ukaru-du," he says, lips curling over a feral smile.

I'm taken aback by his words and as his smile grows wider, I'm certain the surprise is showing on my face. Before I can form the words building behind my eyes, Rego asks, "What happened to Eija?"

"Unfit to lead," Ukaru says, moving to recline on the bed. He studies his fingernails as the displeasure of his words falls on us.

"And Papa-du?" I ask.

"Dead."

I swallow back the pain that rises in my chest. I was not close to Papa-du, but he was always kind to me. I glance to Rego. His head is bowed, hand over his heart, seemingly overcome by the news.

"Any other questions for your chief? Or maybe it's time I ask some of you."

"Ask what you wish," I say. "We have nothing to hide."

"Where have you been?"

"With the star-people," I say.

He nods, eyes roving over those who've come with us who have been wise enough to remain silent. "And these offerings, are they from the stars?"

I nod once, watching the sneer cross his lips. "Do you expect them to be accepted after the last trouble you brought upon us?"

His amber eyes meet mine with a challenge. I ignore it, unwilling to be baited into an argument with him. Ukaru was kind to me before I found Krew, maybe not friendly, but not so outright hateful as he is now. Though his words are plain, I see the malice behind them, the way he looks for a reason to argue.

"What happened to Eija?" I ask.

"I told you—"

"You told us nothing," Rego interrupts. "Does she live?"

Ukaru's lip curls up as he turns his eyes from me. "She lives, if you can call it that. Speak to her if you must, but do not linger. I want you away from here before dawn."

"Uka—Chief," I correct myself. "We return with news, with need."

"Your need is nothing to me. Breathe easy in my kindness, that I have not killed you already."

Rego's eyes are dark as he looks up, saying, "We are Raiders. You can do no such thing."

"You *were* Raiders. Now, you are strangers to us, sand drifting on the breeze."

I can feel Rego as he starts to shake beside me. I put my hand on his shoulder and pull at him. "Let's go."

We file outside, the others surrounding us for an explanation for what happened as they don't speak Raider. Hiro says, "That felt tense."

"It didn't go as planned," I say.

"I picked up a little of it," Karina says. "Raider has roots in Spanish, I think. It's not the same language by far, but there are enough similarities that I could get a few words each sentence."

"What's Spanish?" I ask.

She waves a hand to dismiss me and says, "Forget it. What happens next?"

I look around the tents, my eyes finding Fatboy lingering nearby talking to someone I do not know. I catch his eye and wave him over. He walks to us, his eyes tracing Karina's figure as he does.

I ask, "How long has Ukaru led the Raiders?"

"Nearly a year. Since you left."

"Why?"

"After Eija couldn't do it anymore, and Papa-du fell ill, Ukaru took over."

"The Raiders voted him as chief?"

Fatboy shakes his head. "He's been filling in until we vote."

"There have been two solstices since we left. A vote could have been called at either," Rego says.

Fatboy shrugs. "No one else has shown interest."

I run a hand over my face, annoyance bleeding into my tone as I say, "This is not the Raider way."

"There are many things we now do that are not the Raider way," Fatboy whispers. "But no one questions it anymore. Not after the Banishment."

"Whose banishment?"

I can tell by the furtive glances he casts at Ukaru's tent that he doesn't want to continue speaking out in the open. I ask, "Is there somewhere my friends can wait while we go speak with Eija?"

Fatboy winces, but nods. He leads us to an empty fire pit where logs are positioned in a circle around it. He motions for the others to sit, offering what little comfort he can. Before he can lead us to Eija, I lean close to Rego and say, "I do not trust Ukaru. He may change his mind at any moment, endangering our guests. Perhaps one of us should stay with them."

He nods. "I will stay. I do not know if I can handle seeing what has become of little Eija."

I follow Fatboy to the edge of the tents. He leads me into a small one, unlit and reeking of sweat and unbathed skin. Fatboy lights a lamp in the corner, knowing exactly where to go, as if he's done this many times. He carries it back to me, whispering into the dimness, "Chief, I've brought some company."

Eija is on the bed, or at least, what used to be Eija. She is all bones now, skin stretched over her in too-tight angles and jagged edges. Her cheeks are hollow, black circles under her eyes. Her tanned skin is ashy, her once bright eyes dull and glassy.

"Hey Chief," I say, kneeling beside her bed. "It is Nova."

"Little Star?" she asks through cracked lips.

"Yes."

She tries to spit, though nothing crosses her lips, before moving a bony finger over her eyes. "Cursed child. Come to bring more misery to us?"

I flinch at her words. The Chief was always hard on me, but never cruel. "I've done as you asked. I took the boy to the star-people."

"You killed her."

"Who?" I ask. Gods help me, I know who she means. I just can't say it.

"Who? She asks me who," Eija says, a laugh building in her chest. It sputters out in a thick, wet sound, surrounded by wheezing. "Have you forgotten so easily? Destroyed me and forgotten in the same breath."

I think back to when we left with Krew, the days trekking through the desert, the grasslands, the woods where we saw the airship. Where Nukiki died.

I close my eyes, my head drooping. "I'm sorry Chief, about your wife."

"Ah, so you do remember ripping out my heart."

I didn't know she loved her so deeply, but I should have. They'd only been married a few days when we left, and she could have taken a new mate twice since then. But before they were married, they were friends. And though I didn't know Nukiki well, everything I ever saw from her was built around a kind heart.

I don't know how to acknowledge the pain she feels. I mutter, "Nukiki was a painful loss..."

Her wet laugh keeps me from uttering more. Her voice is gravel as she says, "I died that day. She was everything."

I bite my lip, unsure what to say. Though her pain is clearly still present, could Nukiki be the whole reason she's in this bed, barely holding onto life? "I do not understand, Chief, not fully, and I cannot pretend to. Is there nothing else that keeps you living? What about your people?"

She stares through me, past me, at the corner of the tent. "They are cared for."

"Not well," I say. "Ukaru lives in extravagance, there are no lookouts, the nightly fires are still."

"We sleep at night."

"Since when?" I ask.

"Since we settled here."

"Settled?" I ask. "Raiders do not settle."

"Things change, Little Star."

"You certainly did," I mutter.

A flash of defiance crosses her dulled eyes. "What do you expect? I have nothing to live for. Nukiki, dead. Papa-du, dead. My people…"

"Your people suffer under Ukaru. Fatboy says that none can speak against him, that there was a banishment. Since when do Raiders turn away their own?"

"You do not know what you say. You do not understand the cost of death, never did."

I feel my heart harden towards her in those words. "I understand death as well as anyone. My hands are covered in it. But I keep going, because that is what I must do. The Chief I knew, she would have kept going, too. That's what Nukiki and Papa-du would have wanted. She was the fiercest thing these eyes have seen. Now she is a corpse."

I rise from her side as I see my words falling on unhearing ears. She does not wish to hear these things from me, craving only the release of death. My hand falls to the blade at my waist and for a moment I consider giving what she wishes. Her eyes light up, begging for release, but instead I press my lips tight and turn away. I will not release her from her responsibility.

"Please," she whispers, her voice a breath in a typhoon.

I shake my head but do not turn back to her. "I will not give you the mercy of the blade. Return to life: if not for you, do it for your people."

"It is too much."

I let the words sink into me, but they do not foster pity. I have faced the pain of two worlds and yet, I fight. Life and pain are synonymous. Her excuses mean little to nothing to me. "Die as you are, or live as she would want you to. I will not make the decision for you."

CHAPTER
TWENTY-FOUR

I step from Eija's tent into the hot night air, still and thick as stew. I press my palms to my closed eyes, fighting back the overwhelming need to wail into the night. The first part of Ivy's plan has already failed. We need the Raiders, need their strength. But these are not the people I knew and the strength they had has bled away.

Distant shouting catches my attention and I head towards the sound. As I maneuver through the canvas town, I realize the sound is coming from the fire pit where I left the others.

I come around the corner of a tent in time to see Rego and Ukaru staring each other down. Ukaru has half a dozen Raiders at his back, blades drawn. Rego stands in front of our group of misfits, arms outstretched to prevent any of them from moving on the Raiders in front of them.

"What is this?" I yell.

"Chief Ukaru-du has broken his word," Rego says, making sure his Raider tongue is loud enough for everyone backing Ukaru to hear.

I glare at Ukaru. "You said we could stay until dawn. By my eyes it's nowhere near morning."

Ukaru sucks air between his teeth. "Why would I allow outsiders to rest in my camp? I commanded you to leave or face the blade."

I look at those assembled behind him, realizing these are all Raiders I do not know. They have no reason to believe me or Rego when their chief gives his account. We could not best true Raiders, but since these Raiders have been here a year at the longest, they are likely not yet trained. With the trial winners and the prisoners at our side, we could win in a fight if it came to it.

But I don't want it to come to that. I will not risk the lives of any of these people because of Ukaru's pettiness. I put my hand on Rego's arm, trying to dissuade him from pressing into the altercation Ukaru seems desperate to cause. Rego ignores me, stepping so close to Ukaru that their noses almost touch. There's a ripple in the Raiders behind Ukaru, but no one steps closer.

"You have no integrity," Rego says, more venom in his tone than I have ever heard. "You make the Raiders weak. You are no chief."

Ukara bares his teeth and says, "Like it or not, there is no other."

"I would call a vote of no confidence—"

Ukaru laughs, cutting him off. "We are long from the solstice, old man."

"Aye, we are. As I said, I *would* call for a vote, but since we are months from a solstice, there is another way to remove you."

I step forward, saying, "Rego, no," but he waves me away like an annoying child.

"You challenge me?" Ukaru asks. "Are you so hungry for death?"

He's right, I think. Challenging him is a mistake. Rego has trained as a Raider, certainly, hunted for the family when he was younger, but now he is challenging a man who is twenty years younger, a strong hunter, with a temper that drives him near madness. If Rego were challenging Ukaru to a battle with wit or tongue, he would not lose. But he isn't; no, Rego challenged Ukaru to a fight to the death for the right to be chief.

"Don't do this," I say.

Ukaru says, "It is done. I accept your challenge."

"Do you still have a fight pit or have you disgraced our ways even further than I know?" Rego asks.

Ukaru's eyes narrow. "We have a place that will serve our purpose. Our fight begins at first light, as tradition dictates."

Rego shakes his head, finally sparing a glance to me. "They don't even have the fight pit any longer. How many times did we dig the pit at each encampment, knowing it would only serve us a few weeks?"

"Countless," I say. My voice is thick, fear gripping me with strong hands.

"And yet this pup dishonors us so," Rego says. "When I am chief, I will return the Raiders to their former glory."

He turns from me then, turns from Ukaru, and walks past the star-people into the grass beyond. There he sits and turns his face skyward. I can't hear him, but I know he calls to his goddess for help.

The Raiders are not religious, as a group. We are made of many people with many histories. We honor all the gods as much as we honor none, favoring whomever we choose, regarding none above the others. I have always appreciated this about the Raiders, though I have no god of my own. But tonight I find myself hoping Rego's goddess is real and strong and listening.

Ukaru and his cronies are gone, but they do not take the tension they brought with them. Instead it is left to fester in the air around us, souring our already dour moods. Though the others do not speak Raider, do not know what has transpired, they are not fools. They know our plan has failed, even if they aren't certain to what degree.

I sit on a log by the fire pit and drop my head to my knees, hugging my legs and making myself as small as I can. A moment later, I feel someone sit on each side of me and arms spread across my back. When I raise my head, I find Valeska on my left and Hiro on my right. Zeb and Sarah stand in front of us, Drev and Karina behind. They've formed a circle of protection around us.

"What's going on?" Valeska asks. She doesn't try to comfort, doesn't use a saccharine-sweet voice to ease the words out. Valeska is practical, sharp, true. And though she asks in a way that allows me to explain without condemnation, she knows all our plans have gone awry.

"Our plan would have worked, if the chief hadn't changed," I shrug.

"The old chief wasn't an asshole?" Hiro asks.

I smile, glad for his company yet again. "She was, but not in the same way. She was fierce, doing whatever she needed to protect her people."

"Dead?" Valeska asks.

"No," I say, shaking my head. "Broken."

"So we leave without Raiders. It could be worse," she says.

"That's what I thought, but now…" I trail off, glancing through the darkness to Rego.

They follow my gaze and Hiro says, "Rego wasn't having it."

I bite my lip, letting my eyes slip down to my shaking hands. "He challenged Ukaru. Winner becomes chief."

"That's not so bad," Valeska says. "If he wins, he can bring the Raiders with us. And if he loses, we're no worse off."

A tear slips down my cheek. "He can't lose, Valeska. He mustn't."

Hiro swallows, and even before he asks I know he already knows the answer. "What happens if he does?"

"It's a fight to the death. So he wins, or he dies."

THE NIGHT IS LONG.

Darkness lingers, surrounding me with its shadowy embrace, stretching black fingers over the gaping wound of my heart. Rego will die.

The night is short.

Dawn barrels over the horizon, blinding streaks of red and orange overtaking the purple of first light, bringing hope as its companion. Rego must live.

Rego stands from where he held his midnight vigil, stretches long and lean against the light of the rising sun. He walks towards us and I aim a soft kick at Hiro's ass and Drev's leg as they lay on the ground outside the fire pit. The others are already awake, yawning and stretching as they watch him approach.

His skin is glowing in the light, his smile as bright as ever I've seen. This is not a man who fears the morning, but one ready for whatever comes. He squeezes my shoulder as he passes and I turn to follow him with my eyes, realizing he aims to meet the messenger waiting at the edge of the tents.

It's Fatboy, his brows curled into question marks as he looks from Rego to me. I've closed the gap and am close enough to hear when he says, "Ukaru waits at the pit. I've come to take you there." He pauses for a second and adds, "Unless you'd have me tell them you were already gone."

Rego smiles and says, "No, thank you. I aim to take back the Raiders and save them from the perversion the false chief has inflicted."

Fatboy nods without a word and turns away, leading us through the tents to the other side of the encampment. There is a divot between two natural rises and it is here they have dug a fresh fight pit. It isn't large like those we've had before, no more than a couple feet deep compared to the standard we've always held—the depth of the dead, six feet.

Ukaru waits for us, the whole of the Raiders at his back. There's thirty maybe, half the number that Eija led. I see faces I recognize among them, though they are few. A woman at the edge of the assembly nods a greeting, a man in the back gives a smile, but for the most part they keep their eyes averted. They do not want to be here.

Rego jumps down into the pit and for a moment I see the man he once was, in the years before I knew him. Ukaru steps forward and drops into the pit, leaving a few feet between them. A woman steps up, Caita, and I'm glad to see someone familiar. She is a hunter like Ukaru, like me, but her prey was always fruit or nuts she was able to gather. I never recall her returning with meat. Though I do remember the faces she brought to our family. Caita is a proper life-bringer.

"Chief Ukaru-du," she says, "name your second."

Ukaru calls a barrel-chested brute to stand at the edge of the pit. The man is huge, thick arms and legs like logs. Thick red hair covers head, face, and chest in wild curls. His skin is tanned from the sun, but his natural coloring looks to be pale, like mine.

With a smile, Ukaru waves a hand for Rego to choose his own. Rego says, "Nova-du."

There's a gasp among the crowd by those who know us, who know that I have not brought life to the Raiders. Rego has blasphemed in his use of the title with my name. Still, I step to the edge of the pit and fold my arms across my chest, projecting the ferocity I do not feel and daring anyone to challenge him.

"Rego-du, choose your weapon," Caita says.

"We fight with the blade," Rego says, "as a Raider should."

He throws off his robe and pulls a blade from his belt. It is short and sharp and I hear it singing for blood as sure as the sun is shining. Ukaru pulls his own blade, longer than Rego's, but not so long as to disqualify him.

"Seconds, ready?" Caita asks. The brute and I nod and Caita asks, "Fighters, ready?"

Ukaru and Rego nod and without further fanfare, they circle. Ukaru is the first to strike, jabbing hard towards Rego's midsection.

Rego sidesteps with little effort, extending his hand towards Ukaru's with such speed, I almost miss it.

Ukaru pulls back his arm with a yowl and I see a line of blood well up on his forearm. The cut is shallow, but it seems to rattle Ukaru. He pulls back from Rego and falls into a defensive position. He's lost the smile he wore when they started and now seems to be taking Rego seriously. Pride and hope swell inside me and I realize Rego has a better chance than I thought.

Now that Rego has drawn first blood, Ukaru is more reserved in his strikes. He swipes forward a couple times testing Rego's guard, but both times he's met with a parrying blow. Still, he doesn't make the same mistake twice, refusing to give Rego another opportunity to strike him.

The crowd watches them trade blows, and though the star-people behind me cheer for Rego each time he gets in a good hit, the Raiders remain silent on their side of the fight pit, as in tradition. This fight is for them, for the future of the Raiders, but I'm not certain all the new people realize the magnitude of what's happening. I'm not surprised. Though we dug a pit at every stop, in twelve years I never saw it used.

Rego yelps in pain and my eyes fly back to him. I only looked to the crowd for a second, but it was long enough. Ukaru has sliced through Rego's leathers and left a deep gash in his side. Rego clenches his arm against it to staunch the blood flow, but stars above, there's so much of it.

"You need to get him out of there," Karina says.

I jump, so focused on the bout I hadn't noticed her approach. "I can't stop it."

"You have to," she says. "He's going to die. Get him out now and I might be able to save him."

I don't spare her a glance, unwilling to risk taking my eyes from Rego again. "To the death. Those are the rules."

She snorts. "Since when do you care about the rules? You're really going to let that bastard win?"

"I don't care if he wins—"

"But you care if Rego loses."

I grit my teeth, but they do nothing to fight the tears threatening to overflow. The last thing I want is to lose Rego. But this is the way of the Raiders.

Ukaru lands another blow, slicing through the meat of Rego's shoulder. Ukaru retreats, showing a sliver of mercy where others might have pressed their advantage. Rego staggers back, legs shaking, tries to lift his blade. But he can't. He falls to his knees, drops the weapon in the dirt beside him.

Ukaru's wolfish grin spreads over his face. He raises his arms in victory as he walks around the pit, letting the moment linger before he takes his final swing. When he walks towards Rego, it's with a swagger in his step.

"Let this moment serve to remind those who oppose me that I will not bow to anyone, I will not cower in the face of death. I will master it and any who challenge me!"

He raises his blade above Rego. Ukaru stabs at Rego's heart but my blade deflects it. There's a sudden scream on the air and it takes a second to realize it's me. I knock Ukaru's blade from his hand as I catch him by surprise. I will not let him kill Rego. I will not let him or anyone else take and take and take from me.

Not without a fight.

I stalk forward, hands clenched at my side. The blade in my right hand feels like an extension of me, sharp and singing for blood.

Ukaru slinks back, sputtering. "This is not our way."

"What do you know about our way?" I yell. "You've broken our way over and over since you've been chief." I slash up with my knife, using it to point at the crowd behind him. "That's why you've brought all these new lives in. Not because you wanted to give them a family, a life as a Raider, but because you wanted subjects to rule who didn't know you were doing wrong."

"You are banished," he spits as I close in on him. "Never return to us."

I laugh, unable to stop myself. "You cannot banish me. You are not my chief."

There's a thud in the dirt beside me as Ukaru's second drops into the pit. I feel him moving behind me but I do not take my eyes from Ukaru. The big man is a distraction, a jumprat promising chase while Ukaru is the snake waiting in the grass.

"Give up now and I'll let you leave alive. I'll even let you take Rego, if he still has breath," Ukaru says.

My lips curl into a sneer. "You don't have much choice, Ukaru-du. I'm the one holding the blade."

A whistle cuts through the air and I spin left. The second's blade cuts the space where I was, a hair's breadth from me. I continue my spin, using the momentum to push my blade into the man's side. It hits true, digging into his flesh, but I don't twist the blade, don't drive it towards his vital organs.

"I do not wish to hurt you."

He bares his teeth and in stuttering Raider tongue he manages, "I protect the chief."

In the old tongue I say, "My quarrel is not with you."

The big man tilts his head, his lips giving into a smile. "It is a treat to hear those words, even from the mouth of someone I have to kill."

"It doesn't have to be this way," I say as we circle one another. "He's using you, but I'm willing to let you live."

His grin grows wider. "Let me? Aye, girl, such kindness. You'll not find it in me. You may have scratched me, but you'll not get another chance."

I shake my head. "Remember this when you go beyond."

I stab out, quick, slicing a gash on his arm. I dance away from him before he has a chance to swing his weapon. He's a brute, undoubtedly strong, but he can't hurt what he can't hit, and I am fast. I've trained with the Raiders more than half my life, whereas he has lived among them a year. The poor thing hasn't a hope.

He charges towards me, looking like the buffalo we hunt on the plains. I dodge and spin and weave away from him with ease. Each time I move from his advance, his face flushes brighter, anger getting the better of him.

Each time I glide away from him, I check the pit's bank. Karina and Drev attend Rego. I can't see what's happening, how he is, but I watch a streak of blood spread across Karina's forehead when she wipes the sweat from her brow.

The second and I have only been dancing a minute or two, but already he tires. My blade hits him thrice more before Hiro's voice cuts through to my ears: "Behind you!"

I dive forward towards the second and roll into a ball. He slices down with his blade and knicks my shoulder, sending a sharp sting through me. There's blood, but not much. He didn't hit anything important.

Springing up on the other side of him, I spin to see both he and Ukaru on my heels. Looks like the chief has given up on his second burying me on his own, has given up on his offer to leave unharmed, and is ready to end my life at the tip of his own blade.

"Two against one," I say. "I guess that's the only way you think you can best me."

Ukaru's eyes flick to the star-people behind me, to the body on the ground. "I had no trouble killing Rego on my own."

His taunt hits home. My gut tells me to strike out, to attack for what he said, but I hold back. It isn't my ferocity that I need right now, it's Rego's patience. I may be able to dodge the second's clumsy attempts to skewer me, but Ukaru is a seasoned hunter. It will take more than bravado to win against him.

Something scrapes against my boot and I look down. Rego's blade is still where he dropped it. I grab it, wielding it with my left hand. Though I am not as skilled with this hand, Rego made sure I could fight with two blades if the need arose.

They move to the sides to close me in and split my attention. I will need my focus to fight Ukaru, so his second needs to die first. I run to the right. The brute braces himself in the dirt, planting his feet and lifting his blade to meet me. The moment before I reach him, I shift my trajectory towards the pit's edge and let my feet take purchase on the higher ground.

Everything seems to slow in those heartbeats. Surprise registers on his face, but he swipes out with his blade trying to catch me. His blade slices just outside my deltoid muscle. It is but a scratch and I ignore it.

Side by side with him, I strike. My blade's song is satisfied, coated in red spray as it cuts into his carotid artery. The blood spews from his neck even as he drops his weapon and moves to cover the gash in his neck. I feel the warmth of it as it covers me in its dark mist.

I come down from the wall, feet landing back in the pit. The second no longer a distraction, I set my eyes on Ukaru. His wide eyes survey me as the blood drips down my face. I meet his gaze with a smile. Planting my feet in the earth behind his dead brute, I point a knife in his direction and nod my head for him to make his move.

"Stop this."

Eija stands above us at the pit's edge. She is frail, leaning on Fatboy for support, but some of her sharpness seems to have returned. Her command sparks the air like a match, igniting a fire in my bones. I drop to a knee where I stand and say, "Yes, Chief."

"This doesn't concern you, Eija." Ukaru's voice is unusually gentle when he speaks to her. "Go back to your tent."

Her eyes flash as dangerous as the daggers in my hands. "I've spent far too long in that suffocating canvas. Meanwhile, you've robbed my people of the dignity we Raiders keep."

Ukaru steps forward until he's directly in front of her, looking up into those dagger-sharp eyes. "You gave up on us. You gave away your role as chief over some stupid bitch that went and got herself killed."

"Don't you dare—"

"Or what?" he spits. "I am chief now. You are nothing."

Quicker than my eyes can follow, Ukaru's blade swings up. It slips between the ribs, puncturing her heart, and he twists, twists, twists.

CHAPTER
TWENTY-FIVE

Eija convulses while Fatboy holds her, repeating her name like a chant. He lays her on the ground, moving with more gentleness than I've ever seen from him. Her shaking body stills and her eyes go dull while he cries, "Eija, Eija, Eija."

I don't know what Ukaru expects when he turns to me, smile spread across his face. I close the space between us in two strides. My knife swings towards him. He throws his arms up to block. His blade is still lodged in Eija's chest and his forearm can do little to stop my advance. I miss his neck, but the tip of my blade catches him just below the collarbone. I press forward, letting it dig into his skin.

Ukaru shoves me away. I throw myself towards him again. Rage boils inside me. I reach for the anger, burn it for fuel, let it consume every part of me. I spin towards him, my knives dancing so fast they blur the air in front of me. I slice into him with my right blade. He tries to twist away from me and I lash out with my left. It moves through his side as if he's made of butter.

He howls in pain, high and keening. *It's a dirge*, I think, *his lament.*

But no, his cry is for himself, not for the things he's done. Not for those he's banished. Not for the hurts he caused Rego. Not for what he did to Chief.

I grit my teeth as I push forward. Ukaru tries to back away, holding his side as blood dribbles from his wound. His legs hit the edge of the fight pit and he falls backward, sprawling on the ground.

He holds up his blood-covered hand and cries, "Mercy."

I shove his hand aside and bury my blade in his windpipe. Ukaru gurgles as blood and spittle come to the corners of his mouth. After all this, he's finally stopped smiling.

"I am a Raider, a death dealer, Nova-gra. I do not give mercy."

It takes several minutes for Ukaru to die. The old Nova would not stand by and watch as he suffocates, as he endures this slow and painful death. But that girl is not here and I stand over him, watching every second of his death.

After Ukaru takes his last breath, I turn my eyes on Fatboy. I do not acknowledge the Raiders behind him, knowing that our whole plan will be determined by what happens in the next few minutes.

"Build a pyre here, in the pit. Burn the bodies. Send them to their rest."

Fatboy doesn't hesitate, nodding his acceptance of my words and saying, "Yes, Chief."

He grabs a couple Raiders I don't know and they head off to gather wood while Hiro comes to the side of the pit to haul me up. I'm bone tired and ready to fall over, but I wave away his help and turn to the Raiders. They've heard Fatboy's words and are whispering among themselves, but as soon as I step towards them they go silent.

I fidget with the button in my pocket, the one Ivy gave me to disable the cameras. I don't want them to hear my words. "Many of you know nothing of me except that I killed Ukaru. For some, you've never known the true ways of a Raider, only what this false chief taught you. I will not hold you to any oath you swore to him, any promises you made by his campfire. You can leave this place with my blessing."

"Where would we go?" someone asks.

I shake my head. "I cannot say. North, south, east, west—no matter where you go, there will be challenges. But you can go, if you choose."

"And if we stay?" another person asks.

"Then you honor the ways of the Raiders, the true ways. We return to our path, traveling the land, sleeping during the day, living with only what we can carry in our skiffs. We train you to fight, to win. We train you in stealth that you can be as silent as a blade of grass in the wind. You will hunt, you will gather, you will serve your family as needed."

"With you as chief?" a mazulla person says, stepping in front of me and folding their arms.

Caita steps forward and says, "She won the right to be chief."

I hold up my hand towards her and give her a nod of thanks, but turn back to the mazulla Raider. "If you'd like to take the right from me, you can try." When they don't reply, I look past them and add, "That goes for any of you. Now is your chance."

No one moves, speaks. After a moment, I turn back to Caita. "You would call the fight for me?"

She nods, her lips curled at the edges. "Aye, Chief."

"Though I broke up the challenge before Ukaru could kill Rego?"

"I would've sided for Ukaru and seen you to the pyre myself, had he not called down his second. In doing so, he agreed to accept you as a new challenger. Though if you hadn't defeated him, I would have been next to try, for what he did to Eija."

"I'm glad to know you would have honored her. She deserved better than she got."

I look to the star-people still standing by the edge of the pit. Karina still kneels beside Rego's body. I'm terrified to speak with her, fearing what has become of him. I watch her for a moment, trying to gauge what is happening by the lines of her face.

She looks up as if sensing my gaze. She meets my eyes with a smile. My heart seems to stop beating, stilling in my chest long enough to recalibrate so that when it restarts it beats out one name: Rego.

I stagger forward until I can see him. His eyes are closed and he's covered in blood, but his chest rises and falls. That is enough.

Hiro wraps an arm around my shoulders and I slump against him, letting my exhaustion overtake me. He settles me onto the ground beside Rego and the star-people form up around me.

"Sooooo, that was intense," he says.

I laugh, the sound high and unnatural in my ears. It fizzles in my throat as tears come to my eyes. I gulp back the laugh, the tears, the mass of emotions tangled inside me. Putting my hand on Karina's shoulder, I say, "Thank you."

"Don't thank me yet," she says. "He's alive because Drev thought to bring a med-kit, but he's not in the clear. We need to get him somewhere sterile to avoid infection. Real medical equipment wouldn't hurt either."

"We don't have access to it."

Karina curses. "I forgot what it's like down here."

"The ship would help, at least as far as cleanliness goes," Drev says.

Valeska nods to the Raiders. "Are we going to need to fight our way out of here or will they let us go now that their chief is dead?"

"Their chief isn't dead," I say. I look around at the star-people and say, "It's me."

SIX RAIDERS LEAVE. I DON'T ASK WHERE OR WHY, JUST LET THEM wander away with blessings and full packs. Of the twenty-two who remain, I only know four of them: Fatboy, Caita, Numi, and Owen.

I was never close with any of them, but each shows me acceptance as their new chief and I'm grateful for their support.

I send Zeb, Valeska, and Sarah back to the ship to tell Rachel what's going on and have the ship brought closer. While they're gone, we move Rego into ~~Ukaru's~~ my tent and try to make him comfortable. I toss out some of Ukaru's excess, his frilly pillows and decorations, leaving only what we need for Rego's care. Karina and Drev stay with him while Hiro accompanies me to speak with the Raiders. I have a lot to tell them and only a little time.

We gather at the pyre and watch it burn, flames licking the sky above. Though we do not worship a single god, I call for blessings from all who may listen, that they would take Eija to join Nukiki in whatever world may be after this one.

The Raiders move from the funeral to the cooking fires and it is here I go to speak with them. "There is much that needs explained. I left the Raiders a year ago to help a star-man return home. And I did, but I went with him." There are gasps among them, but I press on. "We've all seen the ring around our world, but the stories tell us it is the home of the gods. It is not. I have been to the ring. It is full of people, like us."

A ripple of uneasiness courses through them, but Hiro steps forward. "It's true. That's where I'm from, and contrary to popular belief, I'm not a god."

I look at him and sigh, rolling my eyes. "They don't understand you, Moose."

"You called me Moose!"

"You're about as bright as one," I mutter. Turning back to the Raiders, I say, "My friend tells you he is from the ring. As you can see, he's nothing special."

They laugh at this and I take a breath in relief, hoping that what I'm about to say won't push them away again. "Some of the star-people use our world for entertainment. They watch us and pit us against one another. They are cruel. Not all, but some. And I want your help to destroy them."

While they eat, I explain as much of the story as I can. Some of it doesn't make sense no matter how many times I replay it in my head, and saying it aloud doesn't help either, but I do my best to help them understand.

When I finish talking, the Raiders grumble and talk for a few minutes before Caita says, "Your will is ours, Chief."

"No, not about this," I say. "I need you to make this decision for yourselves. You've chosen to stay, you wish to be part of the Raiders, and I intend to honor that loyalty. But this is not part of being a Raider. This is bigger, harder, and it's for our whole world. Some of you will not live through it."

Fatboy is the first to rise. He says, "When Chief Eija asked us to volunteer to go with you to the City of Trials, I chose to stay with the Raiders. I was wrong to do so, afraid of what it would mean to leave. I will not make that mistake again. Wherever you go, so do I."

He steps behind me, soon followed by Caita, Owen, and several whose names I don't know. Numi and a few others linger, unsure. She asks, "What happens if we don't go with you?"

"You continue our path until I return or someone brings you my bones."

Numi asks, "This is worth your life?"

I nod. "For the people who come after us, who live when even our memories are lost. They deserve freedom from the star-people's eyes. They deserve to be more than caged beasts viewed for entertainment."

She looks to those alongside her, meets each person's eyes, then turns back to me. "Then we are with you, Chief. Lead us to the star-people and let us save the future."

CHAPTER
TWENTY-SIX

The Raiders settle onto *The Disorderly Glory*, though it takes some effort to coax them aboard. They've never seen a ship like this, just like I hadn't until Rachel's appeared in the sky, so their curiosity does more to get them on the ship than anything I could say.

Rachel turns her private quarters over for Rego's care. Karina and Drev make good use of the limited supplies on the ship, but try as they might, Rego is still unconscious. He needs a doctor to check his wounds. The trial winners know field medicine and can keep him from dying, but it's only a temporary fix and he needs something permanent.

We fly north, leaving the heat in favor of chilly spring mornings. We've been traveling a day and a half when we spot a floating city on the horizon. My heart soars at our luck. If it holds, Rego may get the help he needs by nightfall.

It's too difficult to make out which floater it is, but Rachel is hoping for her home city, Aeroport. In addition to finding a doctor, she wants a chance to replenish supplies before returning to the farm.

"We'll need to get ahold of Herol at some point anyway," she says. "It's always good to have a guy like that on your side."

Herol Hamrick has been running Aeroport, along with another sky-pirate named Sage Delaney, for the last eight months. Once Mayor Nigel came to the good side, he helped disrupt the child abduction ring and implicated multiple people on various floaters. Two of those were on the Aeroport council, and Herol didn't appreciate that at all. With swift and deliberate justice, he made sure Bardlo Sutherland and Lu L'Amour met the ends they deserved.

"He's a good man," I say, thinking back to the little time I spent with him.

Rachel laughs. "I don't know if anyone has ever called him that and I wouldn't recommend you say it to his face. He's wily, conniving, and dangerous." She pauses for a second before saying, "But yeah, he's good."

It isn't Aeroport on the horizon, but a junker city called Copperhill. They sift through the waste the larger cities drop, fueling and feeding themselves on other peoples' trash. Rachel knows the family who runs it and says we'll be welcome. They don't have a full-fledged doctor on Copperhill, but Rachel says there's a woman who lives there named Davie and she'll be able to help.

I'm uneasy about the stop, though I can't pinpoint why, so I go looking for Hiro to see if he has any concerns. I find him sleeping below deck, curled up between two Raiders.

I'm still learning the names of the new Raiders, but I believe the woman is Folly and the man is Gareem. If these two are an indication of Hiro's "type," I can see why he didn't like Captain Alik. She was wire-thin, while Hiro seems to prefer larger frames.

I try to slip away unnoticed, not wanting to rouse him after what I assume was an invigorating morning. Instead, I bump my knee into a crate as I turn away and let out a hiss of pain. Hiro sits up, alert. He catches sight of me and scrubs a hand over his eyes, his shoulders drooping a bit as he relaxes.

I mouth, "Don't get up. I'll catch you later."

But it's too late. He slips out from between the furs they've laid across the floor and moves towards me. He grabs some pants from the floor and slips them on, but not before giving me a glance at all he's got. No small wonder, I must say. Still, I can appreciate the toy without wanting to play with it.

He glances back to the two still curled in the furs and smiles conspiratorially to me. "If you get some free time, I highly recommend seeking them out. Ten out of ten."

"You're an animal," I say, swatting at him.

"I've been called worse. But seriously, they know how to have a good time and you seem like you could use that."

"There are so many other things to think about right now."

He shrugs. "That's the problem, right? There's always something new to worry about. It's okay to give yourself a break from saving the world."

I open my mouth to argue, but instead I say, "This isn't what I wanted to talk about."

He shakes his head, but smiles. "What's up, Squirrel?" I roll my eyes and he says, "Right, sorry, *Chief* Squirrel."

"It's about Copperhill."

"Oh, yeah, it's a terrible idea."

I furrow my brows, unsure how he knew my question. "So you don't think we should go there?"

"I don't think anywhere but the farm is a good stop. We need to get the Raiders back and start figuring out the next step. But I'm a skeptical bastard. Your aunt thinks it's safe. Do you trust her judgment?"

"She's no fool," I say.

"Lots of smart people do stupid things, especially where familiarity is concerned. How well does she know the people that run the place? And how long has it been since she's been there?"

"I don't know."

He nods. "Maybe you should ask."

"I don't want her to think I'm questioning her. She's the Captain."

"And you're the Chief. She may own this airship, but you've got a responsibility to the people you lead to make sure the best decisions are being made. You're on equal footing with Rachel and if she's the leader you think she is, she'll understand where you're coming from."

I nod, step onto the ladder leading above deck, but Hiro takes a step backwards. I ask, "Going back to teach them a few more things?"

He smiles in that broad Hiro grin. "I'm going back to see what I can learn."

RACHEL IS LEANING AGAINST THE STERN OF THE SHIP, OVERSEEING THE work her crew is doing. She never seems to give them commands, but they do what she needs all the same. It must come with time, with working together so long you anticipate the needs of the ship and her crew before they arise.

At least, that's what makes sense in my head. In reality, I can't imagine being around people so long they understand my needs as well as I do. Sometimes I don't understand them myself. Even living among the Raiders, I was never close enough to any of them to be understood in such a way, aside from Rego.

I sidle up next to her, looking out over the back of the ship. I blink, surprised at where we are. To my left, hidden in a small copse of trees, is the homesteader's cottage. Kavis. With everything that has happened, I'd all but forgotten about her, forgotten my promise to return. Gods, it seems like a lifetime ago that I stood dripping wet in front of her fire, my spirit buoyed from watching Thoa and Krew playing in the rain.

I wonder if Kavis still makes clothes for the Raider children, binders for the mazulyr, even if no one comes to trade for them. Does she wonder about me? Or perhaps she thinks I'm dead, like so many others, so many at my hands.

"You okay?" Rachel asks.

I shake my head. "Not really."

"What's wrong?"

I laugh, the sound hollow in my ears. "More than I have words to say."

"You're not on an easy road. But at least you know where you're going."

"I have no idea where I'm going," I say. I'm unsure where these words are coming from, why they've chosen now to be said, but there's truth in them.

"Don't discount what you've already done, kiddo. You played a big part in changing things down here. There's a hundred kids who would thank you for what you started, if they had the chance."

"You did all the work. You, Coco, Herol...gods, even Nigel."

"Wouldn't have happened without you bringing us all together. That's the thing you do, Nova." She grabs my arm and turns me towards the deck. "You have this unusual gift to unite people. Just look around: pirates, Raiders, star-folk, trial winners from gods know where—they're here because of you."

"I'm just, I'm tired, you know. I keep wondering what the end of this looks like, when the dust settles. How many people will die because they followed me and how will I ever live with that? Sometimes I think the only reason I haven't gone mad from all this is because I haven't had time to fully think about it. There's always something else to conquer, someone else to kill. At some point, it has to stop."

"You can worry about that when you get there. If you let it draw your focus now, you'll be adding to what you're already dealing with and that won't help anyone. Least of all these people," she says, waving at those milling about the deck. "And when it's all done, you'll go find yourself a quiet place to rest where you can mourn every loss, every hurt, every heartache."

"What comes after that?"

Rachel shrugs. "Once you've done that, you get to decide what's next, see what kind of life you can have after all this. But no matter which way this wind blows, you can't give up."

"Sometimes I want to."

"We all do. That's part of life. Doesn't mean you can. I swear, if you even think about giving up, I'll kick your arse."

I smile at her. "Thanks, Aunt Rachel."

"Anytime."

I start to step away before remembering that I came to talk to her about Copperhill. I look ahead to the junker city we're approaching, then glance back over my shoulder to Rachel. Somehow all my nerves about the place seem to be settled. Maybe it's the easy way Rachel regards the place and the fact that I trust her, but I decide to let it go. There's no point worrying about something out of my control.

WE ARRIVE AT COPPERHILL AT DUSK. AFTER RACHEL DOCKS *THE Disorderly Glory*, she calls everyone together and says, "We're going to go meet the people who run this place and arrange help for Rego. It's best if only a few of us go at first so they can see we mean no harm. Stay on the ship until we return."

I translate her words to Raider and am thankful when I see heads nodding. I may have only been Chief a couple days, but the Raiders code of honor makes my word law. Even if my word happens to be Rachel's word this time.

Rachel leaves her first mate in command and I realize I need a second of my own. When Eija was chief, she had Papa-du for advice, but I don't have the luxury of a previous chief in my camp.

"Caita," I say, "you'll take the lead while I'm away. If you need to speak to the others, go to Rego's room and speak with Karina."

"She speaks our tongue?" Caita asks.

I shake my head. "As a child does. But more than the others."

She nods and I join Rachel and Hiro on the dock. "Glad you could make it, Squirrel."

"Surprised to see you wearing pants, Moose."

Hiro laughs as Rachel's brows rise. She says, "I do not want to know what that's about."

"You sure?" he asks, his bright Hiro-grin in full effect.

"Quite."

She moves a few strides ahead of us then and I wonder if Hiro makes her uncomfortable or if she doesn't like him. Rachel isn't one to back down, even from silly banter. As I see her hand slip to the gun at her hip, I realize maybe she's nervous about this stop after all.

Rachel leads us along a circular path that climbs the metal hill that must be the cause for the city's name. Now that we're here, I realize "city" might not be the right term for this place. There are no houses, no markets, and no people so far. The smell is a strange mix of oil and antiseptic that attempts to cover a deeper, sour scent. It isn't foul, not exactly, but it isn't pleasant, either. It reminds me of soggy leaves and dark earth, the end of life before the cold season.

There are walls of junk, scrap metal, and unnameable things I've never seen before lining the path. In places the walls are taller than we are, in others they shrink to only a piece or two that might look like art if it were somewhere else.

We reach the top of the hill and I'm surprised there is not a building, nothing to mark the place but more junk. I ask, "Where is everyone?"

Rachel points down to the metal circle under her. She lifts a foot and bangs it down with as much force as she can. She does this three times, then steps back from the circle and rests her hands on her hips. I notice they aren't far from her weapons, but she doesn't reach for them.

There's clanging coming from below the circle that sounds like metal footsteps. When the sound stops, the circle slides to the side and a gun barrel slips up over the edge. "Who is it?"

"Rachel MacGale, from *The Disorderly Glory*. My home city—"

"Aye, aye," the voice says, a smile coloring their tone. "I know who you are, Captain."

A head comes out of the hole wearing a grin almost as infectious as Hiro's. The mazula person is salt-pale, a white mass of curls pushed back from seafoam eyes. As they climb out of the hole, I notice their skin is almost entirely covered by slate gray coveralls, leaving only their head and hands visible.

"Hiya, P.J.," Rachel says.

P.J. pulls Rachel into a hug, picking her up. "Good to see you again, Cap. Who're your friends?"

"This is my niece, Raider Chief Nova Kennedy."

P.J. whistles. "*The* niece?"

Rachel nods. "And this is Hiro..."

She trails off as she signals Hiro and I realize neither of us know his full name. He smirks at us as he leans forward to shake P.J.'s hand. "Hiro Komatsu. Pleasure to meet you."

P.J. shakes his hand as they compare their megawatt smiles. They ask, "Not from around here, are ya?"

"Not so much," Hiro says.

P.J. shrugs and dismisses Hiro's non-answer, turning back to Rachel. "You wanna come down and see the others? I know Omy will be thrilled to see you."

"I'd love to, but we have a situation on my ship and we'd like Davie to take a look."

P.J. nods. "I'll get her."

"Just so we're clear, Peej," Rachel says, "we've got a lot of

people on my ship right now. I don't want you to be caught
unawares."

"Trust 'em all?" P.J. asks.

Rachel and I nod, but Hiro remains still.

P.J. says, "Good enough for me. Head on back and Davie will
meet you there."

We head back the way we came through the junk stacks. Rachel
has lost her nervous edge and whistles as we walk.

"How many people live here?" Hiro asks.

"Eight," Rachel says. "Five adults and three children."

"Oh okay, so there are families here."

"There's *a* family here, yes."

Hiro's brow furrows for a second as he seems to work out her
words. "So wait, there's *a* fam...oh...ooooooohhhhhh, okay, got it."

I look between them, confused. I start to ask what they're
talking about, but a banging noise on the path behind us catches
my attention. I turn to see a square metal box barreling towards us.
The top is open with a flatbed on the back. There's a woman sitting
inside the box, waving her hands about as if—

"Oh, no," I say, shoving the others off the path.

We land against a metal statue roughly shaped like a chiger-
beast. Hiro holds up his arm to inspect a cut stretching down his
forearm, a thin line of blood on his arm.

"It's not bad," Rachel says.

"Um, excuse me," he says, tone thick with indignance, "but
there is *blood* on my arm. Blood. On my arm."

I ask, "And? You've seen blood before. Lots of it."

"Yeah, but not my own blood. It's gross."

I roll my eyes as I help Rachel dust off. She landed in a
flowerbed, one of several scattered under and around the heaps of
metal, and her breeches are filthy. I ask, "What was that, anyway?"

"Davie," Rachel says. She starts down the path at a jog, trying to
catch up to the strange machine that sped past.

We reach the airship right after her, but she's already had time to climb up the slipway and start an argument with Rachel's first mate. Rachel waves at them and yells, "Let her through. Take her to my cabin."

With Rachel's words they help Davie onto the ship. We climb up after her, but she's already gone in the few seconds it takes to get onboard. Rachel stops to talk to her mate, but I move past their tiff and head towards the cabin. I want to see Rego, to know he's taken care of. Rachel may trust this woman, but I don't. I have yet to meet her aside from her knocking me on my ass.

Stepping into Rego's room, I can smell the unrightness of it. I know Karina has been taking care of him, cleaning his wound and changing his bandages, but there's been little else she could do and even at a distance I'm certain he has an infection.

Drev and Karina linger on one side of the bed, Davie on the other with her back to the door, to me. I slip in behind her and ask, "Can you help him?"

Davie jumps, spinning to me, and says, "Holy hells, girl. You scared the crap out of me."

I get a good look at her, now that she's not trying to run me over. She's shorter than me, but not by much. Her brown hair is short, cut just below her ears, with chunks of gray at her temples. Her eyes are on the green side of hazel with gold around the outside, sparkling with intelligence. She holds her hands in front of her, fingers dancing like she's playing an instrument no one else can see.

"Sorry."

She says, "Don't be sorry, just don't do it again. Thank the Abyss I didn't have a scalpel in my hand."

The Abyss? I wonder. *That's a prayer I've never heard.*

I move around the side of the bed and get my first look at his wound since Karina patched Rego up. The stitches are neat, better than I could've done, but the skin is inflamed, red and yellow all around them. Davie gives a slight push on Rego's skin, barely touching him, but the wound weeps and he lets out a pained moan.

"I'm sorry," Karina says. She paws at red-rimmed eyes, dreary from lack of sleep. "I did the best I could with what I had."

"The stitching's good. Don't fault yourself for that. Sometimes this happens and there's naught you can do about it."

"Can you do anything?" Drev asks.

Davie tilts her head, halfway nods. "I'm going to try. But we need to get him to my lab."

"Lab?" Hiro asks. He's just walked into the room, but at her word his hand reaches for his blaster.

"Aye, lab. I'm a scientist. Or at least, I try to be."

"What's a scientist doing on a junker like this?" he asks.

"Minding my own business until you showed up. You want my help or not?"

I put my hands against Hiro's chest and push him out of the room, growling, "We need her."

"There are scientists on the space station, Nova, with labs and experiments and the whole mess. Scientists just like her. I've seen what they do, I've seen..." he trails off, shaking his head. He swallows and, with a voice softer than I imagined his could sound, he adds, "They take people in those places and they never come back."

I hear it then, what he's not saying, what happened above that originally led him to my father and the Chasseur. "Who did you lose?"

He presses his lips into a thin line, his jaw as hard as stone. He looks over my head, into the room where Davie and Rego are. When he meets my eyes again he says, "I'm just trying to protect you."

I nod. "Thank you. You're a good friend. But this isn't the station, Hiro. It's not the same."

He sighs. "I hope. I really do."

He turns and climbs the steps to the deck without another word. I haven't seen that side of Hiro before, the serious part, the part that hurts. He's holding onto something painful and deep while wearing a grin to make sure no one notices. I want to follow him and force him to talk to me, or at least to let him know he *can* if he wants to, but I need to take care of Rego first.

I slip back into the room and say, "Sorry about that."

Davie shakes her head. "Stop apologizing. Nobody's got time for that." She hooks her thumb over her shoulder and says, "We movin' him or not?"

"Whatever you need."

A smile spreads across her face and she says, "I was hoping you'd say that."

CHAPTER
TWENTY-SEVEN

Davie has Rego rolled onto a board and loaded onto her machine. I'm instantly worried about his transport on such a thing, especially after what I previously saw of her driving. She tells me I can ride with her, and though the thought makes my stomach churn, I climb inside the metal box so I can stay close to Rego. Karina tries to come as well, but I insist she and Drev need to get some sleep instead and they can catch up to us later.

The return trip up the hill is much slower than Davie's descent. She drives with care on the streets—though to be fair, it would probably be more accurate to call them walkways. The space between the metal walls is so narrow the sides of her vehicle scrape them several times. Still, she moves with caution and does her best to avoid jostling Rego. We're a little more than halfway to the top when she veers off the path and through a cut in the metal wall that I hadn't noticed. It leads down another path just wide enough for her metal transport.

The path leads around the side of the hill through its own set of metal walls, though these are more like heaps than the tall things we passed through earlier. The hill seems to be covered in metal no matter which way I look, but it seems as though we've come around to the back side from where we met P.J.

The trail stops at a wall—a real one this time, that reminds me of the walls on the space station—that stretches off to both sides without a discernible end. Davie presses down on the wheel she's using to steer her metal box and it erupts in a blaring sound that reverberates off the metal around us.

In answer to the noise from her machine, part of the wall ahead of us starts to lift up. I see boots underneath, followed by long legs and thick hips, a full bosom that I struggle to look away from, and finally the door lifts so I can see the whole of the woman who pulls the chain that allows us passage. She's pale like P.J., but her blonde hair is golden instead of white, pulled back into a ponytail, though wisps of it have come loose to frame her face. She smiles as we pass and I notice a dark freckle just below her bottom lip.

We pass into the space beyond and lights click on along the walls as we pass. I turn around to see the beauty closing the wall behind us. Davie must read the look on my face because she smirks and says, "Gorgeous, eh?"

I nod and, pride obvious in her voice, she says, "That's my wife."

"Lucky you."

She laughs. "Oh, girl, you have *no* idea."

A minute later we stop in front of a regular door. It opens and P.J. comes out with another man. They walk past us and go straight for Rego. They unload him with ease, keeping him steady on the board Davie put him on. She holds the door open for them as they carry him inside and waves for me to follow.

The room beyond the door is huge. There are two rows of tables covered in glass bottles of various sizes, papers strewn about, and a blackboard with white writing on it covers one wall. The wall opposite has six narrow beds with pale green linens lined side by side. P.J. and the other man do not take Rego to one of these, but instead take him to the back of the room where another bed is off to itself. This one has plastic covering it and lamps on the floor around it.

The put Rego here and attach straps to his arms and legs. Panic surges through me and I ask, "What are you doing?"

Davie puts a hand on my shoulder. "Don't worry. The restraints are just a precaution. We're going to sedate your friend before we start working on him, so when he wakes up disoriented, we want to make sure he doesn't do anything to damage the wound further."

I take a deep breath, nod, and watch her move about the room gathering supplies. I remind myself, *Rachel trusts them and I trust Rachel.*

"Would you like some tea?"

I turn to the voice and find the beautiful woman, Davie's wife. Her voice is sweet as sugar, eliciting a smile despite the circumstances. "I...I'm not sure."

"You can't do anything to help," she says. "Let me take you to the waiting room while Davie works. She'll move fast and have your friend fixed up in no time."

"I should stay."

She smiles. "What's your name, dear heart?"

"Nova."

She repeats it before saying, "I'm Leona. I'm Davie's wife."

"She told me."

"My wife is brilliant and kind and will do everything she can to help your friend. But she needs room to concentrate and quiet to work. Let's give her that."

She takes me by the hand and leads me out of the lab. I want to protest, but what Leona says makes sense. We walk past Davie's vehicle to a door I didn't notice before. She pulls a chain and the door opens in the middle, half sliding up and the other half sliding down. We step into something akin to a cage and she closes the split door behind us.

"Have you seen an elevator before?" she asks.

I think back to my first time in one of these strange cities and the glass box that carried the wealthy from floor to floor. "Yes, in another floating city."

"Oh, right," Leona says. "You're with Captain MacGale, so you've likely been to Aeroport."

I nod as we descend, though this is not like the elevator I rode before. Leona controls this one with a pulley system that lowers us further into the hill. I look through the cracks in the door at each floor we pass, wondering what they have stored in these various places.

When we come to a stop and step out, Leona takes me into a massive room that looks like a cave. The walls and floors are brown, dirty. I kick my foot against the ground and create a cloud of actual dirt.

"What is this place?"

"This is our gathering spot," she says. "We come here to relax, to talk, to cool off after a row."

"You live here?"

She leads me to a bench cut into the wall. "We do some of our living here, but we have rooms upstairs, if that's what you mean."

"How many families live here?" I ask, retracing the conversation Rachel and Hiro were having earlier.

"Just one," she says. She must see the confusion on my face because she smiles and pats my hand. "We're polyamorous. There are several people involved with one another."

I remember Ivy and her two lovers from the Chasseur. "My sister is in a relationship with two people."

"Ah, good. Some people have trouble understanding."

"I'm not sure I understand entirely."

She chews the corner of her lip for a minute before asking, "Have you ever been in love?"

The question catches me off guard and I have to fight the lump that forms in my throat. I loved Thoa. I don't know if I loved Krew, or if I could've loved him if given the time. I don't know if I'm going to find anyone to love that compares to what I felt for those two men last year. My voice is thick when I say, "Yes."

"You lost them?"

"Things didn't work out the way I thought they would."

"That happened to me, too, before I met Davie. I was involved with a man who meant the world to me. But it didn't work."

"What did you do?"

"Cried a lot," she says, but her voice trills in a laugh. "It hurt, but it hurt less over time. And then I met Davie and Max."

"Max?"

"The man who helped carry your friend. My husband."

"So you have a wife and a husband?"

She nods. "They were married first. I came to live here, to help with the city, and ended up falling in love with them. Luckily for me, they loved me as well."

I take in her words as she excuses herself to get our tea. I stare at the cavern while she's gone, surprised at how natural it looks. From the top of Copperhill, I assumed this whole place was built from metal. But here, inside the depths of this place, it's almost as if they scooped up a piece of the earth and set it to flying. There are stalactites hanging from the ceiling, drops of water gathered on their tips and falling into a pool below. The pool trickles out into a stream that cuts through the center of the room.

There's a serenity to this place. I let my mind wander as I watch the stream bubbling through the room, thinking back to all the times I sat by a brook with Rego, Raiders at our back and the open land ahead, ready to explore. There's a pang in my gut at the thought of him, worry rearing up despite the peace around me.

Leona returns with a steaming yellow cup with blue flowers painted on the side. I smile at her return, grateful for the distraction from my worry about Rego. I tap the side of the cup and say, "This is lovely."

"Thank you," she says. "I make them to sell when we're near

other towns. We all have little area of expertise to help cover the costs to keep this place afloat."

"Who are the other people who live here?"

"You met P.J., right? They are Max's lover. And there's another woman, Omy, who shares my bed on occasion."

"Oh," I say, cheeks flushing. I hadn't expected her to be so forthright with their bedroom arrangements. "I'm sorry. Is it okay for me to ask about these things? I don't want to make you uncomfortable."

She waves away my concern. "We aren't shy about who we are and who we love. You can ask whatever you'd like."

"I don't want to ask anything too personal."

"I'll tell you if you do. I have no issue expressing my boundaries."

"Well, it's just, I've seen jealousy at work. Hells, I've felt it. But no one here gets upset with this arrangement?" I ask.

I remember what it was like to have feelings for both Thoa and Krew, the confusion and guilt that came with it. Thoa made it clear that he was unwilling to be part of that kind of relationship, and his opinion made me close myself to the idea because I was prepared to do whatever it took to be with him.

"Jealousy can be an issue when you're first trying to figure these things out. It's something that has to be overcome, like any other issue."

"You make it sound easy."

She shakes her head. "Not always, but it's possible as long as you're open about your needs and expectations. My relationship with Davie and Max is built on loving one another. I love them individually and as a pair. They love me. Their love for other people doesn't diminish their love for me. If anything, it makes it more special that they have such a huge capacity to love."

"I can't imagine having a relationship like that."

But I can imagine it. I have imagined it. I just didn't think it could ever be real.

"It isn't for everyone, but it works for us."

I pick at my fingernails for a minute, trying to sort out how these ideas make me feel. "How did you know it was right? For you, I mean."

"The same way anyone else knows they're in love: when I looked at Davie, and when I looked at Max, I couldn't imagine living without them. I knew I'd be miserable if I tried."

I swallow hard, saying, "I don't know if I'll ever be in love again. At least, not like before."

"You won't," she says. "Love isn't supposed to be the same every time. What you felt for that other person was what you needed at that time. And the next time you fall in love—and you probably will—it will be different, right for you in the next time. Don't go looking for the same thing and comparing everyone else to your other love. Not if you want to be happy."

I nod, unable to say anything. Her words have struck against my heart like flint to steel, sparking a hope I'd smothered when I lost Thoa all those months ago.

We sit in amiable silence for a long time, sipping mint tea and staring at the water ambling through the room. I follow the path with my eyes and see it collecting in a metal pool at the lower end of the room. I wonder if this place is some sort of filtration system to keep fresh water flowing for them without the need to stop. I'm sure all the floating cities have them, but I'm not sure anywhere else has something so elegant, so soothing.

Leona sighs, drawing my attention. She's looking off into the distance, but then her eyes focus again she says, "We've probably given them enough time to work if you want to head back to see your friend."

I nod. As we walk back to the elevator I say, "Thanks Leona, for distracting me."

She smiles. "Anything for a friend."

"But we just met."

"Like I said," she shrugs.

Rego is asleep, knocked out by something Davie gave him. She walks me through the process of what she did to help him, but her words are jargon, crashing in and out of my ears without leaving any real impression. The only part that sticks with me is that she thinks she got to him in time, that the infection didn't have time to fester and spread.

I wait for a long while, hoping his eyes will open, but they don't. Davie tugs at my arm and as if reading my mind she says, "He won't wake up for awhile. His body has been through a lot. Let's go talk to Captain MacGale and see if the ship can stay overnight."

"He'll be better by then?"

She winces. "I can't say he'll be completely healed, but he'll be better than he is now. We can pump him full of medicine all night to fight the infection so it doesn't return."

I nod and let her lead me out of the room and back to the elevator. Leona is waiting there for us and gives me a small smile. "All right?"

"He will be," Davie says, leaning over to kiss Leona's cheek.

We take the elevator up this time, instead of down into the cavern. We don't pass nearly as many floors going up as we did going down, so we reach our destination in less than a minute. Leona and Davie lead me out into a long room with sage-green walls. There are paintings everywhere, no rhyme or reason to their placement, but clearly done by the same hand.

"Those are lovely," I say, pointing to a landscape depicting a dark lake and distant mountains.

"Thank you." I turn to the small voice and find a boy of no more than ten. He has dark hair and eyes, like Davie, a dimpled chin.

Davie puts her arm around him and says, "Eric, this is Nova. She's here with Captain MacGale."

He holds out his hand and says, "Pleasure to meet you, Miss."

I shake his small hand and give him my best smile. "The plea-sure is mine, Eric. You painted all these?" He nods, eyes down-turned. "They're wonderful. You have a gift."

"That's what we tell him," Leona says, rubbing his shaggy head.

He swats her hand away with a smile and she scoops him into a hug, both of them laughing. The display is so genuine, so sweet, my heart nearly melts right in my chest.

It suddenly strikes me that there isn't anything I wouldn't give to have this life. I want all my loves in one place, sharing a life. I want to share all I am with the people I love without worrying about making someone angry or hurt or jealous. This is what I'm meant to be.

"Hey, there you are," Hiro yells. He holds up a hand from the other end of the room where he sits with Rachel, Folly, and Gareem, the two Raiders I found him with earlier.

"Go ahead," Davie says. "Make yourself at home. I'll find you if there's any news of your friend."

I thank her and join Hiro and the others. Folly passes me a thick slice of buttered bread and I tear into it, realizing my stomach is growling so loud they can all probably hear it. Rachel hands out mugs of tea to warm our hands. I hold it to my nose and breathe deep, letting the scent of lemon fill my nose. "Thank you."

"You're welcome, Chief," Folly says. Her voice is as warm as the tea and nearly as sweet.

"How's Rego?" Hiro asks. He swallows a gulp of tea with a satisfied *mmmmm*.

I take a sip of the tea, nod, and say, "He's asleep for now, but it seems like he's going to be okay."

Hiro says something else, but I don't make out his words. My head seems heavy. I look around the room and everything seems to blur together. I try to speak, but my tongue is fuzzy, too big in my mouth. I feel the mug slip from my fingers and everything around me goes dark.

CHAPTER
TWENTY-EIGHT

I wake up in a hammock, nearly falling off to escape the teeth snapping at my face. Dreams, dreams, never ceasing, no matter what else becomes of me. The hammock sways to and fro, taking on the motions of the airship.

Airship.

I sit up, knocking my head against the rafter above me. Shaking off the pain, I roll out of the hammock and find my feet. My head is pounding and I still feel groggy, but I make my way out of the quarters and onto the deck. The sun is high overhead and I hold my arm up to block some of the light.

Rachel has her back to me, staring off into the distance. I make my way towards her and grab her by the shoulder, spinning her to face me.

"Oh, good, you're awake."

"What is going on?" I ask.

She frowns, as if the words on her tongue taste sour even to her. "I'm sorry. I knew you'd fight me about what we needed to do, so I took you out of the equation."

There's a roar from below deck, ferocious as a wild beast. I watch Hiro come up from below deck and I can see the rage boiling through him even from this distance. "What the hell?"

"Him, too," Rachel says with a nod.

"The others?" I ask, thinking of the star-people and the Raiders.

She shakes her head. "Most of them were still on the ship or wandering around Copperhill. They didn't know anything was wrong."

"What happened?" Hiro asks as he climbs to stand beside us.

"MacGale drugged us."

"I'm sorry," she says, holding out her hands to temper him. "I had to."

"Why?" he growls.

She sighs. "We didn't have time to linger, not if we're going to amass the forces we need to make Ivy's plan work."

"Rego," I whisper as I realize what she's saying. My whole body starts shaking and I can't form the words to say everything I'm feeling.

"What about him?" Hiro asks.

"He's fine, or at least he was when we left."

Hiro's eyes go wide. "We left him?"

"I gave them directions to the farm. They're going to meet us there."

"You trust them to do that?" Hiro asks, scrubbing a hand over the dark stubble on his head.

Rachel says, "I do, but I know you don't, so Karina and Drev stayed with him."

"Two people against their eight?"

I put my hand on Hiro's arm to try to calm him. "Two trial winners against a family with no training. If they had to, they could take them out."

"But they won't need to," Rachel says.

I spin on her, shoving my finger in her face. "You don't get to talk, MacGale. What you did was unacceptable."

Hiro puts his hands on my shoulders, now trying to calm me. "Rego will be fine."

I meet his eyes and take a deep breath. With a nod I say, "They'll take care of him."

Rachel lets out a deep breath, the corners of her mouth lifting in a relieved smile. "Thank the gods you see reason. I was so nervous you'd be pissed."

I clench my fists at my side, trying to remain calm. I don't need a fight between the Raiders and the airship crew, and I'm afraid that's what would happen if I erupted on Rachel right now. "I'm furious. You took away my choice, my chance to say goodbye if something happens. And if something does happen to Rego while I'm not there, I will never forgive you."

"Nova—"

"No," I say, cutting her off. "I may understand why you did this, but that doesn't mean I'm okay with it."

"I did this for you."

"I don't give a damn why you did it, what your intention were, or whether you think you were in the right. Rego is my family. Rego. Not you. *He* knows me. *He* trusts me to make the best decisions without forcing his choices on me. That's what real love is like. What you did was selfish."

She opens her mouth as if to speak, but closes it without words. Instead she turns back to the horizon, staring at the snow capped mountains in the distance.

Several moments pass in silence before Hiro asks, "Where are we going?"

"The Hole in the World," Rachel says.

The words spark recognition in my mind. I've heard them before from Rachel's lips. "Isn't that where you were going to sell Krew?"

She winces. "Maybe."

"Why are we going there now?" I ask. "Planning to sell us, too?"

She cringes, but doesn't acknowledge my dig. "I was talking to P.J. about what happened with the Raiders and the banishment. They said they saw a group of Raiders headed north, about seven months ago. They thought it was weird because they were going north before winter instead of the reverse. Based on their trajectory, P.J. thinks they were headed for the Hole."

I nod, looking off towards the mountains. "You really think we can find them?"

"I don't know," she says. "But I think we need to try."

"How much time is this going to add to our trip? Ivy is waiting on us."

"The people at the farm need the extra time as much as we do. Your sister is trying to plan an invasion into a heavily fortified space station. She only has a couple people who have a clue about what she's trying to do, while the rest of us can only hope to make her plans stronger by adding more bodies to it."

"How long?"

"Two weeks, maybe three."

I clench my hands at my sides and take a deep breath. When I release it, I let all my frustrations go with it. "Okay."

"Okay?" Hiro asks.

I nod. "She's right. We need the bodies. That's what we're out here for."

"This is a mess," he mutters.

"Aye, but it's not the worst situation we've faced. I trust you can amuse yourself for the rest of our travels?"

He grits his teeth, fighting his urge to argue. "Yes, Chief," he bites out. He turns on his heel and stalks away.

I puzzle after him as I watch him leave. He is not a Raider and owes me no allegiance, but he gives it all the same. Perhaps his words held true when he joked that we were meant to be best friends. What else would make him acquiesce to my decisions?

I turn my eyes to Rachel and heave a sigh. After a moment I say, "Don't screw it up, MacGale. We're on borrowed time now."

JUST OVER A WEEK HAS PASSED AND THE HOLE IN THE WORLD IS ON the horizon. It's a circle of purest white, almost like fluffy clouds, with a crackling pink ring lining it, sparking into the air around it. It hangs in the middle of the sky, forests of deep green edging the bottom of the circle, but seeming not to touch it. Along the top and to the sides of the pink ring are storm-dark clouds, unmoving. I stare at it in sheer wonder, unsure how such a thing came to be in our world. Formed by the hands of man, though I can't guess as to why. It's a sight to behold.

Rachel has been there a handful of times, but I do not ask her about the thing hovering in front of the ship. I have not forgotten the choices she made on Copperhill, and whether they were for good or ill remains to be seen. Whatever the end result, my trust in her is eroded.

When I think about the trust I'd placed in her, I find myself shaking my head and shaming myself as a fool. I hadn't seen the woman for a dozen years when her crew picked us up. They killed one of my party, planned to sell at least one more, and these plans were only stopped when she found out Thoa was the long lost heir to Aeroport. Even after we were on the same side, she refused to help me save Rego and Thoa from their imprisonment at Gearhaven, instead leaving on a mission with Coco and her uncle. A successful, good mission, to be sure, but a mission that separated us once again. After all that, why did I fall into her confidence so easily?

And yet, she's my family.

But so is Rego, and she left him behind, I remind myself.

Something about her actions wriggle in my mind, worming around, but I can't quite take hold of it. Something about it doesn't feel like Rachel. She knows what Rego means to me. I don't understand what convinced her to leave without him.

Hiro finds me pacing below deck near Tinora's cage. Again. He's caught me down here twice before. I can't explain why being next to her room helps me focus, but somehow I'm able to focus all my frustrations, all my rage, simply by being in proximity to her. Strangely enough, I don't direct it all *towards* her. I've got plenty enough reserved for her, but knowing she's captive in that small room lets me put it aside, at least temporarily.

"Hey Squirrel," he says, leaning back against one of our last crates of food. He's wearing leathers again today, a gift from his Raider paramores. His hair and beard are filling out a bit, dark against his skin even after these long days tanning in the sun. More and more he looks like the Raiders he cavorts with.

I rub my hand over too-tired eyes and ask, "What's up, Moose?"

He smiles at the nickname every time I say it, but he's stopped commenting about how I've caved to him by using it.

"Thought you might wanna head up with me." I give him a quizzical look and he rolls his eyes. "We're almost to the Hole."

"Any idea what it is yet?"

"Not a clue," he says. His smile is goofy and innocent, not the sly grin he reserves for sweet talking and clever games.

I follow him up the steps. Despite the ever-present crease in my brow and the machinations constantly whirling through my mind, I find myself smiling as I ascend, joyful even. I'm sure Hiro is part of the cause. I haven't allowed myself a friendship like this before. The Raiders wouldn't let me in, aside from Rego, and he became my family. Once we left them behind last year, though I made friends along our journey, none of them were close, soul-baring relationships. I shared things with Thoa, Krew, Coco, Baz...but this is different. This is something special, precious to me, and something I wasn't sure I would ever have. I love Hiro in a way that is different than anyone else I've ever known.

My head pops above deck and I'm thrilled to finally be able to see what this thing is. I've wanted to ask Rachel or her crew every time I've laid eyes on it, but my stubbornness kept the words from my lips. I've only spoken to her as needed to keep the necessary peace. I don't think I'll ever be able to look at her the same again.

The Hole in the World is so close that I can't see the dark green of the forest as a border now. Instead, it stretches around us like a sea of pine, fir, spruce, and cedar—a coniferous forest that blankets the world evergreen. The tops of trees scrape against the bottom of *The Disorderly Glory* like ghostly fingers scratching, digging hungrily into the skin of the living. They are lonely, hungry, and searching for something to satisfy them.

Like all of us.

The crew man their positions in an eerie quiet, Raiders and the few remaining star-people huddled along the deck in clusters that point but say nothing. I think back to the forest that Rego and Nukiki refused to enter and wonder what they would think of this place. Looking around I see several Raiders crossing fingers over their eyes, warding against evil, and I suppose I have my answer.

There's lightning to the west, near enough to light up the sky all around us, but it doesn't seem to change the Hole itself, never crossing the sparking pink that encircles the white. Though the whole sky is aglow with blinding streaks of purple-white, the circle in front of us doesn't change. It doesn' even reflect the glow about us.

I find my hand at my eyes unbidden, crossing them like the other Raiders. But whatever this thing is, whatever fear it is wedging inside me, I will not cower.

I straighten my back and stare straight ahead as the bow of the ship plunges into the white mass. I expect it to part like clouds or wisps of smoke; instead, it surrounds us like a liquid, filling in the empty spaces as it engulfs us completely.

As the white reaches me, Hiro's hand grasps mine. Whether it is for my benefit or his, I do not know. Our eyes meet for the briefest second and then he is gone. The whiteness blocks him out, blocks out everything around me. I can't hear, but I feel his hand trembling in mine and know he is still there, still grounding me.

The moment seems to stretch on forever and I can't decipher how long we linger in the white before the air around us finally clears.

CHAPTER
TWENTY-NINE

T here is nothing but white above and all around. We aren't
swimming in it like when we first came through, but it's all
we can see.

"What the hell is this place?" Hiro asks, an awe that borders
reverence in his tone.

"I don't know," I say, "but I'm starting to regret not asking
someone before we got here."

Rachel turns around and looks at those crowded on the deck of
her airship. "We're through decontamination and we'll be making
our descent as soon as we're cleared."

"Descent?" Hiro asks.

We move across the deck still hand in hand until we reach the
edge and peer over. Though we are surrounded by white—a dome
above and around us—below is pure darkness. The earth is split
open, not the perfect circle of the decontamination field we came
through, but near enough.

"It's literally a hole in the world."

"Not what I was expecting," Hiro says.

As we watch, lights deep within the hole begin to light up.

They're small at first, a dozen pinpricks of red in the black below us, then two dozen, three. They come on in succession, climbing along the walls in rows that light the way down. When the ones at the top come on, all the red lights in the hole flicker off, then come back on a bright white.

Rachel yells something to her crew and I feel the ship start to lower. I watch as we drop below the evergreens that were scratching the ship only minutes ago. Now that we're under the decontamination field, the consuming white of it is gone and I can see the land around. Still, there's *something* out there blocking me from seeing it clearly and the trees look as if they're behind a frosted glass.

Then they are gone and all I can see is the dark earth surrounding us. I stare at the walls as we pass each light, as that is the only place to really see them. The walls are shiny, not quite metallic, and remind me of the black rocks we burned for fuel in the contraption we rode to Nigel's mansion on Gearhaven.

The thought of Nigel immediately sends my mind to Thoa. I wonder what he's doing, where he's gone, if he's safe. I wonder if he's happy. I wonder if he's already moved on.

I squeeze Hiro's hand, thankful he's still at my side lending me his strength even as he takes consolation in mine. The lights above turn off as we descend and it sends a feeling of doom shuddering through me. Below I hear the clanging of metal and a grinding sound, but there isn't enough light to see what's happening.

A few minutes later, we stop moving. The grinding kicks in again, above us this time, and I look up to see a slabs of metal moving together from each side of the hole, their teeth sliding together and cutting out any light left from above. There are three of these doors closing above, some sort of protection against the outside world, I assume. They're able to control who gets in, and who gets out.

As soon as the metal doors close, the airship's crew starts

moving in a frenzy. Captain MacGale shouts her commands, but the Raiders and the remaining sky people have moved to surround me. I look around at these people and take in the sight of those who choose to follow me.

Valeska stands with arms crossed over her chest. She looks around us, eyes narrowed, and I realize I've barely seen her since the Raider camp. I'm about to ask where she's been, but a mazula Raider approaches and Valeska throws an arm over their shoulders. I don't know this Raider, what they've been through before finding us, but I'm delighted to think Valeska has found someone to care about. Rage burns hot in her and I hope this person will be able to temper it a bit.

Zeb leans over and Sarah whispers in his ear. She still clings to him like she's afraid to let him out of her sight. Maybe she is. After what happened to her father, it isn't unreasonable to think she'd worry about losing everyone else.

The Raiders look around this strange place with clenched fists and gritted teeth. I can see the uneasiness in every twitch of muscle, every narrowed eye. But they don't speak of their fear, unwilling to betray the bravery attributed to Raiders. They will face this and anything else they must. Warriors to the end.

I say, "We are here to find the lost Raiders, those banished by the false chief. I will ask them to return to us and join us in the fight to come."

"What if they say no?" Fatboy asks.

I sigh, saying the words that have haunted me this last week. "I will compel them as their Chief. I hope they will choose as you have done and return with us willingly, but we are running out of time and I will command them if necessary. If you see any of them, tell them that the new Chief wishes to speak with them and find me immediately."

I see the crew putting the slipway down and lock eyes with MacGale. She motions her hand towards the exit. In the old tongue

I call out, "Is there anything my people should know before they go into this place?"

She shakes her head. "This place is accustomed to a variety of visitors. Most vendors speak Raider and will barter if they have things they wish to trade."

I nod. "When should they return to the ship?"

"I'll buy a six hour dock. We can meet back and see where we are with finding the Raiders."

I relay the information to the Raiders. We couldn't bring everything they had at their encampment, but we do have the skiffs and tents stored on the ship and most of them were able to bring a few personal items. Most are delighted to hear that they can barter with the vendors and they head below to retrieve any belongings they wish to sell.

At the edge of the slipway I turn to Rachel and ask, "What will you be doing, in case I need you?"

"The crew and I will be off ship as well, buying supplies and having a break. It's been awhile since they've had a few hours rest."

"You're not planning to help me find the Raiders?"

She hesitates, then shakes her head. "I'll listen for news while I'm out, ask a few people I know, just in case. But I didn't think you'd want my help."

I nod. She's not wrong. It might be easier with her help, but that doesn't mean I want it. I'd rather search for them on my own than ask MacGale for anything.

I step off the ship and onto the clanging walkway. Hiro follows behind, a comforting presence as I move off into the unknown. There's a person ahead of us, hand raised. They wave us over and ask, "First timers?"

I nod as we move towards the door they're guarding.

"Ever used an elevator?"

"I have, but the others haven't."

They nod. "I'll get them an escort."

"They need someone who speaks Raider."

"No problem." They wave a badge in front of a scanner on the wall and say, "I highly recommend the level fourteen pleasure centers and the Floor of Feasts on level twenty-one."

"We're looking for some Raiders," I say. "Would've come in a few months ago."

They shrug and say, "We get Raiders passing through all the time."

"These would've been southern Raiders, never been here before."

They smile and say, "Sorry. I'd help you if I could, but there are hundreds of visitors each month. If they stayed, they could be anywhere."

"Thanks anyway."

"Enjoy yourselves," they say as they raise their hands to speak with the next group approaching.

I look behind us and realize there are at least six other ships within eyesight of where Rachel's airship is parked. I hadn't noticed them on our way in, or maybe they've also just arrived. Either way, I can see what the greeter means. There are too many people in and out for them to keep track of.

As we step through the door, Hiro puts a hand on my shoulder and says, "I'd be glad to check out level fourteen for you."

I think back to what the greeter told us and I have to laugh. "You want the pleasure center all to yourself?"

"Oh, do you feel pleasure? I thought you only used your body to house all that rage you're storing in there."

"I mean, I *can* feel pleasure," I say, searching for a way to contradict his words, though I know they ring of truth. I huff and say, "It's not like I've had a lot of time lately for that sort of thing."

Hiro flashes his too-bright grin. "Yeah, Squirrel, sure. It's not like we've been floating on a ship for a week without a way off or a lack of things to do."

"I've been busy."

"Brooding," he says. "But you know, we all have our specialties."

I purse my lips. "Brooding isn't the only thing I'm good at."

"Of course not. You're great at stabbing, plotting, hating everyone…" he says as he ticks each item off on his fingers.

With a laugh I say, "I don't hate *everyone*. You're exaggerating."

He nods. "Another one of my specialties. But seriously, Nova, you need to make time for yourself. It doesn't have to be at the pleasure center or anything like that, but just an hour or so to relax and turn off your brain. You've got a lot going on and it wouldn't hurt to reset on occasion."

As we step into an elevator already full of other people, I make note that we are docked on the twentieth floor, out of fifty. Several buttons are lit up, but I decide to go to the top and start on the first floor and work my way down. We don't have any clues about where the Raider might be, so this seems like as good a plan as any.

I sigh and whisper to Hiro, "What you're saying makes sense, but I don't have time for all that."

"Make time for the important things," he says. "And you, kid, you're important."

He squeezes my shoulder and exits with some of the other passengers. I call, "Where are you going?"

He turns back to me wearing his mischievous grin and waggles his eyebrows. I look at the number on the side of the floor. Fourteen. With a laugh, I watch him walk down the hall before the doors close to take me higher.

As we go towards the upper floors, I think about what Hiro said. Part of me knows he's right. I need a rest from all the doom and gloom before I break. But the rest of me knows I'll get time away from all this soon enough, when it's over. Until then, I can't lose focus. I can't afford the distraction, as much as I might like it. I don't have the same luxuries as the others.

I exit onto the first floor and start down the hall. The walls are carved out of the same black stone as the landing area. Every twelve feet or so there are mint green doors pressed into the walls, each with a number on them. Residences, I think. There's no one around to ask.

I walk to the end of the corridor and back, then press the button for the lift. I look around one last time, surprised at how much this place reminds me of the space station. Everything is the same, the uniformity broken only by the gold numbers on the doors or the occasional decoration hanging nearby.

It seems to take a long time for one of the lifts to arrive, and when it does there's a family inside. They exit into the hall and start towards their home.

"Hello, sir," I say in the old tongue. The young father turns back to me, shakes his head. I try again in Raider, but still he smiles and shakes his head.

"Je suis désolé," he shrugs.

I don't know his words, but the language sparks a memory of sitting in the homesteader's cottage, listening to Kavia transition in and out of languages as she told me stories. I say, "Bonjour."

The man's face lights up and he starts speaking so fast I can't make out any words. I pinch my fingers together and say, "Only a little. Un petit?"

"Ah," he nods.

I try to remember the words in his language, but it's been a long time since I've heard it, much less spoken it. "I'm looking for," I say, pointing to my eyes, "mes amis."

"Your friends?" a little girl says in the old tongue as she pops her head around her father's hip.

"Yes," I say, smiling down at her.

She bites her lip, looking me up and down. Her tiny voice asks, "Are they Raiders, too?"

I nod. "I think they came here a few months ago. I hope they stayed."

"Raiders don't stay long," she says.

I sigh. "Not usually, no. But if they aren't here, I don't know where else to go."

The little girl looks up to her father and rattles off several sentences that I can't follow. Her father's brows knit together as he glances back to me, but then he gives a terse nod and starts to walk down the hallway.

I take a step after him before noticing the little girl hasn't moved. I ask, "Should I follow?"

"You can follow me."

I glance at the father's back, then down at the girl. "Isn't your dad afraid I'll steal you?"

"No way. Mommy works at the docks, so everyone there knows me. If you tried, they'd arrest you."

She takes off walking and I trail behind her. "Where are we going?"

"I'll take you to the Raider boy I know from school. He doesn't like me, but maybe he can help."

"You have a school here?"

"Of course," she says, giggling. "How else would we learn?"

Her words strike me in their simplicity. Of course there's a school. It's not like star-people attacked and murdered their family, they escaped into the night, and then were taken into the ranks of the Raiders to be taught how to stalk, steal, and murder.

"What's your name?" I ask as we climb onto the elevator.

"Kesley. What's yours?"

"Nova."

"That's a weird name."

I grin. "Maybe I think Kesley is a weird name."

She wrinkles her nose. "There are three girls in my grade with the same name. It's not weird, it's boring."

"I've never met anyone named Kesley," I say. "I think it's nice."

"Never?" she asks. I shake my head and she says, "Huh. Have you been a lot of places?"

"Quite a few."

She thinks this over and says, "And you're really old, so you should've heard it before."

I laugh at her words and ask, "How old do you think I am?"

Kesley shrugs and says, "At least forty."

"I'm twenty-one!" I sputter.

She shrugs again as the elevator stops. "That's still pretty old."

I follow Kesley off the lift onto the sixth floor. The walls and doors are the same here as above, distinguishable only by the numbers painted on them. She walks to the end of the hallway and knocks on number forty-two.

A boy opens the door, eyes narrowing when he sees Kesley. "What are you doing here?"

"This is Nova," Kesley says, waving to me. "She's looking for Raiders."

The boy's eyes drift to me, then back to Kesley. "Why?"

"I don't know," she says. "I just brought her to you because I don't know any other Raiders."

The boy glares at her and she sticks her tongue out at him before turning her back to us both and skipping back towards the elevator. I feel a smile lift my lips as I watch her go. She has big Hiro energy—confident and carefree.

The boy looks me up and down as if trying to decide if I'm some sort of trap Kesley has left for him. Finally he frowns and says, "Wait here."

He closes the door and I lean against the wall, waiting. A moment later the door opens again and a dark-eyed woman steps into the hall. "My son says you are looking for Raiders."

I nod and stretch out my hand. "Hi, I'm Nova."

She narrows her eyes and doesn't reach for my hand. "What do you want with them?"

I pull back my hand and try to ignore her hostility. "I'm looking for Raiders who came here a few months ago. They were banished by a false chief and I've come to seek them out."

"I ask again, what do you want with them?"

I tilt my head, taking the woman in. I don't recognize her or her son, but she has the bearing of a Raider, a chief even. "They were my family."

"You lie," she says, shaking her head. "Speak truth."

I grit my teeth together, losing my patience. "I don't see how it is any of your business."

She gives me the same glare her son gave Kesley. "Then I guess you don't need my help finding them."

She moves back inside the door and moves to close it, but I stick my foot inside to hold it open. "Are they here or not?"

"Move your foot before I rip it off."

I feel a growl building in my chest, but before I can say anything else I hear, "Little Star? Is that you?"

I turn towards the voice coming from down the hall. It's deeper than I remember, but I recognize it and the man approaching sends a swirl of emotions through my gut. I haven't seen him since before we set off over a year ago. He is broader now, his shoulders wider. His hair is short as it always was, but now he has a patchy beard where before he could not grow one.

"Leer," I say, a smile spreading over my face.

"What are you doing here?" he says, wrapping me up in an embrace.

"Looking for you."

He steps back but keeps his hands on my shoulders. "It's good to see you. Come in."

Leer pushes past the woman at the door, seeming not to notice the snarl she gives. He leads me into a small room with a sofa and chair. The apartment is bigger than those on the station had been, but being inside still feels me with anxiety as if I've returned to my prison in space.

We sit, Leer still smiling at me. "I wasn't sure you'd make it back."

"Nor I. But we did."

"We?"

"Thoa and Rego are alive," I say.

He nods. "I'm glad. After we found Nukiki, we weren't sure any of you remained."

My throat tightens at the thought of Nukiki, of Eija. Before I find the words to speak about her loss, Leer puts a hand on my knee and nods. Understanding seems to pass between us and for a moment we sit quietly, sharing each other's pain and loss. Soon the moment passes and Leer's smile broadens. "I can't wait to see Rego."

I wince, my mind going to the floating city where he waits, all alone. "They aren't with me, but I'll be meeting them soon."

"Bring them here," Leer says. "There's plenty of room and jobs for anyone willing to work."

"Everyone is happy here?"

He shrugs. "You can't make everyone happy. But many are. Most, I think. It wasn't easy, after the banishment." He looks up through dark lashes and asks, "Do you know about that?"

I nod. "I was at the camp last week. I spoke with Eija."

"Poor girl," he says, shaking his head. "She was never the same."

Time seems to stop for a moment. Finally I say, "Leer, it's wonderful to see you, but I don't have a great deal of time. I need to speak to your chief."

"You did," the woman says from the edge of the room. "She was unwilling to help you, but still you are here, in her home."

Leer looks between us, realizing for the first time that there's a problem. "Ah, yes. Nova, you've met Zulie?"

"Not officially," I say. I do not hold out my hand this time.

Leer swallows hard as the tension in the room builds. "We met Zulie and her Raiders after Ukaru banished us. She was leading them here."

"Ah, so you were with a different band of Raiders. That is why I didn't recognize you."

Zulie nods but doesn't speak. Leer says, "She was with Chief

Ikarov until they grew too large and he wanted to leave the oldest and weakest behind."

I grind my teeth at his words. I'd heard tales of bands splitting once they reached a certain size. Raiders are all branches from the same tree, after all, bringing in new members and growing until there's no other way but to split and start a new band. But I thought they split evenly, branching a new family that could support itself. I've never heard of a chief sending away those who struggled to care for themselves.

I look up into Zulie's dark eyes. "You wouldn't let him?"

"How could I?" she asks. "He was sentencing them to death. I challenged him for chief."

"And she won," Leer says, smiling. "She led them here—and us, too, after we joined with her—making sure those who couldn't survive the travelling were cared for. Those who wanted to leave were released to a new chief."

"How many of our band remained?" I ask.

"A couple dozen. We were tired after what happened with Eija and Ukaru, and this was a way to get out of the life of a Raider. We've started building something here, Nova. Families are growing."

I close my eyes and press my fingertips against my eyelids. This isn't how things were supposed to go.

"What's wrong?" Zulie asks. "Not enough for whatever you wish to sacrifice them to?"

I laugh then, not because there's anything funny about this situation, but because there's nothing else to do. It bubbles out of me in manic waves for several seconds before giving way to sobs. I'm barely able to stutter out, "I've come all this way for nothing."

Leer puts an arm over my shoulders and pulls me to his side. "What is it, Little Star?"

And I tell him, start to finish. I tell him of losing Nukiki, of the airship and the floating cities, the missing children and rescuing Thoa and Rego from the Mayor of Gearhaven, I tell him of the tower battle and my time in the space station. When I get to the part about Ukaru killing Eija, he gasps and covers his mouth. A tear slides down his face as I explain how I killed Ukaru and became chief, but how Rego was nearly killed.

When I look up to meet Leer's eyes, I find Zulie's instead. She has softened as she listened to me, as if she understands better than most. Perhaps she does. She has sacrificed for her people, done what she needed to protect them. My life is only sacrifice, only lived for others.

I swallow, saying, "We came here for the banished, to bring them back to the farm. We're going to attack the star-people and punish them for their injustices, but we needed their strength. How could I command that of them, knowing that they're happy here, that they're starting families of their own?"

Zulie releases Leer's hand and kneels in front of me. We look into each other's eyes for a long moment and I see something there that is more than a fierce Raider, more than strong leader. She is a care-giver, a mother to the motherless. And when she looks at me, she sees a hurting child.

She wipes my face with her palms. "You can't command that of them, but you can ask."

I look into her eyes and see something I hadn't noticed before: compassion. She is their chief because she wasn't willing to leave the broken on their own. Her heart is for her people.

"Why would they follow me? I am not their chief."

"You don't have to be," she says. "They don't follow for that reason alone. They'll follow someone they believe in, someone who believes in them. Is that you?"

I nod. "I think so."

She presses her lips together. "Go back to your ship. When you *know* so, come back to us and we will help you."

I open my mouth to protest, but stop the words from coming out. She is right. I cannot ask them to come with me until I can do so with a clear heart.

I rise from their sofa and they walk me to the door. Leer embraces me again and whispers, "I hope to see you soon, Little Star."

Zulie runs a thumb across my cheek as I pull away from her husband. She says, "Don't worry. We will."

CHAPTER
THIRTY

I meander through the corridors, stopping at random floors to wander through and see more of the Hole in the World. The walk clears my mind and lets me relax, even as I weigh what's next.

There aren't any other Raiders in the corridors that I walk, but I pass a couple of Rachel's crew as I'm nearing the dock.

"Back to the ship already, Chief?" one asks.

I nod. "I need to think."

"Good place for it while everyone else is off," the other says.

They continue on their way, laughing and smacking at each other's arms while they walk. The interaction makes me smile. It's nice to see the camaraderie after the seriousness we've endured of late. Maybe Hiro has the right of it.

I make my way onto the airship and across the deck to the steps that go below. I'm not sure what it is about the space below deck where I pace, but I know that's where I need to be. Though I'm alone on the ship, I still find myself moving with as much care as possible. Something about this ship seems to expect reverence from me. Perhaps because it is not mine, and with everything going on with Rachel, I no longer feel at ease here.

Passing the cargo and moving to the place where my feet have worn the boards smooth, I notice light coming from under Tinora's door. It isn't uncommon, as she's recently been allowed a lamp in her small room. But the light seems to illuminate the edges of the door as well, as if it isn't closed.

I sneak closer to it and see that it is indeed cracked open and the lock lies on the floor by my feet. My body stills as I work to regulate the shakiness in my hands and the blood pounding through my ears. Everything in me wants to pounce forward and kill Tinora while I have a chance. Though I promised Rachel I wouldn't, I don't know that my promise to her means anything now.

Instead, I listen. There are noises within, though I can't make out any words. I try to make out the conversation for several seconds before understanding hits me and I realize what I'm hearing.

Steeling myself for what I'm about to walk into, I clench my fists in front of me and pull the door open. Tinora is on her divan, naked and reclined as a red-head bobs between her legs. She sees me standing in the doorway and smiles wide, lifts her hand to wiggle her fingers in a wave. As if enjoying herself more with an audience, she begins to moan in rhythm with Captain MacGale's movement.

"You're kidding me," I growl.

Rachel spins around at my voice, eyes wide in surprise. Now that she faces me, I see that her shirt is unbuttoned as well, revealing more of her than I ever wanted to see.

"We're busy right now," Tinora says, stretching her arms above her head. "Or we were before we were so rudely interrupted. Maybe come back later?"

Tears are falling down my cheeks and I feel a pressure building in my chest. I scream at her, "She tortured me. She tried to kill me."

"Nova, let me explain," Rachel says, holding her hands out in front of her body to try to placate me.

"Explain? What could you possibly say?"

"She's not who you think she is. There's more to her than that."

A laugh cuts through my tears. "I know exactly who she is. But you...I have no idea who you are."

"I know things have been strained lately—"

"Strained?" I ask, cutting her off. I rub my palms over my face to wipe away the tears that betray my emotions.

Rachel is buttoning up her shirt now, straightening herself as if we can talk this out. Tinora doesn't bother dressing or even covering herself, as if she thinks her nakedness bothers me. It doesn't. In fact, I'd probably enjoy seeing it if she wasn't such a bitch.

I shake my head as I stare at her with disgust. Then I remember the part of this that stings the most. Not for me, but for the woman waiting at the farm. "What will Permilla say?"

Her jaw clenches. "She doesn't need to know."

Her reaction confirms my fears. Permilla hasn't given permission for an open relationship. That sweet woman has no idea. "You're supposed to be in love with her, but you don't have the decency to remain loyal to her for the few weeks we're gone."

Rachel's eyes shine with anger. "Don't bring her into this."

"You brought her into this. I'm not the one cheating on her."

Rachel clenches her fists at her side and says, "I've had enough of your high and mighty attitude. Just because you've destroyed your own relationships doesn't mean you have to ruin mine."

My hand whips across her cheek before I realize what I'm doing. Her head jerks to the side with the slap and she puts her hand over the red mark coming up on her cheek. She huffs at me and says, "You little bitch." She glances back to the naked girl behind her and as an afterthought she adds, "Jane was right about you."

Rage boils through me and my hand goes to the knife at my belt. Before I can draw it, I think of the last time I pulled my knife and the lives that ended because of it. I take a deep breath work to remind myself that I don't want to kill my aunt, even as my blood sings for her blood.

She smirks at me as I fight to pull my hand free of my blade's hilt. She sees a victory here as I back out of the room. I don't care if she counts this as a win. I won't be baited into a fight that can only win one way. Until now, I didn't think she would want that either.

I trip on something as I step outside the door. I bend down to see what it was and find the padlock. Rachel must see me pick it up because she lunges for the door just as I move to close it. She bucks against it with all her weight, but I hold it closed and slip the lock into place. As I snap it closed, I find myself smiling for the first time since I found her here. Victory is mine.

AFTER THE ENCOUNTER WITH RACHEL AND TINORA/JANE, I sit on a crate and listen to Rachel pounding on the door for nearly an hour before she grows tired and I grow bored. I'm certain one of her crew will let her out when they get back, and perhaps it will mean trouble for me and mine when they do, but I can't bring myself to let her out. Besides, the only key is locked in the room with her.

Rage still burns under my skin and I can't seem to shake it. There's still about four hours paid dock time left, so I leave the ship and go to find Hiro on level fourteen. Exiting the elevator I immediately notice that this floor is different than the others. There are no doors on each side of the hall. Instead, there's a single door at the end of the hall with a frosted glass window with the words "Pleasure Center" printed in the old tongue, Raider, and at least a dozen other languages.

I open the door and step inside. I don't know what I was expecting, but the compact white room was not it. There's a short line and I step into it, slowly creeping towards the front of the room where a woman waits with a clipboard and pen. She's an older lady, faintly wrinkled across her forehead and near her mouth, her dull gray hair still clinging to a few strands of black. When I reach the front, the woman doesn't look up as she asks, "Are you eighteen or older and here without coercion?"

"Yes," I stammer. "I'm looking for a man."

She waves her hand and says, "They'll address preferences at the next counter."

"No, wait, I mean I'm looking for a friend."

"Whatever flies your ship, honey. Hold out your hand."

I do as she wishes and she presses a device against the tip of my middle finger. I feel a pinch and then her machine beeps twice. "Clean," she says, stamping a piece of paper. She hands it to me and nods to the door on her left. She looks up when I don't move and says, "You're good to go, hon. Enjoy."

Unsure what else to do, I step through the door. There are several counters inside, each with its own receptionist. I slip into the shortest line and wait until my turn to speak with the gentleman at my counter.

He reaches forward and I hand him my slip of paper as he says, "Hello, mx. How can I help you today?"

"I'm looking for a friend," I say.

He smiles and says, "A rare find, indeed. How many partners would you like and do you have a gender preference?"

"One male. He came in here a couple hours ago. About six feet tall, well-built, dark hair, dressed like a Raider."

"Ah, I'm sorry mx, but we do not make room assignments in such ways. Could you be less specific?"

I sigh. "Um, yeah, okay. I guess I want male."

I'm just looking for Hiro, I think. *Nothing more.*

He nods and says, "Perfect. How will you be paying?"

"Oh," I mouth, my cheeks flushing.

"We accept trades if you do not have the coin."

I turn out my pockets but there's nothing in them with value. My cheeks flush as I say, "I'll show myself out."

"That would work." He points at the knife at my hip. I look at the blade Coco gave me and bite my lip. He seems to sense my hesitance, saying, "You can return later and purchase it back, after you've finished your business at the Hole. It'll sell for three silvers," he says, looking down at his clipboard.

I nod and remove the knife from my belt. I can get the coin from the airship, or borrow it from Hiro when I find him.

The man smiles and hands me a ticket stub. He points at the door at the end of the hall and says, "Enjoy."

"Why do people keep saying that?" I mutter as I walk through the door.

This corridor is as long as the others I've been in, longer perhaps. There are doors here, like on the residence levels. Outside the doors wait men in various states of undress. There's a myriad of skin tones, hair and eye color, sizes and shapes. I walk by the first two pairs without realizing what's happening.

The third man on the left calls out to me. "Come visit with me for a bit."

"Ignore him," another says. "I'm more fun."

I think, *This isn't what I was looking for.*

But another voice, a voice that sounds remarkably like Hiro, whispers in my head, "Are you sure about that?"

I can only fool myself so much.

I slip my fingers into my pocket and check for the button Ivy gave me. I do not want the star-people to see what I'm about to do. Some things should be private. Besides, they've seen enough of me.

With a sigh, I clear my mind of everything around me, everything I should be dealing with. Instead, I focus on being present in this moment. I know what comes after this when I return to Leer and Zulie. I'm ready to finish my task. But like Hiro said, I deserve a moment when I'm not weighed down worrying about whatever comes next.

Halfway down the hall, there's a man who catches my eye. His dark hair is grayed at the temples, silver in his sculpted beard. Unlike many of the other men, he's fully clothed and doesn't reveal anything but his head and hands that look more than capable of anything I might desire. He's shorter than the men I'm typically interested in, his body rounded in a way that makes me think of Bets.

I sigh at the thought of her. We danced around each other for weeks, stuck in each other's gravitational pull. When we finally collided, it was magic.

It takes effort to pull my mind from her. Even in our brief time around each other, I could tell she was special. I wonder what might have happened if I hadn't left that night, after. If I would have stayed, would I be on the space station now, wrapped in her arms?

Refocusing on this moment, I turn away from the man who makes me think of Bets. I can't live in the past anymore than I can worry about the future.

I scan the other side of the hall for a different distraction. I catch eyes with a blond god, his smirk a little too much like Hiro for my tastes. Beside him is a bare chested man with skin the color of tree bark and arms as thick as branches. The way he holds himself makes it clear he knows how to do his job and makes me feel foolish for considering anyone else.

I step towards him and am about to hand him my ticket when I hear a voice say, "You sure about that?"

The words daze me, just as they did when they were in my head. But these are not in my head. I turn towards the voice, knowing who I'll find before I see him. I know that voice as well as I know the beat of my own heart.

Thoa.

He's leaning against the door behind me. Gods, how did I not see him? Now that I do, I can see no one else. He wears a white shirt with half the buttons undone, loosely tucked into a tartan. I've seen him wear it once before, in the tower battle, when we had to tell our secrets.

Though I stare at him, I can't make my legs move closer. There's something about seeing him here after I've said goodbye, after I've closed my heart to the possibility of him, that nearly rips me in half.

He holds out his hand and asks, "Do you have a ticket for me?"

My fingers unclench from the stub in my palm. I'd forgotten I had it. Thoa steps forward, somehow managing to saunter in just those two strides. Instead of taking the stub from my palm, he puts the tips of his fingers on the soft part of my arm near the elbow and traces the ghost of a touch down my skin. I shiver, unable to stop the desire that rises in me unbidden. Such a little thing, that touch, but the fire it ignites is an inferno.

My eyes travel up the rest of him until I stare into his azure gaze. I don't know what I'm looking for, what I'm expecting to find, but it wasn't the ember of need that I see glowing there. He chose to leave only a few weeks ago, said he didn't feel anything for me, but the spark is undeniable.

He raises his brows as if to ask permission. I nod, consent to whatever he's asking, though there was never any chance I'd say no to him, no matter what he asked of me. He smiles and takes my hand, pulling me towards his door. When we step inside and his hand falls away, I realize the ticket stub is no longer in my hand.

Thoa walks into a dim room. There's a lamp in the corner emitting a soft glow, a sheer red cloth draped over it. He moves to the bed, the only place in the room to sit, and pats the mattress for me to join him. My body trembles as I cross the room and I fight the instinct in me to run, to get away from him before I lose myself again. But I know I'm already lost to him. I was his long before this moment, I'll be his long after.

We sit side by side, not quite touching, living in the *what ifs* that always seem to haunt us. After a moment, he says, "What are you doing here?"

I laugh at the simplicity of the question. "I could ask you the same."

"You could, but I think it's pretty obvious." I turn to him and raise a brow. He shrugs and says, "Working."

"How did you end up working here?"

He sighs. "I went to Gearhaven with Nigel. He's trying to find help with the floating cities, but he doesn't have the clout he once did."

"Well, that happens when people find out you kidnap children."

Thoa winces, but doesn't comment. I'm not sure if he truly doesn't remember that part of Nigel or just doesn't want to. "Anyway. The city came this way to trade. Nigel was going to ride back towards the farm, but I opted to stay."

"And be a sex worker?"

"Don't say it as if there's shame in it, Nova."

"I'm sorry," I say. "I didn't mean it like that. I'm just surprised to see you here. There are probably tons of jobs around this place."

He smirks. "I like this one, Nova. People are nice, and everyone knows what to expect. Besides, anything I did before the station, anything I might have done..." he trails off, pointing to his head. "It's mostly gone."

I slip my hand over his, entwining our fingers in the hopes of taking away some of his hurt. They took so much away from him, so much away from both of us.

He holds out his palm where my ticket rests. "It was selfish of me to call out to you. But I saw you going toward Donovan and, well, I was a little jealous."

I glance at him, the sheepish grin on his face. I try to keep my face calm, though my insides are somersaulting. "Jealous? That doesn't sound like the new Thoa."

"Does it sound like the old one?"

"A little. But that Thoa was in love with me."

He swallows hard, holds my ticket out to me. "If that's who you're hoping to find in here, I can't help you. But you can still take your ticket back and go to another room. I would understand. It isn't fair for me to think you'll be okay with this."

I bite the inside of my cheek for a second before asking, "So you want me to take my ticket back?"

He shakes his head. "Not really."

I turn to him, stare up into eyes whose equal I've never seen. Slowly, I say, "I understand this is just a job to you."

"Nova—"

But I cut him off. "I understand, and I'm okay with that. But I'm not going to another room unless you tell me I have to."

He brushes his fingers against my cheek and I close my eyes involuntarily. I feel my lungs expanding, drawing in a deep breath as if I can hold this moment inside me. I hold it while his hand rests against my face, hold it til my lungs burn. And then his lips are on mine.

They're soft, softer than I remember though it's only been a few weeks since I felt them against mine. But I don't have long to think on their softness before they move away from mine, trailing over the lines of my jaw, crawling down my neck. They feel warm against me, but still send a chill racing down my spine, leaving my skin tingling in their wake.

His hands roam my back, pulling me against him. I gasp as they slip under the hem of my shirt, relishing their roughness against the soft skin of my back. He may not be a Raider any longer, but his hands still hold their callouses, still speak of long nights on the hunt.

And hunt he does. His lips explore my skin and each time Thoa finds his prey, it elicits a shaky gasp from my barely-breathing lungs. I feel him smile against me each time he finds such a place. This may be his job, but that doesn't mean he doesn't enjoy it. And he's definitely good at it.

Deft hands remove the fastenings of my killing leathers. His mind might not remember wearing these, but his fingers do. His hands slip down to my hips and he pulls me up, out, letting my leathers fall to the floor as he spins me onto his lap. He pulls me against him, hard, his kilt riding up until there's nothing between us but the past.

AS HE ROLLS ONTO THE BED BESIDE ME, PANTING AND FLUSHED, I CAN'T stop myself from staring at him. This is how it was always supposed to be. Me and him, fighting and loving each other, forever.

We don't talk as I get dressed. I feel the wall rebuilding between us, but I don't know if it's because of him or me. Maybe a bit of both.

His hand on my waist guides me behind a curtain at the back of the room. There's a door for me to exit and I'm thankful I don't have to walk the corridor past the men again.

"This was fun," he says.

Glancing over I see him smiling and I'm surprised at how much it hurts me. This was fun, but it was more than that, to me anyway: this was the life I was supposed to have but never will. But I can't say that, so instead I nod. "Yeah."

I step outside and turn back to face him, preparing my heart for another goodbye. Though I know what he'll say, I still offer: "You could still come with us."

He shakes his head, his eyes turning wistful as he says, "You know, I keep thinking about what it would've been like if Rachel had brought us here, if we hadn't gone on to Aeroport and the City of Trials. We could've stopped fighting anytime and let ourselves be happy."

My throat constricts as I listen to him and I forget to breathe. He says, "But that's the thing with 'what ifs'—you can let them be anything you want, imagine every scenario under the sun, but they're rarely equal to reality." He looks back to me, a sad smile on his lips. He leans over and kisses my forehead and whispers, "Goodbye, Little Star."

With those words, he said goodbye to me. With those words, he told me so much more.

Thoa remembers.

CHAPTER
THIRTY-ONE

I 'm in a wide room and there are doors everywhere I look. This must be a neutral place where everyone leaves. Somehow seeing all the other people departing makes my time with Thoa seem less. It shouldn't, I know, because we were all here for the same thing. We all paid the same price.

Still, I let myself fall into the trap of believing there was more to it than that. He warned me he didn't have feelings and was just doing his job, but a small part of me—no, not a *small* part, all of me —thought it had to be more than that. I had an encounter with him that could've been a fond memory, but instead it tarnishes with each step away from his door.

My footsteps echo through the hall: *Thoa remembers, Thoa remembers, Thoa remembers.*

I grind my teeth as I try to send the thought away. So what if he does? It still doesn't change his feelings, or lack thereof.

There's a small group ahead, gathered at a door as they say goodbye to one another. There are two women, one reed thin and towering above the others, the other short and thick-hipped, running fingers along the bare chest of the smiling, one and only, Hiro. A man stands behind the women, black hair draped over one eye and thumbs hooked in the waist of pants that hang indecently low on his hips. Hiro has his hand cupped to the man's cheek when another man comes out of the room. The new arrival presses past the other three and wraps his arms around Hiro in a fierce embrace.

As I approach, I hear one of them ask, "Can't you stay? I have a very big bed I can share until you get a place of your own."

"I guarantee you could find work," the tall woman says, her eyes sliding down his body like sap over treebark.

"I'm sorry, loves," Hiro says, flashing his devastating grin. "Would that I could, for I should love nothing more than to spend my days and nights with you."

My eyes roll of their own accord, the smile coming to my lips both genuine and snarky. I put my hand on his arm and he turns to me, his smile going even wider as his brows raise so high I'm afraid he'll lose them in his hairline.

He puts an arm around my shoulder and says, "There you are, dearest. Did you enjoy?"

I shoot him a glare and give a noncommittal, "Mm."

"I see." Turning back to his companions, he says, "I'm off, darlings. But I promise to stop by again next time I'm in the area."

"Three seventeen," the short woman says. "That's my room number. Don't forget it."

As we walk away, Hiro pulls a thin shirt over his head and sighs, but says nothing. I wait as long as I can, which isn't very long, before asking, "Okay, what the hell happened back there?"

Hiro's face takes on an innocence that doesn't suit him. "Whatever do you mean?"

I laugh. "How did you get the four of them swooning over you like that?"

"How indeed," he grins. Then he adds, "What about you? Where are you coming from, little lady?"

I raise my eyes at the new nickname and he winces a silent apology. "I was visiting an old friend."

"Do I know them?"

I scrape my tongue across my teeth, weighing my words. "You've met."

He smiles. "I saw him, you know, when I was making my selections. Honestly, I was tempted to choose him. Thoa is a fine specimen."

"Why didn't you?"

"I wasn't sure if it would bother you and I didn't want to risk it. We're best friends, after all. There's a code of honor with regard to exes."

I nod. "Thank you. It...it would've bothered me."

"I could've wooed him, though, just so we're clear."

"I have no doubt," I smile. "But it means a lot that you didn't. I know he's moved on, but at least I don't have to spend time each day with the people he's moved on *with*. I guess I need to move on, too."

My throat is so dry I nearly choked on my words. Even when I thought I was moving on, there was still hope that one day Thoa's memory would return and he would love me again. Now, his memory has returned, or at least some of it, and he still doesn't love me. There's no longer any hope left to hold onto.

He squeezes my shoulder and asks, "You okay?"

It isn't the question I expect from him. Hiro is the kind to ask, "Did you screw?" or "How was it?" or "Is his dick as big as mine?" But he doesn't. Because even as a rake, a scoundrel, he still regards his friendship with me as more important than the mischievous facade he portrays. Hiro wears a suit of scandal but inside he's all heart.

The least I can do is give him the truth. "I don't know."

He lets his hand slip into mine as we walk to the elevator. Though he says nothing else, that little action is enough.

We get off on the sixth floor and go to Leer and Zulie's door. When I knock, the young boy answers. Though he still stares daggers at me, he lets me in without a word. Hiro and I follow him into the living room where Zulie sits with half a dozen other people. She smiles when we enter and waves me over.

Zulie stands and leans over in a half hug. It's a strange thing, considering how we met only a couple hours ago. She presents me to the others and says, "Everyone, this is the chief I was telling you about."

Echoes of *Chief* repeat in greeting throughout the room. I dip my head and say, "Well met."

Zulie says, "These are the local chiefs, those whose Raiders stayed in the Hole. I hope you don't mind, but I told them your story."

I nod. "If we are to defeat the star-people, everyone should hear and know the truth."

One of the chiefs, a hunched woman with wrinkles criss-crossing over her cheeks, stands and asks, "Do you truly believe we can win this fight?"

My lips pucker as I weigh my words. I need these people to follow me, but I will not lie to them. "Not easily. But yes, with enough people on our side, we can win."

"How many is enough?" another asks.

I shake my head. "I don't know. They have a lot of people up there, good and bad. We'll need to try to keep the good ones from getting hurt while fighting the bad."

Zulie says, "What they're doing is wrong. Now that we know, we can't let it stand. This fight is about more than any of us as individuals; this fight needs all of us."

"I will gather my people," the hunched chief says, rheumy eyes meeting mine. "We place our trust in you, Chief."

The other chiefs follow her from the room, nodding to me as they go. When they're gone, I say, "Thank you for your words, Zulie."

She nods. "It isn't over yet. The chiefs have agreed to call their Raiders, but you'll still need to convince them."

I swallow. I hadn't realized there was another level of approval. "When will they come?"

"Leer and I have already called for our Raiders. They're meeting us in the community room downstairs in an hour."

An hour. That should give us plenty of time before Rachel's ship casts off. We're so close to meeting our goal, I can almost allow myself to feel relief. Almost. But as Hiro squeezes my hand and smiles, I can't help but wonder about the things that could still go wrong.

———

THE HOUR PASSES IN EXCRUCIATING SLOWNESS AND ALSO WITH THE speed of an airship speeding through the sky. I spend the time thinking about what I want to say to the Raiders, how I will convince them, but now as I stand to speak, words fail me.

I stare out at faces in every skin tone imaginable, looking into eyes of brown, black, gray, blue, green, hazel—every hue possible. They stare back warm and hungry and bored, here only as a courtesy to their chiefs. I need to get their attention.

"Tell me the tale of Zappho Curiosity," I say, remembering the rhyme my mother told me when I was a child, "who fell from the stars to vanquish the sea. He turned back the tides to flow the right way, to give us the land for our children to play."

There are scoffs and sniggers in the crowd, but some are listening. I press on. "Tell me about his affair with the moon, how she floated to earth on a hot air balloon. Tell me about her beauty and grace, how the world was enchanted with her loving face.

"I don't want to hear of their terrible plight, when the sun became jealous and came down to fight. I won't listen to how he pulled them apart, or the cruelty he showed when he carved out her heart."

I place my hand over my own heart now, unable to resist thinking about how the star-people tore me and Thoa apart. This rhyme is as much my story as it is Zappho's. I swallow and recite the final verse: "I long for the words to make me brave and strong, for in Zappho's world, these cold nights are long. But somewhere above is a savior for me, and that savior's name is Curiosity."

There's silence in the room for a second as my words linger there, ready to be plucked from the air and heard or discarded. Finally, a man yells, "You brought us here for this? To hear a child's rhyme."

"It isn't a story for children, friends," I say, my voice quieter than it should be. But the room is still, as if the very walls are waiting for my next words. "We may tell it that way now, but I believe Zappho's story is a true one."

The man starts to push his way through the crowd towards the exit. A few others make to follow, but I say, "I've been to the stars."

They stop in their tracks and turn back to me, unsure what to make of me. So I tell them my story, start to end. And just as it softened Zulie's heart for me, many of those assembled seem to hear the truth in my story and sympathize with me.

"I cannot command you to go with me, to fight against the star-people who watch us for entertainment, who let us slaughter one another for their amusement while weeding out the strong among us." I press a clenched fist to my chest and say, "But they have not seen the strength of Raiders in our fullness. They have never known the fierceness of our blades. So I ask you now, to join me against them. To stand and fight their tyranny. Don't do it for me— do it for the Raiders who come after us, for the world yet to come."

I wait.

There's ringing in the room, or in my head, I don't know. But it seems to go on forever.

Then the hunched chief steps forward and draws a blade from her hip. She flips it from her hand and it sticks in the floorboard by my feet. In a booming voice, louder than her body looks like it could contain, she says, "You have my blade, Chief."

There's a flurry of movement after that. People drop throwing knives, swords, whips, cudgels, scimitars, daggers and all manner of things on the floor, promising their weapons for my fight. I am honored, I am surprised, I am relieved.

"When do we leave?" Leer asks, his smile broad.

I look over the assembled Raiders and wonder how we'll fit them all on Rachel's ship. I guess I'll need to let her out of Tinora's room to figure it out. The thought of them sends a fire through my gut, but I push it away. I don't have time to be angry. Leading these people is more important.

"Gather your things and say goodbye to anyone you leave behind. Meet me at the docks in an hour."

"Yes, Chief!"

The exclamation resounds through the room and for a moment I'm certain I can feel the words vibrating through my boots. For so long I stood as an outsider with the Raiders, no true title, no true family. But here, among these brave warriors, I am home.

CHAPTER
THIRTY-TWO

Nothing went wrong.

Some of the Raiders went their separate ways, but it was only a drop of water compared to the monsoon the star-folk will face. For the first time in a long time, my spirit feels light, buoyed by the progress we're finally making.

While the others get ready, I borrow some coins from Hiro to retrieve my knife. For a second, I consider asking where he got on-world money, being a star-man and all. But then I remember he's Hiro and things like that don't matter. Things always seem to go his way.

Getting the knife was as easy as the gentleman had said. I'm surprised by how much relief I feel when it's back in my possession. With my blade at my hip, I'm ready to go back to the airship and face Rachel. I'm still angry about what happened earlier, but my blood isn't boiling as hot as it was. I will attempt to have a conversation with her without raising my voice or my blade, and as long as Tinora isn't there, I think it's at least possible.

I get off the elevator at the twentieth floor and head towards the docks. Hiro meets me when I step out of the corridor. His jaw is clenched, but his expression is conciliatory. He holds his hands up as if to calm me but my pulse quickens at the gesture.

"It could be worse," he says as I push past him.

I stare wide-eyed at the empty dock before me. *They've moved*, I think, because it's the only explanation. I spin to the man at the door, the same one who'd been there when we arrived. "Where is the *Disorderly Glory*?"

He winces as he says, "They pulled out about an hour ago."

"But they've still got at least an hour of dock time."

He shrugs. "They forfeited their time, said there was a change of plans."

A slew of curses pours from my mouth as my knees buckle and I hit the ground, hard. I sit there, staring at the dark walls of the dock, while Hiro kneels and tries to comfort me. But there is no comfort. This is my fault. If I hadn't confronted Rachel, if I hadn't locked her in Tinora's cell, if I'd just minded my own damn business, if it wasn't for Tinora…

The walls are black, the floor is gray, when I find Rachel, that bitch will pay.

Tinora Jane will be paid back. She'll scream when her head goes crack, crack, crack.

For a moment, more than a moment, I'm back in my little room on the space station. I stare at the same point on the wall for a long time, a year or a second or three months. I don't know. My will seeps away and I'm lost to my thoughts, lost to the fantasy of destroying the women who have ruined all we've done here.

There are voices around me, but I don't hear what they're saying. Arms tug at me and I swat them away. I don't want them. It doesn't matter if I'm standing or sitting or here at all. Without Rachel's ship, we can't get back to the farm. We can't signal Copperhill to get Rego and Karina and Drev. We can't fight the star-people when we're too busy fighting ourselves.

"I think I can help."

The words drift down into my brain, floating like a feather

through the fog. I know the voice, the man speaking, but my brain can't figure out why I'm hearing it. Nigel isn't with us.

The Nigel-mirage kneels in front of me and grabs the front of my shirt. It shakes me. Figments of my imagination shouldn't be able to do that. Through bleary eyes, I see the hallucination haul back his hand and—

"What the hell?" I howl, my hand going to my burning cheek.

I draw back, blink a few times, and focus on the man smiling in front of me. This time when his lips move, I hear him: "I've wanted to do that for quite some time, but you know, I'm a gentleman."

I grit my teeth and growl, "I'm going to murder you."

He lets go of my shirt and stands, straightening into an infuriatingly dismissive stance. "I wouldn't recommend it, love. I'm here to save your ass."

"What are you talking about?" I ask, scrambling to my feet.

He steps back from me now that I'm up, eyes wide as if he wants to hide behind something. He arm jerks towards the dock and I look, giving him a moment's reprieve. There's a massive ship ahead, far larger than Rachel's, its blue and white sails furled against dark wood and bronze. At the bow is an intricately carved man, naked, with golden wings spread out behind him. Along the side of the ship in large, flowing letters, it reads: *Curiosity*.

My jaw hangs open. He couldn't have known the story I would tell the Raiders. I didn't know it myself until the words tumbled out. Besides, Nigel wouldn't name a ship after something I said. It has to be a coincidence. Or, as Rego would say, it's a sign from the gods.

And though I've never believed in any of them, I say a silent thank you to Zappho Curiosity. He may not be a god, but that doesn't mean he isn't looking out for us.

"Thoa radioed Gearhaven," Nigel's saying, and despite my dislike of him, I listen to what he says. "We were near enough to get the message. Luckily, I still have a few friends around the town and I was able to make arrangements for you."

"He said Gearhaven left, and you with it," I say, remembering how he ended up here.

Nigel nods. "We did, but we hadn't gone far. The new mayor likes to move slow, pretending he's a big city. Arrogant fool."

I laugh, surprising myself. The thought of *Nigel* thinking someone is arrogant is unbelievably funny.

Not to mention the relief that suddenly fills me. We can fit everyone on that ship. We can get to the farm and meet with Copperhill and I'll get Rego back. And it's all thanks to that garbage person, Nigel Weatherfield.

THEY ARRIVE IN TWOS AND THREES, MOST CARRYING LITTLE MORE THAN the clothes on their backs and the weapons strapped to hips and backs. A woman with onyx-dark skin and short ivory curls walks beside a large gray and white beast with eyes the color of the sun-soaked sky.

Her top lip curls up in a smile when she sees my expression. "Don't worry, she's tame. Unless I don't want her to be."

I laugh, or try to, but it sounds strained even to my ears. I watch the beast's tail swish back and forth as they board Nigel's ship.

"Chief?"

I turn back to see the man who'd questioned me in the assembly, the one who *didn't* commit his weapon to me. I plant my feet and put my hands on my hips, staring at him.

He presses his lips together and nods towards a group walking towards the *Curiosity*. "I questioned you on their behalf."

I look at the two boys jostling to get onboard. They're young, fourteen or fifteen, if I had to guess. Young like Ivy, Sarah, Wolfie, Edith Ann Roody, Krew's sister, Zazira. This fight is for the young, to give them a chance for a better future.

"They've never been in a real fight," he says. "We've been here years now, so long I don't know that I remember what it's like out there."

"I understand you want to keep them safe," I say, but he shakes his head and cuts me off.

"I want their lives to be better. But I can't teach them that from inside this place. So I let them choose what they want to do, and they want to go with you. They believe in you."

"What do you believe?" I ask.

He sighs. "I believe in the blood running through their veins. They were born of the strongest Raider, the strongest Chief I've ever known. She died of a fever," he says, his eyes distant and cold. "And now you tell me there are people looking down on us who could've saved her? The thought of those bastards makes me sick."

"I'm sorry for your loss," I murmur, though the words taste like sawdust on my lips. I wonder how many more times I'll have to say those words. "I will give you vengeance if I can."

"Vengeance doesn't matter to me. I join you for my boys, and because I'm a Raider, and you are the Chief. But I'm warning you now, if you're sending my boys to their deaths, I can't be held responsible for what I do to you."

His words are sharper than the blade at his hip, slicing through the armor of righteous justice I've used to gird myself. Though my plans have hinged on vengeance, he makes me feel foolish for even thinking about it.

"What's your name, Raider?" I ask.

"Delano."

"I'd like you on my council, Delano. I need to be surrounded by those who speak plainly."

He sucks air through his teeth for a second, then gives a nod. "As it pleases you, Chief."

I watch him walk towards the *Curiosity*. I haven't spoken to anyone else about the council yet, but with over a hundred Raiders, I'll need to have leaders among them to keep things organized. But that's something I can worry about once we're airborne.

As more Raiders come through, I see several that I recognize from my old clan. I wonder if they are surprised to see me leading as I am, considering the last time they saw me I was on the verge of being outcast. If they are surprised, none of them show it. Instead they smile and greet me as an old friend, as their new Chief, and as Nova-du.

The ship is loaded with Raiders at the hour mark as I instructed, but I wait anyway. For stragglers, I tell myself, though I don't believe it. There are no stragglers among Raiders. It is not our way. Still, I wait.

Standing at the top of the slipway looking out towards the door, I feel a sense of loss settle over me. A hand touches my shoulder ever so gently and I turn, expecting Hiro, but it's Nigel's gaze I meet.

"He's not coming," he says. His tone is sad, but matter-of-fact.

For the first time I realize that he loves Thoa, too.

I nod, not trusting my voice to respond. I let Nigel lead me away and we set off from this place. Once again, I let my heart say goodbye to Thoa. But this time, I know it will be the last. The realizations hits me with such force it takes my breath away, leaves me clinging to the railing as we soar higher, putting distance between me and the one Raider I can't win with words—or anything else.

THE COUNCIL AND I STAND ON THE DECK EIGHT STRONG, A SACRED number among the Raiders. Along with Delano, I've chosen Zulie, Leer, Fatboy, Caita, who called the fight between me and Ukaru, and two former chiefs, Amana and Jinx. I spoke with all the other chiefs to offer them a place on my council, but two of them thought it was time for other voices to have the chance to lead, and the others were relieved to have the responsibility fall to someone else, as they'd only taken the mantle when there was no one else to lead.

"This council shares my burden," I tell the Raiders. "Speak with them as if it were my ears, listen to them as if it were my lips. We are as one."

Echoes of "Yes, Chief!" surround me before they break off and return to their work. Nigel was able to get the ship, but he had little in the way of a crew, so the Raiders have been learning to fly. The thought of it sends a chill through me. I'd never seen an airship before we set out for the City of Trials, and now my people are flying one. Traditions be damned.

We are nearing the farm, a day away, when Caita finds me on the bow. "Good afternoon, Chief."

"Hello, Caita." Her brows are knit together as if she's worried, so I ask, "Something on your mind?"

She bites her lip for a moment, then rushes, "Just curious how you will lead the solstice choosing tonight, without the bonfire, the ceremonial staff, or the mated tents."

Her words catch me off guard. *The solstice choosing?* I hadn't realized tonight was the solstice, but even if I had, the idea that people would want to choose a mate the night before we reach the farm, only a short time before we go to battle where some of us will die...

"Is it wise to observe the solstice, with everything else going on?"

She forces a smile and says, "Wise? I don't know, Chief, but the Raiders are expecting it. With all the other uncertainty, giving them something familiar seems like a kindness."

"You're right," I nod. "I hadn't considered that."

"Papa-du's staff was on the other ship," she says, her tone a mix of bitterness and anger.

My fists clench at the thought of Rachel and what she's done. "I will get it back. Maybe not as soon as I'd like, but MacGale can't run forever."

Caita nods and says, "I'll ask around and see if we can make do for now."

"We could hang curtains through the sleeping hall to give some privacy for after the choosing," I add. "The unmated will sleep on the deck tonight."

"That just leaves the bonfire."

"Bonfire?" Hiro asks, throwing his arm over my shoulders. "Planning a surprise party for my birthday?"

"It's your birthday?" I ask.

He shrugs. "Shouldn't you already know that? I mean, you are the one throwing my party."

Caita looks between us, confused, and I realize we were speaking the old tongue. But Hiro was answering something he heard in Raider. I turn to him and ask, "Can you speak Raider now?"

"A bit," he replies, beaming. "Folly and Gareem have been giving me tongue lessons."

Caita snorts and I mutter, "I bet they have."

"So what's up with the bonfire for real?" he asks.

Caita and I tell Hiro about the solstice ceremony and what we're planning for that night. Despite his own preferences regarding relationships and monogamy—or lack thereof—Hiro is a captive and respectful audience. At the end of our explanation, Caita raises her brows to him and adds, "It's also a night to declare the new Raiders we've added to our ranks."

Hiro blushes and I'm certain it's the first time I've seen him show anything but ridiculous confidence. He says, "I like the Raiders, I just don't know if I'm cut out to be one."

Caita taps two fingers over his heart and says, "You already are."

I DON'T KNOW HOW HIRO MANAGES IT, BUT HE FINDS US A BONFIRE. Well, more the size of a cooking fire, but better than nothing. He drags a brazier across the deck—leaving sizable scratches in the polished wood—a satisfied smile plastered on his face.

As the sun settles at our backs, we light our miniature bonfire. As the ship moves through the darkening skies, it flickers like a match in a windstorm. Still the Raiders gather around it as we share food and stories and songs.

When Caita brings me a makeshift ceremonial staff, I can't help but smile. She has taken a broom and turned it into a fine thing. The bristles are bunched and braided, decorated with beads and threads of gold and violet. Each bunch twists in to form the petal of a flower with the polished handle becoming the stem. The wooden stem is carved with our story, the tale of how the many bands became one, and all the carvings lead to a little star.

"It's beautiful," I say.

Caita points at Zeb and little Sarah across the ship. "One of the new Raiders made it."

"He did a fine job."

"He's a fine man," she says, her gaze still following him.

I smile. "Will he be chosen tonight?"

Her eyes drop. "I'm sure there are many who would choose him."

"Will you?"

She laughs, but doesn't answer. Instead she points at the staff in my hands and asks, "Do you remember the words?"

I nod and hammer the staff against the deck. Silence falls around me and I say, "Tonight, we honor the sun who gives us the day, who withdraws so we may have night. Like the sun, we give ourselves to whom we choose as we share the right to wed. Like the sun, we turn away as we desire, offering instead a period of rest."

I shake the staff, listening to the rattle of the beads. Before I can continue, the hunched chief steps forward, wrinkled and smiling. "Chief, it is your right to choose first. Who will you have as your mate?"

The question takes me by surprise, and though I smile for the assembly, I whisper to the old chief, "I wasn't planning to choose anyone."

"But you must," she says, leaning close so only I can hear. "The Chief must have a mate or no one else can."

I think of Eija and her wives. She always chose first, but I never realized she had to choose a mate. How did I not know? But then I remember the way I shied away from the ceremony, using Rego as a way to avoid choosing a mate. Small wonder I didn't realize it—I didn't care enough to learn the ways.

A sudden thought strikes me and I feel sick to my stomach, wondering if they're allowed to say no, if I choose them. The thought of forcing someone to wed me makes me want to puke.

Hiro pushes through the crowd, leaving Folly and Gareem behind. He leans in close and says, "Pick me, Squirrel."

"But Hiro—"

He shakes his head. "Don't lecture me. I know what this means, for both of us."

My mouth is dry as I hold out my hands to him. The words get stuck for a moment, but finally I ask, "Will you walk with me through sunlight until the solstice marks the end of our path?"

He takes my hands and replies, "Let the sun guide us, Nova-du."

And with those words, Hiro and I are mated.

CHAPTER
THIRTY-THREE

The rest of the mating ceremony passes in a blur. I point the staff at my council and let them choose, then at the others gathered around, if they are old enough to have a mate. The couples trickle off the deck two at a time, going to share the night with their new loves.

Caita chooses Zeb, as do two others after he refuses her, but he turns his back to all. I know he does this for Sarah, so that he can be the father she needs while she's grieving, but I wonder when he will allow himself some comfort as well.

When only the youth and the unmated are left, the ceremony concludes and Hiro and I retire below deck. My whole body is shaking as he takes my hand and escorts me down the stairs. There is a gentleness in his movements, as if he is afraid I will run like some frightened creature. Perhaps he is right. I am frightened.

We go into the room I've been given, a perk of being Chief, and he closes the door behind us. Gods, it's *our* room now. What have I done?

I turn and look at him as he leans against the door. He folds his arms across his chest and says, "So, you ready to consummate this thing?"

My mouth drops open, but words don't come out. His face breaks out in his megawatt smile and he says, "Gods, I wish you could see your face right now, Squirrel. You look absolutely mortified."

When he laughs, it sends a surge of relief through me and I laugh in response. "I mean, I wasn't happy about it."

He rolls his eyes and says, "You're the only woman alive immune to my charms."

"Thank all the gods for that."

Hiro crosses the room and sits on the bed, patting the seat beside him. I sit beside him and he takes my hand in his, suddenly serious. "Look, I know you weren't prepared for that tonight, and I didn't see a way around it. So I did what I had to, as your friend. But also, I want you…" he says, his voice strangely hoarse.

"Hiro, please," I interrupt.

He rests a finger against my lips and says, "Let me finish."

I nod, dreading what will be left of us when he says whatever he needs to say.

His eyes meet mine as he says, "I want you to understand, and I'm sorry to say this on our wedding night, but I have zero desire to have sex with you."

A genuine laugh bubbles up and I can't decide whether to hug him or punch him. I decide to punch, pull my hand from his, and hit him in the arm. "You should be so lucky."

We sit for a moment as the ease of our relationship settles around us like a warm blanket on a cold day. After a few minutes he sighs and says, "I can't believe I agreed to give up sex for the next six months."

"Whoa, dude, you can still have sex."

He looks me up and down and says, "I appreciate the offer, but like I just told you…Zero. Desire."

I wave away his words and say, "You committed to loving me until the next solstice. That doesn't mean you can't have sex elsewhere, as long as your mate consents."

He raises a brow and asks, "Do you consent?"

I take a second to relish holding this over his head. With a smile that rivals his, I say, "Ask me tomorrow."

WE SEE THE FARM AROUND NOON ON THE SEVENTH DAY AFTER LEAVING the Hole in the World. Despite the crowded conditions accommodating so many Raiders aboard the *Curiosity*, spirits are high. The solstice ceremony went well, even for me and my marriage of convenience.

As we close in, Nigel approaches me on the bow. "Just spoke with someone named Davie from Copperhill."

My heart hammers against my ribs as I ask, "Is Rego okay?"

Nigel nods. "She said he's recovering well. They're a few miles south scouring some wreckage while they were waiting for us. She said they'll head up this way once they pull in their haul."

This is the best news I've had in days and I feel some of the tension melt from me. Rego is well and will meet us later today. In a matter of minutes, I'll get to see Ivy and my dad, Coco, Krew, Baz and deliver more Raiders than they ever imagined would join us. Ivy's plan is going to work.

We set down in the field south of the farmhouse and disembark, making our way through the grass while the sun beats down upon us. There is no need for stealth in this place, so the Raiders are doing something they normally reserve for night by the fire: they're being noisy. Scattered songs sail past my ears, laughter and yelling and joy. I'm so delighted by the hope this sight brings, it takes me a minute to realize there's something wrong.

My hand slides to the knife at my hip as dread settles over. Hiro leans closer as we walk, asking, "What's wrong?"

I purse my lips as I turn around, surveying the field we're in and the land around it. The last time we were here, it was full of children at play. They trailed after the airship, chasing us as we flew out. So where are they now when they should be running to meet us?

"Where is everyone?"

While I keep moving towards the farmhouse, Hiro signals the council and with a quick word, they manage to stop the progression of the Raiders.

But I keep going. My pace quickens as I approach the empty porch. A few feet away, I see the first real sign of trouble—the door is ajar and there's a smear of blood on the door frame.

I'm in the door with my knife drawn before I realize I've closed the distance. The table and benches are turned over, dishes and silverware scattered across the floor. The acrid scent of burning fat and metal and earth clogs the room, making the air thick and near unbreathable. I run my tongue over the roof of my mouth, unable to get rid of the taste of it.

And then I find her. Aunt Abby, or what's left of her. She's wearing her apron, like always, a dusting of flour on her cheek. Her head and torso are as they should be, but her arms and legs...gods...

Her arms are separated at the shoulder, elbow, and wrist. Each of her fingers are sawed from her hand. Same with the legs. The parts are burnt and stacked beside her on a serving tray with a dead flower in a vase and a card with my name on it.

I pick up the card with shaky fingers, but can't force myself to read it. Instead I dwell on the question running rampant through my mind: *What have I done?*

Hiro finds me pressed into the corner of the kitchen, dry heaving. Everything is out of me already, but my body won't stop. He pulls me against his chest and I sag against him.

"Let's get out of here."

I shake my head. "I need to clean her up," I say, but really I can't stop wondering what we'll find at the next place. I can't do it anymore.

"N-Nova?"

I turn to the small voice. Edith Ann Roody is peeking out from a floorboard. When she's sure it's me, she pushes aside the hidden door and climbs up, along with Zazira and Wolfie. I grab them all and pull them against me, letting their shaking sobs overpower my own heartache.

Hiro ushers us all out of the kitchen and we sit in the grass outside the house, breathing in the fresh air that doesn't quite cut through the stench of burnt flesh still clinging to my nostrils.

"She pushed us into the crawlspace," Edith Ann says, when her sobs have subsided enough for words to make it out. "Then she covered the door and wouldn't budge. She's the reason we're alive."

Her words dig into me, reminding me of my own mother. She let herself be caught and killed so Rachel and I could get away from the star-people. I only hope these children aren't haunted by Abby's sacrifice as I have been by my mother's.

"Chief," Delano says, stepping towards us, "there's something you need to see."

No, I think. *I don't need to see anything else.*

But I get up and follow him towards the barn. He leads me to the side away from the farmhouse and stops. I look around, expecting bodies, but there's nothing but tall grass. Then I look at him and follow his gaze to the side of the barn.

In red letters the color of dried blood, it says, "Come and get them."

There's an arrow pointing down to a barrel resting against the building. As I step closer, I realize there's something there—a bundle of strawberry blonde hair. Ivy's ponytail. And sitting on top of it is a tracking bracelet.

The notecard from the kitchen is still in my hands, though I didn't notice I was carrying it with me. I look at the card with my name on the outside in swooped, fancy handwriting and a red kiss-print on the inside, a single name signed at the bottom. I place the card on the barrel, trading it for the bracelet. Picking it up, my eyes tracing its curve, the raised bump along the edge. I run it through my fingers, pass it back and forth between my hands.

"You can't," Hiro says.

I don't know when he arrived. He steps forward, reaches for me, and I see my name forming on his lips as I slip the bracelet on my wrist and disappear.

EPILOGUE

She disappears as my fingers graze the bracelet entangling itself on her wrist.

I hit the ground, my knees sinking into the wet earth beside the barn. There's a hollowness burrowing through my gut and I can't even begin to think about what this means for the resistance, for the Raiders, for us.

Us? Is that a thing?

No, of course not. I shake it from my head. I think I love that girl; no, I know I do. But this feeling of emptiness without her isn't because I'm *in* love, no matter what foolishness tries to wriggle into my brain while I'm grieving the loss of my best friend. There's nothing more to it than that.

What the hell even happened? There must be something that made her put on that bracelet. She chose to return to the star-people, but why?

I take a deep breath and wipe my sweaty palms against my legs. There's no time to sit around and wonder what to do next. Nova would get up, Nova would act.

Nova is gone, I think.

I swallow against that thought, clamp my lips shut, refuse to give it voice. She may not be here right now, but that doesn't mean she's *gone*. I would know if she was dead. If pre-cataclysm entertainment has taught me anything, it's that the good guys always triumph. And Nova is good.

Besides, she has to come back to me. The Moose can't exist without the Squirrel.

I push myself up and take in the scene, trying to weigh things with logic rather than the multitude of emotions running through me. The writing on the side of the barn tells me part of the story that led her away from here, and though the initial shock of the rusty coloring of it must have given Nova a scare, as I look closer I can see it isn't blood. The message was painted on, so the missing people were probably captured rather than murdered.

At least, they weren't killed here on the farm. So far, the woman in the kitchen is the only body I've seen, and it wouldn't make sense for the Règle to take a bunch of people onto the station just to kill them.

There's a clump of reddish hair sitting there along with a note. It could be Ivy's, which would explain why Nova rushed away, but as I run it through my fingers, I'm not even sure it's human hair. I read the card, but I have no clue who Bets is or why it would matter. There's not enough to puzzle this out.

I don't know how long I stand there trying to make sense of things, but after a while I feel a hand on my shoulder. I turn to find Rego, the man who raised Nova, staring at me with knowing eyes. I don't know when he arrived, but I'm so glad he's here.

"I lost her to the stars once before, son. She came back then, and she'll return again. My Little Star knows the way home."

I nod, fighting back tears that I never would have expected when I met that wily creature a few weeks ago. That damned Raider-girl stabbed her way into my heart.

Rego guides me back towards the ship. I say, "Guess we're screwed now."

"We make a new plan."

"Without Squirrel?"

"*For* her. She might not be here to guide us, but we can make ourselves ready until she is."

"Some of the Raiders might get a little, you know, stab-stabby."

"No," he says, shaking his head. "I'm certain the new Chief will keep fighting for her."

"How does that work, with her leaving? Who gets the ridiculous privilege of trying to control those beautiful fiends?"

"She isn't dead, and since she didn't name someone in the interim, the responsibility goes to her next of kin until she returns."

"You probably don't know yet. Her Aunt Rachel isn't with us anymore, because she's a mega-bitch."

"Good. That only leaves one person then. A good, strong Raider."

I stop short. "Who?"

"Her mate, Hiro. The new Chief is you."

ALSO BY SHELLY JARVIS

Next in Series:

Coming Soon!

The Book of the Golden One:

Duology Boxed Set

Standalone:

TAP

ABOUT THE AUTHOR

Shelly Jarvis began working on speculative fictions thanks to a writing assignment in Mrs. Bettijane Burger's eleventh grade English class, but her passion for writing developed at seven when she wrote a Halloween tale about a witch and a ghost who became best friends.

An avid science fiction and fantasy reader, Shelly spends a large portion of each new day dwelling in other worlds.

Shelly enjoys spending time with her wacky spouse, her wonderful nephews, and her rescue pups, Gimli, Butters, Fergus, and Pickles. She currently resides near Charleston, West Virginia, in the wild and wonderful mountains that have her heart.

Learn more about Shelly, including other books and how to contact her, at ShellyJarvis.com.

www.ingramcontent.com/pod-product-compliance
Lightning Source LLC
Chambersburg PA
CBHW031602240626
47153CB00002B/605